When Jonny con

Home.

John Arthur Cooper.

Hold on through the years,

that's what I intend to do.

Hopelessly devoted

to you.

Chapter 1.

It dropped from the high narrow vertical letter box with two other envelopes and a soft clatter. Irene knew exactly what they were. Vernon's pools coupons, the water rates bill and that letter. The one she'd been dreading and the one he'd been nervously, excitedly, impatiently waiting for. It was typed and bore a red Ministry of Defense frank, not a stamp. She thought of throwing it in the fire but decided if he found out he'd never forgive her and he was all she had.

Jonny was nineteen now and still running old Frank Tomb's corner paper shop. He was doing well, Frank kept the money from the newspapers and Jonny had a free hand to sell anything else he wanted. Fireworks were always popular and were a handy bonus being just before Christmas. These days, on the cold dark mornings Frank didn't surface til about ten leaving Jonny to do everything. He'd get up at four, clean out the grate from last night and start a fire for her then bring her a cup of tea in bed then get rid of the bucket down the yard so she didn't have to go out in the cold. He was such a good son. He'd leave the house about five and be back about eight for breakfast then off again 'til twelve for lunch, He'd bring her two ounces of potted beef or some fish paste from Wooliscrofts on the corner but this letter was going to change everything.

She put the letter on the breakfast table and waited for him.

He always came in the back way, ride down the entry on his bike, turn sharp right and lean the bike on the wall next to the water butt. The butt was a forty five gallon steel drum with the top cut off, it was always full. As a boy Jonny used to tie penny bangers to a stone, light them, wait until it started to 'fizz' then drop them in. It was great fun to watch the explosion thump into the sides of the butt then cause the surface to erupt. Now he was a man. Now he sold fireworks to small boys knowing full well how exciting they were.

Irene didn't have to say. He saw the letter propped up against the sugar basin as soon as he entered the kitchen. She looked. He looked, then he opened it.

Dear Mr. Conrad.

I am pleased to inform you that you have passed the initial recruitment interview and assessment and have been selected to attend R.A.F. Cranwell Officer and Aircrew Selection Centre for a four day further selection process on April 20 of this year.

It is recommended that at this stage you do not give up any work, employment or training that you are currently engaged in.

The college has a direct rail link and a travel warrant for the above date is enclosed with this letter. It is expected that all applicants will attend the college before 1700 hours that evening.

Congratulations and good luck.

Mark Peterson DFC. Camp Commandant. RAF Cranwell
Cranwell
Lincs.

Irene didn't have to ask if it was good or bad. The smile lit up Jonny's face as he re read the letter and looked at the travel warrant.

"I've got through Mum, I've made it. I've got to go for an assessment in April, that's only two months away. I'd better get fit, don't you think?"

"How long will you be away?"

"Four days, it says here, but if you pass you stay."

She was happy for him but dreading him going. This was it. The beginning of the end, she'd be alone, first Arthur, now Jonny. She sat down, almost collapsed down, onto her chair in tears. Jonny put the letter down.

After a moment she got back up. Reaching for the small saucepan of hot milk on the stove she carefully poured it over Jonny's two shredded wheat. He would put his own sugar on then wait until it became soft. That was how he liked it.

"You'll need some smart new clothes."

"I've got some money Mom, will you come with me on Saturday? We'll go to Ordish and Halls in town. What do you think, a suit or slacks and a Blazer?"

"A nice suit will be best with some new shoes and a tie. Now eat your breakfast, I'm making your toast. I've bought some of that new Roses Lime marmalade you like."

"Thanks Mom."

"You won't get this there you know, It'll be canteen food, take it or leave it."

"It's what I want Mom, you know that. Dad knew what I wanted to be, that's why he bought me that Gloster Javelin kit all those years ago. I used to love the Farnborough Air Show when it was on the telly. We both did."

"You're a working class boy from a poor home, don't build your hopes up too much Jonny. Usually it's only rich folk who become Officers and you'd have to be an officer to be a pilot you know. Folks who can afford to send their kids to college or university."

"Things are changing Mum, these days it's how good you are, not so much where you're from or how much money your parents have got."

"I'm not sure." Irene reached out and put her hand on his as he reached for the toast.

"I Don't want you to get hurt or disappointed. If you get through what you going to do about the shop?"

"Leave. It's not mine, it belongs to Frank, if he died or decided to sell I'd be out on my ear, no doubt about that."

"I suppose so." Irene muttered as she buttered Jonny's toast. She could sense her beloved son was itching to go by the speed he ate his breakfast.

"Slow down, you'll give yourself indigestion."

"Can't wait to tell Veronica."

Veronica lived next door, through the back gate. Her dad was an electrician, they'd had a telly for ages. He kept chickens in the small backyard. They really used to annoy Arthur. The cockerel used to crow very loudly most of the night. Albert, - Veronica's Dad - never gave them any eggs. Irene thought that was mean and unfriendly. Veronica was a year older than Jonny but had always chased after him, when she was nine and Jonny was eight she'd tried to kiss him. It frightened Jonny so they fell out for a while but after that they've been best friends for years.

"She won't be in 'til dinnertime now she's working at the Coop."

"Yes I know Mum." Jonny finished the last of his toast, washed it down with the remains of the tea and jumped up to grab his coat.

"Bye, see you later. Oh, do you want anything from the shop?"

"No, it's OK I'm going out to the butchers later, tripe and onions for tea. You won't get that in the RAF." The door slammed as she said it and he was gone.

Chapter 2.

For April it was very cold, especially at seven in the morning on the station platform.

There was a sheet of thick, not very clean glass between Irene and Jonny. He looked so young and handsome sat against the window in the railway carriage. His best suit, new shoes and carefully knotted tie complemented his glowing excited face and shining combed hair. Irene tried not to cry but failed. She fussed unnecessarily with her headscarf and waved as the train jolted slowly away taking with it her love, her only remaining life. All she had now were painful bandaged knees that had to get her up the station steps and the tearful walk home to loneliness.

It was a steam train, only a fifty minutes trip to Derby and then a change to a train for Grantham. Most of the trains these days were new fangled diesels but this was old fangled with separate compartments in the carriages and windows that were let down with a leather strap. If you let the window down you could immediately smell the smoke and steam. It was quite nice, there was no one else in the carriage so Jonny let it down. The cold morning air immediately rushed in like unseen dry water. His thoughts split between his Mum and the RAF. Frank Tomb's paper shop was now in the past. It's comfortable dark varnished wood getting more distant by the minute. It's bell on the door could now not be heard. It's glass display cabinets with the tops so scratched it looked frosted could not be seen. He looked down at his new shiny brown shoes, there was a slight scuff on the right toe cap so he rubbed it on the calf of his left leg. That looked better!

Mum hadn't even washed to come with him to the station. She'd just put her comfortable green thick coat on, her headscarf and old handbag. Her look just matched her mood of loss and depression. There was nothing to make an effort for. Now her life was empty. Jonny's Grandad had given him a real leather writing case containing a Basildon Bond writing pad, envelopes and a Parker fountain pen. Jonny had promised to write to her as soon as he could.

He never thought about Frankie Fletcher. It was as though that night was a dream, or rather a nightmare, no, a dream, because it was what he wanted to do. He didn't care a jot about Frankie's Mom and Dad, Frankie's girlfriend, Frankie's anything 'cause Frankie Fletcher hadn't cared a jot about Dad when he lied to him about the boxes. No, it was the right thing to do. He was a bit sorry for Harry Shaw but from what he'd picked up from bit's of conversations between Mum and Brenda, prison was the best place for him anyway. Course it meant the end of 'The Notes' but life moves on. The clattering of the train over a bridge brought him back to now for a while then the drizzle became rain that ran diagonally down across the window from left to right making the fields and trees appear wetter than they really were. What he'd done to Frankie had made him stronger. It was a secret strength he had, nobody else had done it. He could do it, it was easy, then you just went home, carried on but you knew what power was within you. He had no regrets, he'd done it for Dad.

Dad would be really proud of him today. Mum didn't really understand what it meant to be an 'Officer'. She just hated him going away. She wanted him to manage or possibly buy Frank Tomb's shop, meet and marry a local girl, preferably Veronica, settle down and have some kids. She'd never been on or in an aeroplane. Neither had he for that matter. He thought to himself. No. Dad would have been really proud.

The train started to slow as the red reliable brick of Derby became more prolific. Derby, the home of Rolls Royce and jet engines. The station, with it's cream painted cast iron stanchions and dirty glass roof quickly appeared. Now he needed the nine twenty train to Grantham. Expect it would be a diesel, he thought standing up to grab his leather suitcase. It was a new case, he'd bought it with tip money he'd saved at the shop. All leather with two leather straps. Shiny, new, but built to last. He hated buying cheap. Six pounds it had cost him, the most expensive case they had. Made in Northampton, same as his leather shoes.

It was easier to ask a porter than calmly examine the timetable to find out which platform the Grantham train left from. Jonny's excitement made his new case weigh nothing as he tripped up the wide steps to the bridge then down the other side to platform two. He had a twenty minutes wait. Mum had made him a big breakfast and packed him some cheese and pickle sandwiches so he wasn't hungry. The cup of hot tea was simply to pass the time in the warmth of the cafeteria and it's glowing dark green Esse stove. He couldn't relax, the time on his Timex seemed excruciatingly slow. Then just as he was finishing his tea the train pulled in. It was just two diesel carriages, green and dirty yellow, they looked as though they'd lost their engine, no aerodynamic front or back, it was as though somebody had sawn off a metal tube.

There were about twelve people waiting to get on. This was the start, so the train was empty. The doors were opened by a little button ringed with yellow lights, the inside was mainly plastic with throbbing vibrations that came from somewhere below. Jonny found a seat by the window with a table in front of him, no one else sat in the other three seats. He wondered about Mum and thought about Dad. Dad had never been on a diesel train, they were all steam when he was alive. He hadn't missed much, Jonny thought. An RAF pilot, could he really do it? Dad would have been so proud of him. A light Wedgewood blue uniform with gold wings on his chest. WOW! Would it really happen? The train revved up and jolted out of the sheltered station out into the cold miserable drizzle.

Grantham came and went with a grey blue brick blur, the train to Sleaford was just one carriage that throbbed it's lonely way through the murk along the guiding wet lines. There were some other young shiny men in the carriage. Jonny guessed that they were bound for the same place but everyone was too polite, too shy, too nervous to speak. Then they were there. Blue and white stanchions with white wood skirting coming down from the canopy. Everybody got off and made their way nervously to the exit, not knowing what to expect.

Across the way was a Bedford single decker grey bus with a man in RAF uniform and a clipboard waiting by the door. All the young men on the train headed for the man who had two stripes on his upper arm.

"Name?" The Corporal snapped.

"Jonny Conrad."

He looked down the list and ticked him off.

"That would be John Conrad then?" He looked out from under the peak of his cap.

"No, Jonny."

The corporal said nothing but his eyes moved on to the young man behind him.

"Name?"

"Jolyon Vernon Clay." Jonny heard a very cultured and 'posh' voice behind him reply.

"Come on, get along, we haven't got all day." The Corporal barked. His voice wasn't posh at all.

"Hello I'm Jolyon." Jolyon Vernon Clay put out his hand as he sat down on the seat next to Jonny and smiled. It was a beautiful smile that completed his handsome face.
Jonny shook his hand, it was strong and real.

"Hi, I'm Jonny, Jonny Conrad. Are you here for an assessment?"

"Yes. Hope I pass, had to fight Mother and Father like mad to do this, they wanted, no, expected me to go up to Oxford or Cambridge but I pestered them to death about becoming a pilot. They think it's something akin to being a bus driver.

Something the hired staff do." Jolyon laughed as he settled into his seat. The driver of the bus pushed a very large lever and the concertina doors closed. "If I fail they'll insist I go to Cambridge. Can't think of anything worse can you?" Jolyon answered his question before Jonny could speak. " Still I suppose they did have the infamous Cambridge five there, Burgess, Blunt, Maclean 'et al' so it would be preferable to bloody boring Oxford."

"What's 'et al' mean?" Jonny asked.

Jolyon looked at Jonny.

"'And all', everybody else, haven't you done Latin Jonny?"

"No, it's not exactly on the curriculum of a Technical High School."

"Lucky you."

The bus bounced off, it was three quarters full of fresh male faces and smelt faintly of sick. The gear lever was nearly as big and sloppy as the door opening lever.

"Do you think we'll get separate rooms or a dormitory?" Jolyon asked as he stared out of the now wet window. "Mother and Father wouldn't support me doing this, had to get a scholarship. How about you?"

Jonny followed his gaze as the 'brownness' of a February Lincolnshire stumbled by. Confused by the vibrations of the Bedford bus and the choppy undulations of the road the rivulets of rain made a difficult journey across the window.

"Just applied at the local recruitment office and here I am."

"Good grief Jonny. Are you good?"

 Jonny looked at Jolyon.

"In most ways I'm very good, in some ways I'm very bad. It all depends where you are and what the circumstances are."

"That's a bit deep for a bumpy bus Jonny. Do you think if we stick together we'll end up in the same 'something'? Room, dormitory I've no idea."

"I hope so Jolyon, I like you. What do you think these tests will be?"

"The usual stuff, fitness, hand eye coordination, your vision, see if you're colour blind or not, bit of problem solving, maybe some leadership stuff as they're looking for officers."

"You done anything like this before?"

"Oh yes, at Eton we had a lot of stuff like this, it was disguised of course, a camping weekend, or a competition but really they were looking for leaders."

There was an 'elevation' in Jonny's words, as though he was in a place where many men and definitely no boys had got to yet.

Then they were there.

The bus rattled and waited as the magnificent black iron gates slowly opened. The crest on the front, both intimidating and welcoming at the same time. The Crown, the Eagle, 'Per Ardua Ad Astra' striding confidently around the circle that contained the eagle and supported the crown.

"Take it, that's Latin. What does it mean Jolyon?"

Both young men leaned close to the window to view the gate and beyond. The formidable huge pillars fronting the College Hall seemed to reflect the enormity of the challenges that lay ahead.

"Through adversity to the stars." Jolyon muttered.

"Wow! Do you think England can afford to go to the stars?" It was half a joke, half a comment.

"Why not?"We've taken what we want from the world and abused the world's poor for centuries to get where we are today. Can't see it changing unless we have some visionary social leaders, and that is highly unlikely. It's two o'clock, do you think we'll get lunch?"

"Don't know but I've got some sandwiches we can share if we don't."

"What's in them?"

"Bread and dripping with brown jelly and salt, and some cheese and pickle."

"What's dripping?"

Jonny looked at Jolyon who was now grabbing the handles of his bag as the bus pulled up outside the hall.

"Tell you later."

A tall Sargeant with a stick, a peaked cap, a moustache and a webbing belt with gleaming brass buckles ushered them off the shaking throbbing wet bus.

"Line up inside in front of the reception desk." He barked the instruction just once. It was enough.

All the boys, for that is what they were, entered the great hall with trepidation, in front of them was a large square red carpet. Surrounding them and looking down on them were fierce portraits of great leaders and flyers. Their eyes, almost alive, scrutinised them as the latest hopefuls walked through the door. The Sargeant said nothing but indicated they should walk around the carpet, not on it. Jonny thought that was for the privileged, the elite, the important. Jolyon thought nothing of it.

People were summoned to the desk in two's and their names ticked off. Jonny and Jolyon stepped forward together.

"Room thirty two, sign for your keys, lose them and I'll cost you a pound. Follow the gentleman, supper in the hall at six, dress is as you are. Muster at the kit hut tomorrow at nine for uniform issue." The instructions were issued automatically by a man with hair only on the sides of his head, gold bifocal glasses and a lifetime of commitment to the RAF.

"Well that's a good sign." Hissed Jolyon as they followed an elderly man dressed in informal clothes and a brown apron.

"What is?"

"Uniform issue, seems they want us to stay for more than the four day assessment."

"Maybe? Maybe not, they'll just make us hand it in if we fail, don't think it will be much."

"You mean I won't get a flying helmet today?"

Jonny laughed and pushed his arm. It was the first time he'd touched Jolyon.

"That's on Friday if you pass the maths test."

"Ooh good, I'm really good at maths." Jolyon smirked.

"So am I." Jonny replied.

The room was small with two beds, two service issue wardrobes, one desk and two chairs. It was on the first floor after two flights of thirteen steps each. The man had struggled up, holding the rail with his hand. Jonny thought he was at least in his late sixties, maybe more. There was a window that looked out onto green grass. It was three thirty when they relaxed onto the beds.

"I'm dreadfully hungry." Jolyon droned from his bed. "What's dripping again?"

Somehow Jolyon's up market, 'posh' voice didn't work with the word 'dripping'.

"Congealed pork fat from cooking, underneath you get a brown jelly, so you spread them both on bread sprinkle with salt and there you go."

"Can I try one?"

Jonny undid his case and produced the sandwiches wrapped in separate foil.

"There you go, two for me, two for you. Didn't your mum pack you anything?"

"Good grief no, I don't think Mother has ever been in the kitchen never mind cook anything. These are delicious, you're a very lucky man Jonny. What does your Dad do?"

"Did, he's dead."

"Oh sorry."

"It's OK, he was a labourer in a foundry, he died of a burst stomach ulcer. The doctor said it was caused by stress."

"How old were you at the time?"

"Fifteen."

"Do you miss him?"

"Terribly, he was my best friend."

"As I said Jonny, you're a very lucky man, I hardly know my Father yet we live in the same house."

"Is it a big house Jolyon?"

"Huge, it's a mansion, Bovington Hall in Herefordshire."

"Where's Herefordshire?"

"Near Wales. What were your sandwiches."

"Cheese and pickle."

"Can I come and visit your house one day, I want your mum to make me some dripping sandwiches."

"No, it's a small terraced street house in a poor area."

"That's why I want to come. You must have been very good to get selected from your background. I don't mean that as it sounds."

"It sounds OK. Yes I'm very good at most things I do." The confidence was almost threatening.

"Shall we sleep?" Jolyon asked as he relaxed back on the single bed. The noise of a small jet whistled overhead.

"Don't you think you should take your shoes off if you're going to lie down?"

"Do you think so? I suppose you're right, who do you think cleans these rooms?" Jolyon was untying his laces.

"Us."

"I'll enjoy that, I used to watch the maids at home and often thought to myself 'I could do a better job than that'."

"Maybe it was just work for them and they didn't want to do it."

"Suppose so. Can you remember your way back to that hall for supper?"

"Yes."

Sleep came easily and quickly to the two young boys who thought they were men.

The eighteen young hopefuls stood out in their civilian clothes amongst the packed hall of blue serge. Nervousness and false confidence saw them all draw together on one long table. It was set with a soup bowl resting on a dinner plate and a small bread plate above toward the left hand side. To the right of the dinner plate were two knives and a spoon, to the left of the plate were two forks, one being bigger than the other, and a napkin. Above the plate was a spoon and a small fork. On the bread plate was a small knife.

Jonny stood for a moment as Jolyon sat down, picked up the napkin and like some others tucked it behind his tie so that it fell away in front of him. Others had it simply spread out on their laps.

"You might have to help me here." Jonny whispered into Jolyon's ear as he sat down. Jolyon turned to look at him, it took a moment before he realised Jonny's predicament.

"Put the napkin wherever you feel most comfortable, the spoon on the far right is for the soup, the knife next to it is for fish, then it's your dinner knife. The big fork on the left is for dinner, the smaller fork is a salad fork. OK?"

Jonny nervously glanced at him.

"Yes thanks." He whispered. "Sorry."

"For God's sake Jonny, don't be sorry, the whole adventure is a learning curve for all of us, look around you. Everybody's smiling and gay but we're all shit scared. Never be 'sorry' Jonny, especially in front of the servants." He chuckled as a middle aged lady, most definitely a mother, filled their soup bowls from a large white jug. Another mother followed behind placing a bread roll and knob of butter on the small plate.

Jonny chose chicken pie, sautéed potatoes, peas and cauliflower from the buffet, Jolyon chose plaice.

He watched carefully how others ate, how they held their knives and forks, how they spoke whilst not eating, how and when they drank. Jolyon saw him watching.

"You must have been bloody good Jonny, you're not of their class are you? And most definitely not of my class."

"No, my Mum's working class. The only job she ever had was in a munitions factory in the war, after that she was just Dad's wife and then my Mum. Monday was washday, Tuesday was clean bed sheets day and Friday night was bath night."

"Lucky you."

Jonny and Jolyon looked at each other.

"Come on, let's go." Jolyon rose from his chair and discarded his napkin onto the sweet plate. Jonny put his to the side of the bread plate.

"The little room was surprisingly dark when the lights were out, nothing came in through the curtains and it was quiet.

"Jolyon?"

"What?"

"Were you a happy child?"

"Good lord no. shipped off to boarding school at the earliest opportunity. I was just an inconvenient necessity for the bloodline, an heir for the estate. Mother kissed me on a good day and totally ignored me the rest of the time. A cuddle was not on any agenda, smart expensive clothes were."

"Your parents have an 'estate'?"

"Father sees it as a huge burden he has to dedicate his whole life to managing and supporting. That's why they opposed me joining the RAF, I might escape, up there, beyond the clouds. Can't wait. Night."

"Night."

"Is that it?" Jolyon asked of the storeman.

The storeman was king of the immaculate nissen hut masquerading as a 'Uniform and Flying Clothing' store. He was definitely over fifty years old with a 'well fed' physique, glasses and imperious manner to the young hopefuls who turned up before him. He wore a brown dust coat like impenetrable armour.

"How much more do you want? You're probably only here for a few days. One pair of trousers waist twenty eight, inside leg thirty one, one blue cotton shirt size medium, one blue knitted service jumper, one clip on service tie, two pairs of dark blue socks, one pair of size nine black leather shoes, one blue beret and one PT kit. That's your lot young man."

"What if I get through?"

"Then you come and see me again. Give me your card."

The king duly stamped a square on the white joining card. His counter was covered in the same thick brown polished linoleum as the floor. Behind him were racks of drawers. There were no labels in the brass label holders, he knew where everything was.

"Next."

Jonny moved along and stood in front of him. The man sized him up, there was no need for a tape. A pile of folded kit appeared in front of him, his card was stamped.
Jolyon was waiting for him at the door.

"Back to the room and get changed then."

"Yes, we're in the new entrants lecture room, wherever that is, at ten."

"There's a map in the room. Think we'll make it Jonny?"

"What, the lecture room?"

"No nit-wit, the assessment."

"Of course, if only to piss off Santa Claus back there."

"There's a N.A.A.F.I over there, let's see if we can get a coffee and a cake, I overheard a chap talking. Apparently they do yummy Eccles cakes. I love Eccles cakes."

"Eccles cakes are for common folk Jolyon, not for the likes of you." Jonny joked. "Eccles is a northern town."

"That's why I love them, big, fat and covered in sugar, no pretences just plain pleasure."

"You have to be a communist before you're allowed to eat them."

"I spoke to a chap once who'd been down a mine, will that do?"

"I suppose so, come on it's bloody cold." Jonny moaned. "Why has everyone here got a moustache?"

"'Cause that's what RAF Officers are supposed to look like."

"Fiddlesticks, I'm going to have an iced custard slice."

"How did you do in that test where you had to turn the wooden pegs 'round?" Jolyon mumbled between mouthfuls of Eccles cake.

"Wasn't a test was it? Just a task, finished with loads of time to spare, saw a couple of chaps fumble around a bit, they struggled. Apparently we've got a P.T. test this afternoon, press ups, sit ups, that sort of thing."

"Oh lummy, not very good at that sort of thing." Jolyon groaned.

"It'll be easy, just set your mind to it." Jonny bit into his custard slice trying not to compress one end and force everything out of the other. He bit quickly, it was reasonably successful, he licked away the escaping custard.

"How many do you think?"

"Twenty so I've heard."

"Crikey, better have another Eccles cake. You?"

"The jam doughnuts look nice."

The Sargeant stalked around the lecture room like a well trained sheepdog, baring his teeth and snarling but never biting. His loud boots out of sync with the ambience of the lecture room.

"From now on you will march as a squad from place to place. You will not walk, you will not stroll, you will not amble, you will march. McCallister you will be class leader."

"Yes Sargeant." A tall thin red haired very white skinned young man responded.

"I've chosen McCallister as your drill leader because he has experience in the Air Training Corps. You will obey his instructions to the letter. I want to hear boots on the ground and see arms swinging, preferably in unison and not like a fucking windmill. Is that understood?"

There was a subdued murmured "Yes Sargeant."

"Lunch time from now until one o'clock after which you will assemble in front of the hall in P.T. kit and march to the gymnasium. Is that understood?"

"Yes Sargeant."

"After your tests you will get changed into blue uniform and muster at the parade ground for drill instructions at three thirty. Is that understood?"

"Yes Sargeant."

"Wonders will never cease." Sargeant Terry Nixon muttered as he marched himself out of the lecture room and headed for the Sergeants mess.

"What's tomorrow?" Jolyon asked as they marched towards the food hall.

"According to my secret folded sheet, a reaction test followed by problem solving, followed by eyesight and hand eye coordination tests in the afternoon."

"No talking in the ranks." The thin red head shouted in between episodes of 'Left Right Left."

"Does your secret folded sheet say what we're having for lunch today?" Jolyon whispered.

"Yes - food."

"Wow! Do you think Karl Marx would have sanctioned choices or just one menu?"

"Who's Karl Marx?"

"Oh for God's sake!" Jolyon quietly hissed.

"Squad Halt!" The command was immediately followed by a double rubber soled thump that wasn't totally in unison.

"Fall out." Snapped the voice, most of the class did a correct turn to the right, pause, two three, then broke ranks. Three people turned left.

The dining hall for lunch was not the dining hall for dinner. This was two green painted wooden doors leading into a large concrete framed, cream painted room with Formica topped long tables and corresponding long benches. Soup from two large stainless steel urns was the first course followed by fish, faggots or oxtail stew. At the very end of the stainless steel, steam heated range was apple pie with custard or cheese and biscuits, both if you were really hungry.

"Not exactly the Ritz and no waiters, suppose I'd better get used to how you eat. Eh Jonny?"

"I eat with my mouth, teeth and tongue, the same as you Jolyon."

"Yes but it's not a class ridden oppressive ritual is it?"

"No, it's because we're hungry."

"My people never get hungry, it's vulgar, we pick and graze slowly as though we don't really need it. We're doing you a favour by eating the food you have presented us with. That's why we're stick thin."

"What are you having?"

"The Oxtail stew looks extremely tasty and you get a lot of it, just look how much that chap got. I'm starving." Said Jolyon.

"How hot should I have this iron?" Jolyon was holding the Morphy Richards standard issue iron and looking at the dial. It was ten o'clock at night Jonny had done 'everything' and was lying with his hands behind his head staring up at the cream gloss ceiling.

"As hot as it will go, you've got to create steam through your ironing cloth."

"And why the brown paper afterwards?"

"Dry out the cloth without burning it or making it shiny."

"Complicated this military stuff isn't it?" His 'cut glass' voice cut through everything. 'Perfect for radio communications' Jonny thought.

"Why are you doing this stuff Jolyon? Why are you even here? If, as you say, you're part of the ruling elite."

Jolyon put the iron down to look at Jonny.

"For gods sake pick the iron up NOW! Jonny shouted. The red hot iron had been put down on it's plate. Jolyon reacted instantly and stood it on end.

"No damage." He grinned.

"You've never done this before, have you Jolyon?"

"Not exactly that's what the maids do. That's why I'm doing this, everything seems so wrong, so unfair. One person having to do tedious work all their lives just because they were born poor and people like me not even giving it a second thought. Doing this I can meet real people, people like you Jonny, people who have something more than money."

"And what exactly do I have Jolyon?"

"You have the view from below and that gives you determination. I don't need determination as father can arrange or buy anything I want and I never look down. At least I'm not supposed to."

"Then why do you?"

"Don't really know."

"Last day tomorrow, apparently it's quite brutal. They just tell you up front if you've passed or failed, if it's a fail it's pack your bags there and then, here's your travel warrant goodbye, then they get a letter in the post a few days later."

"And if you pass?"

"You get to spend the night bulling your boots and pressing your trousers."

"Better buy another tin of Kiwi then from the N.A.A.F.I. Goodnight."

Jolyon turned out the light.

The lecture hall had become familiar over the last three days. It was pale green with cream iron framed windows, once a year polished wooden floor with lamps hanging from the steel stress bars that spanned the concrete arches. There was no heating.
A stage with no curtains dominated the room holding sway over about fifty straight back chairs. It was not a place to relax. It was a place of attention and tension.

The Sargeant's boots crunched noisily and quickly through the swing doors. In an instant he was on the stage. It was as though fast movement was essential, he had a clipboard with a single sheet of typed paper on it.

The eighteen boys changed from nervous flippant conversation clusters to statues on the chairs, eyes riveted on the Sargeant..

"Listen up. The following applicants will leave to attend the pay office for travel warrants.

Appleton. Beresford, - "alphabetical order" Jolyon whispered, - Con - Jonny's face drained - stance, Gregory, Phillips, Reynolds and Uxbridge.

Seven faces crumbled into disappointment before putting on a brave face. Friendships that had formed over three days of stress immediately dissolved as they turned to leave the hall.

"All RAF kit and property must be left in the rooms." The Sargeant barked before descending the three wooden steps down from the stage without looking.

"Transport for the station will leave the gate at one o'clock." It was a throw away announcement made as he marched out.

Jolyon winked and smiled at Jonny as they sat down.

An Officer entered the room and everyone stood up.

"Congratulations. You've all just passed a test that will allow the Royal Air Force to really test you. Forget the glamour, this will be the hardest work you've ever done, everyday is a test, an examination. You will be scrutinized and looked at every minute of your waking day. Some of you will not like it. The

RAF will not like some of you but for those of you who make it you will join a very exclusive flying club. The best in the world. Your allotted flying instructor will become your God, your teacher and hopefully your friend. He will demand a hundred and ten per cent from you, any less and he will see through you in a second and you'll be collecting your travel warrants."

The officer had a moustache.

Chapter. 3

There were eleven left on the course. Jolyon and Jonny became close, sitting in adjacent chairs in the classroom, eating together, the conversation never dried up. They made each other laugh, became chums.

"Half term after next week, finish with the trusty Chipmunks, a few days in the classroom then onto the Provosts, a real jet, in my hands, can't believe it." Jolyon spoke as he pressed his trousers. The steam hissed and rose in the small room.

"Yep, solo next week if we're good enough." Jonny replied.

"Solo next week then." Jolyon looked into Jonny's eyes. "Don't be so negative Jonny, failure is not an option, especially in your case. I overheard one of the instructors saying how natural you were, said it was though your mind was above it all, that the mechanics of it all was just a formality, easily mastered, never forgotten."

"Don't like to be presumptuous."

"Tell you what, Father and Mother are having their twenty fifth wedding anniversary bash, it's a big event, Father's having one of the fields near the house re done with hard core for the marquees. Everyone's coming, circus acts, entertainers, music, the works and the food will be the best, Mother and Father don't do things by halves. Why don't you come?"

Jonny looked up from his navigation book.

"Think I'd be a bit out of place. Anyway mum would be really disappointed if I don't go home."

"Rubbish, Mother's invited all the estate gardeners and staff---
--------. There was a pause as Jonny immersed himself in the book again. "Sorry, I didn't mean that the way it came out. I meant---------."

"I know what you meant Jolyon, and it's Ok, You meant that there'll be people there who talk like me and need help at the dining table."

Jolyon put the iron down, went over and sat on Jonny's bed and turned the navigation book upside down.

"No, I mean you're my best friend, I've never had one before and I'd really like you to come."

The two young men looked at each other.

"I'll ring mum tomorrow and ask her if I can go."

The light metallic green Sunbeam Alpine exited the gates of Cranwell just a little too fast. It was four on Friday afternoon as the two joyous young men headed west towards Herefordshire bypassing Nottingham, loughborough, driving into the sunny evening as they navigated Birmingham for Worcester. The car thrust effortlessly through the summer air, stops were only for the toilet and to clear the screen of squashed insects.

"Let's stop at a pub for something to eat and drink." Jonny said as he fiddled with the tuning of the Pye radio.

"What are you searching for?"

"Radio Caroline."

"Doubt it you'll get that here, we can only just pick it up at Cranwell. Try radio Luxembourg."

"That's no good, it keeps fading in and out, I remember as a kid listening to Dan Dare, pilot of the future, must have been an omen, anyway he was always just about to kill the Mekon when it would fade away for two or three minutes, most frustrating."

"Sounds like the trusty 'home service' then."

"It's not trusty, it shuts down at seven. There's a pub, pull in, I'm starving."

"It's not a pub, it's a hotel. Look, The Raven Hotel, in big gold letters."

"It's black and white, so it must be a pub, do you think we should put the roof up?"
Jonny asked as they were getting out.

Jolyon stopped to look at his watch and thought..

"It's seven thirty Jonny, by the time we've eaten it will be nine thirty, by the time we get to Bovington it will be getting close to midnight. I suggest we stay here for the night, that is if they have a room."

"We'd better put the roof up then."

The dining room was large but uninspiring with round tables and straight back wooden chairs. There were nine people eating.

"I'm for the steak and ale pie with chips and peas. How about you Jonny?"

"That's a bit 'bohemian' Jolyon, thought you'd go for the Wye salmon and asparagus."

"You know me, a card carrying communist at heart."

"Rubbish, you speak too posh."

"I'm going to practice speaking un-posh when we go to visit your mum."

"I haven't invited you, she'd be really nervous if you turned up in our street in your snazzie car."

"It's not that snazzie, anyway you said you'd had a Mini-Cooper once. That's hardly dull and boring is it?"

"No." Jonny paused to look at the menu. "I'm going to have the salmon and asparagus with sautéed potatoes."

Jolyon looked at him from under his eyebrows.

The wine was mediocre but the dessert was delicious. Jonny settled for gooseberry pie with Cornish ice cream, Jolyon a bowl of strawberries with clotted cream.

"I'm glad we stopped, I'm feeling tired now after that meal and wine." Jolyon eased back the chair and placed his napkin on the table as they waited for coffee.

"And me, I'm just about ready for bed."

"Be strange won't it?"

"What?"

"Us sharing a bed." Jolyon downed the last of the wine.

"I suppose so, I've never slept in the same bed as anybody before, how about you?"

"Oh yes, brothers, sisters, when we were children."

"I haven't got any, it's always been my own room and my own bed."

"Shall we go up?" Jolyon stood up before Jonny answered. "Ask the receptionist where the room is."

It was up the wide creaking wooden stairs and then at the end of a long carpeted corridor on the right. It had a window that looked out onto the square where the car was parked. There was just one large double bed, a wardrobe, a dressing table and two dark oak chairs, the bathroom, complete with a very old enameled bath with green streaks underneath the taps led off to the left. The room was predominantly yellow with beige curtains.

Jonny used the bathroom then self consciously took off his clothes down to his underpants. It hadn't bothered him in their room at Cranwell but somehow this was different. Anyway he'd always worn pyjamas at Cranwell as the heating wasn't up to much and it was usually chilly. Now he was going to share a bed with Jolyon. He noticed how thin Jolyon was. He was right, he did eat very slowly, picking over his food even though in the end he ate all of it.

Jolyon slipped into the side of the bed by the window leaving Jonny the side nearest the bathroom. The sheets were crisp, clean and cool. There were old fashioned blankets, not the now fashionable duvet.

"What are we going to do tomorrow daytime?" Jonny asked from his side of the bed.

"Well we won't get there til lunch time, Fanny our cook will rustle up some sandwiches and some cider for us, I'll show you 'round the duck pond and garden then we'll have a nap so we're nice and fresh for the festivities which will probably start about six."

"Never had cider before."

"It's our own, Ted the gardener makes it from windfall apples from the orchard, be careful it's dynamite. Fanny will bring a big jug of it with our sandwiches, I'd recommend no more than one glass, it is very more-ish though. Don't worry you'll have your own bed tomorrow night, won't have to share with skinny Jolyon."

Jolyon put out his long left hand and squeezed his shoulder.

"Goodnight Officer Cadet Conrad."

"Goodnight Officer Cadet Clay." They both laughed. Within minutes the wine had worked.

Jolyon paid at the reception with a cheque.

"What's that." Jonny noticed Jolyon handing over a small plastic card with his cheque, the receptionist seemed unsure of what to do with it.

"It's a cheque guarantee card, my bank sent it to me, it's a new scheme, she writes the number of the card on the back of the cheque then it won't bounce even if there's not enough money in my account."

Jolyon didn't have to speak loudly; his cut glass voice somehow flooded the area with sound. The receptionist looked at the cheque, turned it over and copied the number.

"Thank you Sir, I hope you had a pleasant night. Coutts, I've never heard of that bank where is it?" She asked. She was a pretty girl about twenty but most definitely rural.

"London."

"Oh, I'll know in the future when we get guests from London." She giggled, finishing off with a smile at Jolyon.

"Not all people from London will bank there." He smiled back at her as they headed for the door.

"I haven't got a bank account, do you think I should bank there?"

"No." Jolyon started to unclip the roof of the Alpine.

It was the sort of summer morning when the clouds didn't matter, in fact although you could see them, they somehow didn't get in the way of the sun. The road out of Worcester towards Ledbury was a joy, it was as though everything was a colour matched backdrop to the sleek humming Sunbeam.

"Three quarters of an hour and we should be there." Jolyon spoke for the first time in the last thirty minutes but it didn't matter, both young men had been engrossed in the lush beauty of the 'Marches' countryside.

"Actually I'm a bit nervous about the whole business Jolyon, have you told your parents anything about me?"

"Only that you're my chum from the college. I know you Jonny, once you're amongst it you'll rise above it, you do with everything, I've watched you. It's as though you have this knowledge, this position, an unassailable position that no one else knows about or comes anywhere near."

"How on earth did you form that opinion?"

"No idea, but it's right isn't it?"

"Maybe."

"Do you want to tell me about it?"

"No. How many people will be there?"

"Not sure, two or three hundred I suppose. Mother and Father entertain a lot. Both of them were at Cambridge, that's where they met, so there's all their 'alumni' as it were plus all their families."

The road had now changed from one with a white line to a single track lane. The bulging summer hedgerows eager to scrape the car as it cruised by. Summer soft smells pushed their way around the fly stained windscreen. They approached a ninety degree right hand corner, on the left was a large duck pond that followed the road around the corner, The banks of the pond were of almost manicured short verdant green grass contained by a guard of lilies, rose bushes and spent daffodils. The ducks quacked, squabbled and explored their pond for the umpteenth time. Jonny was wondering if the ducks ever got bored with swimming about on the same pond when Jolyon swung the car into a low range of open brick and tile outhouses that led onto the rear of an imposing red brick mansion.

"Here we are, 'home sweet home'." A man in his sixties in working clothes came over to the now silent Sunbeam. He was smiling as he reached up to touch the peak of his cap.

"Good morning Mr. Jolyon, you had a safe journey here I see. No bumps on the way?"

"Morning Ted. No, all safe and sound, a few narrow scrapes in the lane but not a scratch on the Alpine."

"Leave the keys in it Sir, and I'll get young Anthony to give it a wash."

"Is Mother in?"

"She is, tell her I'll be in with the rhubarb in about ten minutes. And who's this with you? One of your flying chums?"

"Sorry Ted, this is Jonny, yes we're on the same course at Cranwell. Jonny this is Ted our gardener."

Jonny moved around the car and put out his hand. Ted looked directly into his eyes then took his hand. Jonny's hand was white, protected by the pigskin flying gloves, protected by the privilege his new position gave him. Ted's hand was brown, well not brown but a sort of faded red with small brown patches and white hairs. His fingernails were brown with soil.

"Pleased to meet you Sir. It's a big 'do' you're here for. Mr. and Mrs. Clay don't do things by 'alves. Leave your bags in the car, I'll get the boy to bring them to your room." His voice was old, the sort of rasping croak that comes with age.

Jonny had never been called Sir before. He wondered what his mum would think.

"Come on Jonny, I'll show you around before we go in."

Jolyon and Jonny walked back out to the road and followed it around the corner. Another road went off to the left after a cattle grid. The pond expanded up to the junction then gave way to summer meadows now transformed into a scene that was nearly a fairground. Several large marquees adorned with flags and pennants sat safely on newly graveled ground. People and vehicles were coming and going, delivering, fixing and preparing for the night's celebrations. Behind them were trucks with animals in them. Opposite the 'T' junction were the large black heavy iron gates of the house, on each of the stone pillars that supported the gates were large black metal sculptured Eagles pouncing with outstretched sharp claws and parachute wings. The gates were shut, but behind them could be seen the grand wide stone stepped entrance to Bovington Hall, a large light blue Mercedes crouched on the gravel in front of the steps.

"I see Father's home as well by the looks of things. Do you like it Jonny?"

Jonny looked at Jolyon.

"So one day all this will be yours?"

"Don't see it like that. As I see it I have to keep it safe, not lose it, not mess it up and then provide a male heir to hand it on to when I pop off. That's why Mother and Father hate me joining The RAF, I might get killed before I have a chance to squire an heir."

"Have you got anybody in mind to help you do that?"

"No, that may be a problem, not too keen on girls, much prefer aeroplanes, all that clothes, hair, make up stuff just to get a free meal ticket for life annoys me a bit."

"I don't think they see it like that Jolyon."

"I don't suppose they do but you have to admit they are obsessed with their hair. Women are always touching and fussing with their hair."

"How long has this estate been in your family?"

"Over five hundred years."

"Quite a while then,"

"Yes. Come on, let's get you settled in your room, it's listed but comfortable."

"What do you mean, listed?"

"There's a picture painted on the ceiling painted by some famous painter, can't remember who. As a result it's listed as of architectural interest, basically it's against the law to paint the ceiling in Magnolia."

Cars were beginning to arrive. They were carefully directed by a policeman wearing his helmet and big white gloves made even whiter by the bright summer sun, towards the hard-cored car park normally reserved for sheep. Cheeky new Mini's with fashionable young occupants, laughing, smiling and joking as they effortlessly alighted and headed towards the big black gates. Respectable Rovers, Humbers tailed by rakish MG's and a gleaming red E type Jaguar with the hood down and confident occupants slowed, then took their place, crunching the stone almost to gravel.

The backyard of Bovington Hall was large, soaked in sun and perfectly aged. It was bordered on three sides by a low range of open fronted buildings. A mottled terracotta tiled undulating heavy roof was supported by stout oak timbers emerging from red brick clumps every five yards. The back wall was the same ancient brick studied with hooks, nails, shelves and projections to put something on or hang something on in times gone by. Some of the bays had old farm machinery, some had a car, some had bags of feed, some had bails of hay. It was a comfortable barricade for the large house. This was Ted's domain, he knew where everything was.

Jolyon and Jonny climbed up the wide stone steps that led to a rear hall that still had a line of black bells on coiled flat springs. Some of the wires still seemed attached to the system whilst some were broken and detached, their pull wires going nowhere. The kitchen was off to the right, it was large, people were busy preparing food, delicious smells escaped into the hall.Ted followed behind carrying their two weekend bags. He deposited them on the floor of the hall, it wasn't his job 'inside', a maid would take them upstairs.

Jolyon opened the large dark oak brass knobbed door and waved Jonny in. Once inside Jonny stopped and stared. On the roof was the most marvellous rural picture he had ever seen. He knew nothing of art but marvelled at the colours, the shades, the shadows, the sheen of the sky. It was like looking at the real sky, how could anyone do that, ducks taking flight from half frozen water, brown bullrushes, frozen dead grass and that pale winter sun. He closed his eyes then opened them again, he could almost feel the winter chill. The walls were fielded light blue with a cream border, roses separated the two colours. A large English oak bed had carved wooden panel scenes from the book of Kells. The floor looked as though it was made from the same tree.

"The bed's a few years old Jonny so God knows what secrets it could tell." Jolyon laughed and pushed Jonny onto the bed, It was deliciously soft and comfortable, the linen sheets and woolen blankets smelt of the recent spring air. For a moment Jonny thought he was going to lie on the bed alongside him but a moment's hesitation saw Jolyon stride towards the tall arched window.

"You've got the best view in the house Jonny. I insisted you have this room, it was mine when I was a boy."

"Where are you sleeping Jolyon?" Jonny asked.

"Next door, we'll share this view." Jolyon looked at Jonny.

The view was of a fairground, all that was missing was a ferris wheel. Marquees, tents and big tops dominated the curious sheep and wondering cattle that were barred from the event by the 'ticking' single wire fence just over the cattle grid either side of the road. The backdrop, lush green pasture partitioned by summer full hedgerows and heavy trees.

"Have a rest, then ring for a maid to show you down, come and find me. I'll be around mingling, it's what I'm supposed to do. Rather be in a Jet Provost but hey duty calls."

"What do I wear?" It was a similar plea to the one at the dining table.

Jolyon looked at him.

"You look good in everything Jonny, before five casual, after five dress for dinner."

"Ok, thanks."

Jolyon left.

Jonny threw himself backwards onto the high sumptuous bed as the door clicked shut, He stared up at the ceiling marvelling at how the painter captured the reflection of the limp winter sun on the still, almost frozen water. He wondered what dad would make of this. Would he be proud of him moving into social circles where the elite danced or would he think he was being a traitor to his class. Maybe he'd talk to mum about it when they had a quiet moment together. It was almost silent, just a trickle of happy voices fell through the imperfect glass of the arched window along with summer sun rays that soothed him to sleep.

Then there was a knocking on the door as it opened.

"Time to go Jonny, official eating time is six thirty in the marquee on the left, so in the infamous words of some infamous sargeant 'hands off cocks, on with socks.'" Jolyon laughed.

"What time is it?"

"Five thirty, the maid has been in and unpacked your bag, your tuxedo has been hung and pressed, it's in the wardrobe, I'll read the paper whilst you shower and dress."

Jolyon epitomised comfortable elegance, his black dinner suit fitted perfectly, totally at ease with a cummerbund and winged tie, he slouched into the large winged chair and picked up one of the three newspapers tidily positioned on the small highly polished walnut table in the corner. Jonny hadn't noticed the newspapers.

Jonny was awkwardly aware of the slight bulge in his Marks and Spencers 'Y' fronts as he swung as quickly as he could from the bed and headed for the bathroom. He hoped Jolyon hadn't seen. He'd done nothing to cause it, it just happened in his sleep.

Jolyon had suggested he wore a cream tuxedo. He'd said he was the only person he knew who could carry it off other than James Bond. He'd paired it with a very pale lilac dress shirt, black tight trousers with a black silk side stripes and black patent leather shoes. A very dark red velvet bow tie finished the outfit. Jonny had baulked at the combination saying it was too gaudy but Jolyon was paying and he insisted, saying that his personality and strength demanded something that people would look at. Maybe he was right? He didn't know all these people, they weren't 'his type' of people, he'd never meet them again, it was just a fun weekend, what the hell. Jolyon said he could pay him back out of his flight lieutenant's salary when he was one, so that's what Jonny was determined to do. One day.

"Are we ready?"

Jolyon and Jonny hovered in front of the large front doors which were wide open. Jolyon's parents emerged from a corridor.

"Jonny this is my father Sir Baltimore Clay."

Jonny proffered his hand which was briefly but strongly shaken.

"So you're my son's flying friend, he's always going on about you. What do you think? Do you think he'll make it, whizzing around in those jet contraptions?"

It was a gruff, elderly but kindly voice that fitted the owner. Tall but now stooped, his face, once handsome, now deeply lined as though the smoke from cigars had curled up his flesh, only the eyes were free from age.

"Jolyon is a gifted aviator Sir. What's more he's a very good and caring person."

The final comment visibly registered with Sir Baltimore who raised his eyes to look directly into Jonny's.

"You're a very astute young man." Sir Baltimore reached out for Jonny's arm.

"Come, on with the show!"

Jolyon butted in.

"And this is my mother Lady Edwina Clay."

Jolyon turned to address the once beautiful but now gracious woman. He bowed his head.

"I can see where Jolyon's compassion comes from."

She looked at him then looked away.

"Flattery will get you everywhere young man." She almost giggled.

"Come, take my arm before we 'appear' I want everyone to think I've got a virile young handsome lover rather than this worn out gentleman."

"And who wore him out?" Jolyon whispered.

"Why me of course." She laughed.

A brass band instantly struck up the Nat King Cole song 'unforgettable' as they stepped through the door onto the wide sandstone steps into the evening light.

"Well Baltimore Clay, am I unforgettable?"

Sir Baltimore Clay looked at his wife of twenty five years.

"Unforgettable and irreplaceable." He tenderly kissed her on the left cheek and the watching crowd erupted.

"Now come on, do your duty make sure I don't fall over or say anything I shouldn't." They both laughed as they headed hand in hand towards the first step and the big marquee.

"Is there a seating plan?"

Jonny looked over at Jolyon and mouthed.

"Yes, You're on the top table with me, don't worry the top table is pretty big, family and close friends."

"I'm not family." Jonny mouthed again.

"We're flying brothers, stop worrying." Jolyon laughed.

"And you're my best friend." Jolyon added after a pause.

The marquee was very large but in the end it was just a large decorated tent. Then there was the inside.

Jolyon and Jonny walked in slowly, a few yards behind Baltimore and Edwina Clay. There were about three hundred people all standing behind their allotted chairs, all dressed as though they were stars in a movie. All along the left hand wall was a waterfall that torrented from the top to the bottom of the marquee, creating a shimmering moving translucent screen on which pictures of the Clays and their family slowly appeared then faded to another picture. Jonny became transfixed by the utter splendour of it.

"Keep walking." Jolyon hissed.

To the right was a solid wall of flowers that scented everything. Behind the top table were large pictures of Bovington Hall, the magnificent front gates, the family crest, the duck pond and the magnificent flowers that bordered it.

Mr. and Mrs. Clay stood momentarily behind their chairs waiting for the staff to pull them out then sat down. All the guests sat down as the silence gave way to murmurs and conversations. Waiters and waitresses appeared from nowhere with large bottles of champagne or large bottles of sparkling water. The show was on.

Jonny sat to the left of Jolyon, to his left sat a fat woman wearing too much makeup and a lot of jewelry, she smiled wanly before turning to the man on her left. The name card read Lady Sylvia Frogmore. Jonny wondered what her connection was and concluded that she or they were probably distant family.

"Need any help?" Jolyon whispered as he spotted Jonny staring at the place setting.

"Think I'm OK thanks." He whispered back.

"Canapés and potato Rosti with salmon and cream cheese or baked figs with cheese for starters. What would you like Jonny, I'm going for the salmon."

"Same as you." Jonny quietly replied as he sipped at the champagne flute.

"Good choice, they're delicious." His voice cut through the hubbub of soft noise and demanded an immediate response from the young nervous waitress.

"Yes Sir."

The food arrived within seconds. It astounded Jonny who stared at the plate. Served on exquisite almost translucent bone china the colourful floral pattern almost exactly matched the colour of the food, the food itself carefully positioned on the plate to correspond with the colours. It was almost a travesty to eat it. Jonny looked around, it was, as Jolyon had told him, they were all picking and fiddling with the food before almost nibbling at it. All the nibblers were thin. That was except for the fat lady to the left who consumed with gusto.

The champagne began to work as the murmurs developed into full blown conversations, laughter and guffaws. Soup, fish course then main, all served on colour matched china. Jonny, like all the other guests, now accepted the complex gastronomic presentations as normal. Dessert was freshly picked Herefordshire strawberries with Cornish clotted cream in a cut glass bowl, take it or leave it. Everybody took it.
The meal and it's after dinner speeches took three hours. At the end of the top table on his right, past Mr. and Mrs. Clay was a girl. Jonny was transfixed. It was as though she was the sun, the rest of the room simply a barren universe filled with dust. Everyone around her sparkled with her light, her life, just her.

Jolyon could not but notice his friends frequent, almost constant glances and outright looks.

"Calypso Fortnum, and before you ask, yes. Come on we're all retiring now to the Big Top to watch the circus acts." Jolyon tugged Jonny's sleeve. The fat lady was still eating chocolate éclairs that had just appeared.

"Yes what?" Jonny asked.

"Yes, Fortnum and Mason."

"Who or what is Fortnum and Mason?"

"Oh for Christ's sake Jonny." Jolyon glanced crossly at Jonny. "Suppliers of fine foods to the Royal Family, Tesco's for the Queen. Course they don't own it now, her great grandfather Charles sold out for a fortune which is still in the family. They also invented 'Scotch Eggs'."

"Never had a Scotch Egg."

"You've never had anything Jonny, that's what I love about you. I'll introduce you later on, you can ask her for one."

"She doesn't look typically English does she?"

Jolyon looked exasperatedly at Jonny.

"Think about her name Jonny, Calypso, it may give you a clue."

The big top was big, but still the champagne never ran dry. Now there was also Muscat De Rivesalte aperitif wine or port for those who preferred.

Jonny led Jolyon to a seat where he could see her, the clowns, the acts, the jugglers, the acrobats, the horses. The monkeys, the elephants. So incongruous to a Herefordshire pasture passed before his eyes but they were all eclipsed. The clapping and applause were just for her, the spotlight was for her but occasionally it strayed to other places. Jolyon noticed.

"Forget it Jonny, girls like her never marry out of class." Jolyon had jumped years ahead. Jonny looked at him.

"What on earth are you talking about?" He said as they and everyone else moved on to another large marquee where the dancing was going to happen. Jolyon prodded him in the back.

"Stick to aeroplanes my handsome friend, far less trouble and much cheaper." Jolyon laughed Jonny didn't.

Jonny couldn't dance. It took him back to Christmas dances at the social club, his dad and Reg playing in 'The Notes' Mum, so proud, looking at Dad, sitting behind Reg and handing him the different xylophone sticks and Frankie Fletcher. The last memory made him immediately switch back to now. The band were playing 'The Anniversary Waltz' as folk drifted in and found themselves seats. Waiters moved silently and discreetly around with the still available champagne, other stuff and cigars. Groups congregated in comfortable seated clusters as the varnished beech wood dance floor waited for Baltimore and Edwina Clay. The guests burst into spontaneous applause as they appeared and moved as one to the Cole Porter foxtrot 'Begin the Beguine'. After a few minutes another couple ventured out onto the floor then the floor was full with splendid couples.

Jonny turned to Jolyon but he wasn't there. His searching eyes spotted him dancing with Calypso, laughing, smiling, totally at ease with each other as they moved around to the music.

'Of course Jolyon could dance. Why wouldn't he?' He thought. Jonny's eyes were glued to them or rather her as he took another sip of the port and lemon. Port and lemon was mum's favourite drink but she only had it on special occasions. Since dad died he couldn't remember one. He'd had two glasses of champagne and that felt enough so it was mainly lemonade. Jolyon was on his second bottle of 'Moet'.

Sir Baltimore came over and sat at the small table.

"Are you enjoying it young man?"

"Yes Sir, I can honestly say I've never experienced anything like it in my life."

Jonny found it difficult pretending to give Sir Baltimore his full attention distracted, drawn to glance at her like a magnet. God, she didn't move, she was liquid, she poured herself into the music. Her dark long hair in ringlets that seemed to cascade around her face and frame it, no matter what she did. Her mouth, simply the balance to her eyes that lit up everything.

"Pretty isn't she?"

Jonny , embarrassed at being so transparent, acknowledged him.

"Sorry Sir, very rude of me."

"Lady Edwina and I were like that at your age, don't ignore it young man, do something about it. You know Jolyon's only dancing with her so he can bring her over and introduce you. I'm a little worried Jolyon's more interested in flying contraptions and other things rather than doing his duty as it were."

Jonny looked directly into the kindly eyes of Sir Baltimore. There was an unspoken understanding.

"I'm sure Jolyon knows exactly what his duty is Sir and I've no doubt he'll do it."

"I hope you're right Mr. Jonny, I do hope you're right. Now get rid of that pop and have a whisky, it's good stuff, not cheap, single malt, single barrel, none of your mixed rubbish." He clicked his fingers at a waiter and within seconds a chunky square glass clunked onto the table. It's contents pale and clear and so smooth to the taste. Like nothing he'd ever tasted before.

"Look after my boy young Jonny, he's not in the same world as you." With that Sir Baltimore moved on.

The whisky made the lights change her skin from olive to gold, made her smile spread all over her body. Made her body ------------. They'd stopped dancing. They were coming back to the table. Jonny stood up as they approached.
Jolyon seemed unaffected by the champagne.

"Jonny, this is------."

"Calypso. I know." He offered his hand and she took it but not in a handshake more of a clasp. She was so beautiful. Their eyes met for far longer than was required.

"And your name is?" Her voice was like wet silk that poured over his ears and suffocated them before it entered his head forever.

"Jonny, Jonny Conrad."

"And are you a flying boy like my Jolyon here?"

"We're both hoping to be RAF pilots, yes."

"Are we going to stand up forever?" She giggled.

"Sorry! Sorry! Please." Jonny gestured for her to sit down. She pulled the chair closer to Jonny and a little away from Jolyon. Her dress was deep red satin. It was simple, as though a loose second skin.

"What can you do Jonny?" She turned her body to face him. He couldn't focus on any part of her. It was almost an ephemeral force that hit him, knocked him back then left him searching for words.

"I, I can fly a chipmunk and play a saxophone." She laughed and put out her hand to touch his knee.

"Would that be a small furry animal or something else?"

"It's a small silver aeroplane."

"And the saxophone?"

"I used to play in a small dance band called 'The Ten Bob Notes.' "

"Do you dance Jonny?"

"No, I can't dance." She looked out from under her long eyelashes.

"You can play a saxophone in a dance band but you can't actually dance."

"Never tried. Never met anyone I wanted to dance with." His eyes silently said 'until now'.

"Can't have that, I'm going to teach you." She took his hand for the second time. This time she didn't let go. Jonny followed his hand. The whisky eased his passage but did nothing for his knowledge of dancing. The circulating relatives and friends from his boyhood memories seemed to do it with ease, surely it can't be hard. The band started up with 'The Tennessee Waltz'.

"Now, a Waltz is easy, just one two three, when I move back you move forward, when I move forward you move back." She took his right hand with her left. "Put your arm around my waist." She paused and looked into his close face. "And don't let go - ever!" Eyes locked for an age then she broke away with a giggle. "Come on - here we go." Jonny floated into another world.

Time just disappeared, the music was inconsequential, the 'other' world was just a backdrop.

"We should go back and mingle. They'll think I'm selfish keeping you all to myself." She quietly said, in his arms and looking into his eyes.

"Think it's the other way 'round, there's a lot of eyes following you."

She gently bit his lower lip, he could taste her.

"But I only have eyes----- for you---- dear." laughing as she quietly sang.

"How come you have such an exotic name?" Jonny whispered close to her ear.

"Mummy and Daddy honeymooned in the Caribbean, you can guess the rest."

"Didn't it matter? Cause a storm? Cause a divorce?"

"Of course not, silly." She laughed. "Our type never divorce, there are far more important things than the odd bit of sex to worry about."

"And what exactly is 'your type'?"

"Daddy says we run the world but we have to manage it, you know, make sure the right government runs the country and they do as they're told."

" 'If I ruled the world, every day would be the first day of spring, every heart would have a new song to sing.' "

Calypso put two fingers gently to his lips.

"There you go, three things, fly a chipmunk, play a saxophone and sing." She laughed and led him back to their seats. Jonny would follow her anywhere.

It was two a.m. the dance floor was beginning to thin out, lights were coming on in the car park and upstairs in the house. Jolyon was nowhere to be seen.

"Would you like to see the listed ceiling in my room?"

Her eyes widened before her face dissolved into a glorious smile.

"Well I have to admit Jonny, that's an original, I'd love to see your listed ceiling. Shall we go now?"

"We'd better thank and say goodbye to our hosts."

Jonny grasped her hand as she stood up, together, hand in hand, they made their way over to the corner table where Sir Baltimore and Lady Edwina were chatting with friends.

"Excuse us Sir," Sir Baltimore broke away from his conversation to look at Jonny and Calypso.

"We're going to retire, thank you so much for a wonderful evening ------."

"Not so fast young man." Sir Baltimore clicked his fingers at a waiter for two more whiskies. "Sit for a moment and drink this, it'll stiffen you up and you may need it."

His eyes travelled between the two young people as his smile conveyed a message.

"Where's my beautiful boy? You know they're always your children whatever their age. Never make the mistake of talking to them as though they're rational adults, they're always children." He laughed as he sipped at the whisky. "How about your father young Jonny what does he say?"

"My father's dead Sir and I haven't seen Jolyon for a while. " There was a momentary silence. Calypso glanced at Jonny.

"Sorry to hear that. Does it still hurt?"

"It was a few years ago, but yes it does, though I did take steps at the time to address it."

"Good, I can see you're the positive type, I hope we get a chance to talk further. Don't forget your promise to look after my boy."

"I didn't realise I'd promised Sir."

"Oh yes, it came just after you'd downed the first whisky." Sir Baltimore watched the happy couple leave the marquee moving with the ease of youth, then glanced at Edwina. 'Twenty five years' he thought to himself. 'Where has it gone?'

Jonny opened the door for her.

"Wow! She circled into the room, her loose dress almost an adoring fan to her perfect body, following it around in an obsessive way. Jolyon couldn't take his eyes away from her for an instant. It was hot in the room, Bovington Hall was not used to heat.

"Lets take all our clothes off and lie totally naked next to each other and look up at the ceiling.

Jonny had never seen or been with a naked woman before, in an instant she was lying on the bed, the weight of her shape only slightly disturbing the bedding. She didn't care about him standing close by staring at her.

"Come on! It's wonderful, it makes you feel cooler, I can almost touch the ice on the water."

Jonny undressed, copying her and just leaving his clothes where they fell, discarded and not needed. Calypso moved up so that he could lie next to her. His large erection expected and ignored as they both looked up at the winter scene above them.

"How does anybody do that?"

"Do what?" She responded.

"Get the colour of the sky, the sun, the clouds so perfect."

"It's a gift Jonny. You're my gift. The biggest and most important gift in my life. You will always be my love but I can never marry you. I'll marry Jolyon, or someone like him because that's what we do, keep it in the family so to speak."

She said this prophecy staring at the ceiling then propped herself up on one elbow to look at him, with her right hand she took hold of him and felt his hardness.

"Now fuck me, make me pregnant if you like, it doesn't matter. Just fuck me and make me yours."

She rose like a fluttering fairy with the sun, barely disturbing the sheets as she slipped out from underneath. Jonny stil smelt of whisky and was deep in useless sleep as she kissed him and tripped silently out of the big old room.

It was ten thirty or thereabouts when Jonny opened his eyes, it took a while to return to the here and now but when he did he reached out for Calypso. She had gone. Just gone, or gone from his life? He'd never had a hangover before, he'd never done that before. He didn't want to do it with anyone else but her and now she was gone. Thoughts and emotions swirled 'round his resting head competing with a thumping headache. An attempt to get up was abandoned.

Jolyon knocked and entered without waiting. He was washed and shiny in clean clothes looking as though he'd simply drank orange juice all night.
"Hey Pilot Cadet Conrad, time to reach for the sky, or at least put your socks on." He sat on the bed. "Where's Calypso?"

"No idea, one moment we were naked studying the ceiling, the next she's disappeared."

"That's Calypso, takes you to the top of the mountain then leaves you there." Jolyon laughed.

"Have you been to the top of that mountain?" Jonny groggily asked.

"Good lord no, far too perfect for me."

"What is for you Jolyon?"

"Come on, shower, shave and lunch before we hit the road."

Jonny tried another question.

"What happened to you last night, no sign of you after eleven?

Jolyon considered it.

"Met a very interesting man, Cambridge of course, he now works for the Foreign Office on the Russia and China desk, very knowledgeable chap, especially about Socialism and Communism we talked for hours. Marxism, Lenin, Stalin, all that stuff"

"What was his name?"

Burghouse, Gerry Burghouse, he gave me his address in London."

Jolyon looked at Jonny as he struggled naked out of the big bed, reaching the bathroom in four big hurried steps, conscious of his company.

Already the big top was down, vehicles and people swarmed over the site dismantling the dream.

The shower made him look better even if he didn't feel it, his youth shone through. Jolyon had brought him some suitable casual clothes from Huntsman's then insisted he wore Church's shoes. He'd asked for the bill several times but Jolyon never produced it.

Jolyon was dozing on the bed looking up at the painting.

"OK I'm ready." Jolyon opened his eyes and inspected Jonny.

"Well don't look so stiff and uncomfortable, relax, slouch about a bit, they're meant to be casual clothes not a bloody uniform."

"They feel like a uniform, an Officer's uniform, I'd never wear a tie on a Sunday morning."

"You are an Officer Jonny, or at least you will be soon, get used to it."
Jonny looked directly at his friend.

"I have no money Jolyon, my Dad was an iron foundry labourer."

Jolyon came close and put his hand's his shoulders. His face was inches away from Jonny's.

"Perfect for a modern Officer, grounded with exceptional abilities." He looked deep into Jonny's eyes before breaking away with a laugh.

"Come, Mother and Father are expecting us in the dining room for lunch."

"Really, do you know Where Calypso is?" Jonny asked.

"God knows, she's just a mirage Jonny, a shimmering hot mirage. Forget her."

Maids fussed around the end of a long polished table. Sir Baltimore and Lady Edwina sat at the end picking at a selection of sandwiches with no crusts on. Another plate presented a large pork pie, cherry tomatoes and a small dish of English mustard. The room housed four large arched windows, a series of descendants portraits in oil on the inner wall and a huge marble fireplace.

"Are! Our pilots have landed. Come! Come! Sit and try this pork pie, it's from Hancocks in Monmouth. The best! How do you feel young Jonny?"

Sir Baltimore was smiling as he delivered his question.

"I think I should have stuck with the Port and Lemon Sir."

"Stuff and nonsense, you just need more practice with the whisky, it has to be exactly the correct amount of water then it's OK. There's a bottle in your bag. Now relax and tuck in, you'll feel better after some food."

A maid proffered orange juice or plain water, Jonny nodded towards the water. Jolyon the Orange Juice.

"Before you ask Calypso left for home very early this morning she asked me to convey her apologies." Lady Edwina said as she reached for a sandwich.
Jonny glanced over to Jolyon, unsure whether or not to ask. He got no affirmation from Jolyon.

"May I ask where is Miss Calypso's home?"

Sir Baltimore replied after glancing at his wife.

"Southern Ireland, she left by helicopter for Luggala, County Wicklow, It's part of the Guinness empire, her mother married into it. Bit of a wild card that one young Jonny, mind you don't crash your aeroplane daydreaming."

"I'll try to stay aloft, above the clouds of romance Sir." Jonny lied, reaching for some pie.

"You drive Jonny, I'm still a little tired from last night."

"Were you up all night then?"

"Yes."

The journey back to Cranwell was mainly in silence and uneventful. The day was balmy, the comfortable car cruised effortlessly, Jolyon dosed fitfully in the passenger's seat. Jonny remembered the way back but his mind wandered, hopelessly lost somewhere between Mom and Dad, an outside lavatory with his pet tortoise hibernating in his box and a helicopter whisking over the Irish Sea to an Irish mansion. A song sprang into his head.

Hey there, you on that high flying cloud
Though she won't throw a crumb to you.
You think one day, she'll come to you."
"Better forget her,
Her, with her nose in the air,

She has you dancing on a string, break it, and she won't care.

He couldn't remember the title of the song. Then suddenly the lights changed to green, there was a furious 'tooting' behind. Jolyon opened his eyes then closed them again as they moved off.

Yes, he'd forget her, being a pilot was far more exciting.

Chapter. 4

The Squadron Leader had a moustache. He was thin with an immaculate uniform. There was no introduction.

"Some of you may have noticed that Chipmunks have a propeller and Jet Provosts do not." The clarity and precision of his voice exactly matched his sarcasm.

"Chipmunks go slow enough to allow you to open the canopy and jump out, hopefully with a parachute should you have forgotten to put any petrol in the tank. However. Jet Provosts are considerably faster and will not allow you to do so without killing yourself and, considering the amount of money Her Majesty's Government has already spent on you, death is not a desirable outcome. Consequently Provosts are fitted with two Martin Baker Ejection Seats. These are excellent devices, British made, and thus extremely reliable. They will whisk you out of your cozy aircraft very quickly should you need to go to the toilet or in any other emergency." His tone softened.

"Tomorrow chaps you will do a dummy run on our dummy seat up a ramp very quickly and back down again more slowly. Good luck."

The Squadron Leader left and after a pause conversations began.

"Are you nervous about tomorrow?" Jolyon was lying on his bed with his hands behind his back, the window was open to an orange sleepy summer sun that was soon to disappear.

"Not really, I'm a fatalist, what will be will be. Look at it logically, as he said, the Airforce has spent a lot of money on us so far so they're hardly aiming to finish us off on an ejection seat ramp, anyway I've heard they only use a single low powered cartridge, not five cartridges like the real thing."

"Suppose you're right, I'll be glad when it's over."

"Apparently if you eject for real and survive Martin Baker give you a certificate and a tie." Jonny spoke looking up from a Jet Provost flight manual.

"I've got plenty of ties, I don't need another." Jolyon laughed.

"In the latest planes, Lightning's and Harriers the seats are rocket assisted, supposed to be less dangerous for your back."

"Think it's the 'and survive' bit that's the worry."

"As I said, what will be will be."

Jonny turned the manual upside down on the table and watched the setting sun. everything beautiful made him think of her.

Ten young men in olive green flying suits carrying silver helmets clambered into the rather tired looking Bedford fourteen seater bus and sat almost in silence as it ground it's way around the perimeter track to the other side of the airfield. Jonny sat next to Jolyon on the dark blue shiny bench seat. The steel gantry got significantly higher as they got closer. At the bottom were three instructors dressed in brown dust coats and one officer in a blue serge tank top and beret. A cold grey wind whipped across the grass bending each blade. Occasional specks of rain were in the wind.

The Officer spoke.

"Good morning Gentleman, as you are aware this morning we are going to give you the experience as near as we can, to what it is like to eject from a jet aircraft. First of all do any of you have any physical impediments or reason as to why you should not do this?"

No one spoke.

"Good, now you're all familiar with the release mechanism of the harness, twist and hit, yes?" everybody nodded.

"OK, this is a low powered rig. We use this old faithful MK4 model seat with only one cartridge in the gun. However you will hit the buffer at the top which is thirty five feet high, don't worry we bring you down slowly." The officer attempted humour but it fell flat, nobody laughed as it was cold and people were nervous."You're all familiar with strapping in procedure and the ejection procedure." He looked around at the ten nodding faces. "At the command Eject! Eject! Eject! Use the top handle and pull it firmly down over your helmet and face. Obviously in real life you have the option of pulling the handle between your legs up but here we're just going to use the top handle. Make sure your head is firmly back against the headrest, whatever you do don't look down, look straight ahead. Even at this low velocity it is possible to damage your neck. The leg restraint system is connected and will work so you will feel what it is like to have your legs pulled tightly into the seat. The drogue gun system and barostat release mechanisms are disabled. Any questions?" He looked around at the apprehensive white faces. "There's no cartridge in the main firing unit at the moment. Perfectly safe now let's have the first victim, - sorry - volunteer." Once again the humour fell flat.

Nobody wanted to be the first.

"Come on Jonny, show us how it's done." Jolyon gave Jonny a playful shove forward. Jonny glowered.

"A willing volunteer, that's what I like. Come on young man sit in and make yourself comfortable, your sponsor here can strap you in." The Officer designated Jolyon by putting his hand on his now damp shoulder.

"Make sure the straps are tight. Don't want him falling out." The Officer checked them then reached for the brass cartridge and the clockwork firing mechanism. In the unit was a spring clip safety pin with a bright red tag saying 'Main Sear.

Jonny sat still looking straight ahead as he heard the brass cartridge clunk into the breach of the telescopic gun and the Officer screwing in the firing mechanism. His body was very close to Jonny's face as he connected up the wire cable to the sear.

"Feel OK young man?"

"Yes Sir."

"Right, the next thing you will hear will be my command. You will pull the handle, there will be a three second time delay as the unit winds down and then you'll be on your way. Do you understand?"

"Yes Sir." Jonny repeated. The nervous group stepped back several faces and waited.

"Eject! Eject! Eject!" Jonny yanked down the top handle with both hands, the canvas panel covered his helmet and visor keeping his head back against the rest. There was a whirring and then a bang then he was high in the air, his feet pinned to the front of the seat, the rig swaying slightly in the wind. Below him faces were craned, staring up, an electric motor took his weight then lowered him slowly to the ground.

"Obviously in real life the harness would release from the seat, the seat would fall away and you would now be dangling pleasantly on the end of a parachute wondering what colour Martin Baker tie to choose. Any questions?"

No one responded.

The officer turned to Jolyon.

"Now, seeing as you were so keen to volunteer your chum, you can be next Cadet -------?"

"Clay Sir. Cadet Clay."

"Right Cadet Clay, hop in, your chum can strap you in."

The Officer moved away to the box of cartridges. Jonny noticed at the bottom of the rig was a metal box with spare sear safety pins. Jonny took one and quickly put it in his pocket. Jolyon noticed.

Cadets who had 'been up' were allowed to sit in the bus, reluctant cadets got cold standing around waiting their turn outside.

"What did you take that safety pin for?" Jolyon whispered to Jonny in the confines of the rapidly steaming up bus.

"Thought it would look interesting on my car keys. I like the red, it's sort of metallic."

"You haven't got a car."

"I'm going to get one."

"What are you going to get?"

"A Mini Cooper 'S', red with a black roof so the key fob will match."

"When are you getting it?"

"When I've got enough money, and thank you but no." Jonny preempted his friend's coming offer.

The bus engine fired up as the last, rather white looking chap clambered up the aluminium clad steps.

"Lunch time. I'm really hungry, how about you?"

"It's Friday so it's fish."

"And chips." Jolyon added.

It was the smell that excited, it meant glamour, power and the future, even if in reality it was just burnt paraffin with a fancy name. The little jet crouched on the hardstanding. Though it was long cold the smell enclosed it and crept out of everywhere. Jonny and his new instructor, a retired pilot, walked out towards aircraft number two eight eight. It was nine in the morning on a cloudy summer's day. Jolyon and his instructor were further down the line. The course, now down to ten, had fidgetted nervously in the briefing, with false smiles and bravado, now they were all trying not to forget any of the pre-flight checks.

Jonny tried not to appear like a 'rookie'. He'd watched the class before touching, shaking, tapping, kicking and peering but there was no other way to do it. Look down every orifice for stuff, move every control surface, check all opening panels are properly shut. Are the tyres up? Are there any leaks? Glance at your instructor for tacit permission to get in. This was it. Jonny's first flight in a jet. Dad would have been so proud of him. His mind wandered to when Dad used to come home on his bike, dirty and tired. Mum would have his hot water and clean clothes ready, then he'd eat and settle in his chair by the fire to doze.

The instructor's kindly calm voice cut through his memories and into his earphones in the helmet.

"Ok Jonny, I'll do everything to get us airborne then you can have a little go. I'll tell you everything I do so try and remember the sequence of what I do. OK?"

"Yes Sir,"

"And Jonny I'm not an Officer so when we're in the air it's Tim and when we're on the ground it's Mr. Barnes, OK?"

Jonny turned to look at Tim.

"Yes Tim, thank you."

"Right Jonny let's get going. The static pre flight in cockpit checks are?"

There was an aura of peace and tranquility in the cockpit, the clouds below them allowed glimpses of England. Jonny thought it all looked so 'rural', towns and villages looked so small, fields went on forever, uneven squares on a multi coloured board game. Jonny had been at the control for ten minutes, correcting the unseen undulations with tender precision.

"Have you done any flying before the RAF young Jonny?"

"No Sir, sorry, Tim."

"Can you drive a car?"

"Yes."

"Did you pass your driving test at the first go?"

"Yes."

"Thought so. Now try and turn us one hundred and eighty degrees to head back for home, try to bank gently to port, don't overbank, you'll need a bit more power to get us 'round so push the throttle forward just a touch. ------------- beautiful. You have a delicate touch Jonny. You'll be fine."

Chapter. 5

Let's go down to London next weekend Jonny, Gerry Burghouse has invited me down, I'm sure he wouldn't mind another guest. He's a bit of a scruffy fellow but a brilliant mind and such an amusing conversationalist."

"From your eulogising about the chap I'm sure he would mind another guest, anyway I've promised to go home and visit mother, I haven't seen her for four months."

"Oh, can I come home with you?"

Jonny looked over at Jolyon, they were lounging in the restroom not due to fly til two o' clock, after lunch.

"What about Gerry?"

"Oh he can wait, he invites me every weekend anyway, your Mom's sounds much more interesting."

"Well it's not. Poor people don't do interesting things, they can't afford it."

"I want to come Jonny, I want the opportunity to experience something real."

"I'll ask her."

It was Friday, although a normal learning / flying day somehow Fridays felt different, happier, everybody looked forward to friends and family time. For Jonny there was an obstacle, Tim had scheduled him in for his first solo. He was the first of the ten students. There had been no real problems during the twenty flying hours leading up to this day. All he had to do was take off, one circuit then land again. The problem would be not making a break for the open skies once he was up there, on his own, free as a bird, he laughed inside at his dangerous clichéd thoughts. Do that and he'd be packing his bag for home, Mom would secretly be glad Dad, wherever he was, would be disappointed.

"What time do you want to leave?" Jolyon quizzed him as he was climbing into his flying overall.

"My flight's scheduled for ten, I'm free all afternoon, how about you?"

"I'm the same, got a two hour slot this morning then we can fly - excuse the pun."

"OK let's aim to leave at three." Jonny suggested.

"Are you nervous? Are you OK hot shot?" Jolyon looked up at Jonny as he was doing up his boots.

"Yes I'm fine, I'm more nervous about introducing you to Mom, especially with your cut glass posh voice, she'll probably curtsey or something."

"Hey best friend, good luck up there." Jolyon patted Jonny's back as he left the locker room.

Tim and an Officer accompanied Jonny to Provost two eighty eight. It sat there on the hard shoulder like a little puppy waiting to be petted and looked at. Jonny launched into the now routine pre flight checks, touching, moving and inspecting, the list ran through his head. A discreet nod from Tim meant 'get in'. A ground crew man helped strap him in, then, on Jonny's say so, removed the three pins from the seat, pushing them carefully and visibly into their storage block, The crewman was a lot older than Jonny, he could see acceptance of life in the man's eyes. This workaday routine was the pinnacle for him. Jonny's circling finger indicated he was going to start up the engine. It felt strange with no one sitting beside him, as though the plane was unbalanced. He wasn't nervous, this was just something to be done, in fact pushing the throttle forward and releasing the brakes gave him such a feeling of power and control. The puppy would jump into the air when he decided it would.

"Hope you've not dragged me out of my office for nothing Tim." Group Captain Peter Truscott was the camp commandant of Cranwell. Cadets rarely got to see him, let alone meet him. To them he was just a ceremonial icon on a parade ground.

"Never had one as natural as this one Sir, seems to somehow know how hard you can push something mechanical, has an empathy for the machine."

"What's his name?"

"Jonny, Jonny Conrad."

"Family?"

"Working class, eight straight 'A' levels from a comprehensive school. A mother but no father, apparently he died a few years ago. Here we go have a look at his landing."

Tim Barnes handed over a small pair of binoculars to the Commandant.

"Ummmm. As you say Tim, perfect, tell Eileen to mark his records 'possible fast jet potential' don't tell him of course."

Peter Truscott turned away and headed back to his office.

The circuit was easy, the lighter weight seemed to make the provost handle differently, just a micro quicker, more eager to please. Within minutes the blackened landing pad was looming up to caress the wheels. As he braked the plane to a halt and killed the engine he could see everyone on the ground was smiling and chatting. He knew it was a pass.

Chapter. 6

"Hood up or down?" Jolyon asked, looking out of the window.

"Oh hood down, every time, people need to see me." Jonny joked.

"Jonny, it's my car, I'm the driver, it's me they need to see."

"Can you fly a Jet Provost on your own? No!" Jonny answered his own question. Jolyon threw a shoe at him.

"Good grief Jonny, are you sure we don't need a police escort going into an area like this?"

"You wanted reality Jolyon, this is it for the working classes." Jolyon's eyes were everywhere except on the immediate road ahead as they entered Casey Lane. A 'bookies' on the corner had large shop windows painted out in dark blue. Men, mostly wearing flat caps and smoking, hung around outside. There were no women but there were two black men talking and laughing. There was a long ugly brick wall on the left, some of it rendered in dirty, sandy cement with cemented broken glass along the top. Behind the wall sprouted the tops of sheds and some pigeon coops, their occupants flying around in fast groups before homing in for food.

"Steady, turn right here." Jonny instructed.

The shiny, silvery green opulent car was out of place in Henry Street. There weren't many other cars parked in the narrow street. It was just two facing rows of small red brick terraced houses with dark narrow entry's giving access to the unkempt little squares of dirt that masqueraded as gardens. Just enough room to tie up a crazed dog, or a ramshackle shed with budgerigars in it. Beyond that was an outside toilet and a roofed 'hole' for the dustbins.

Parked in the Street was a blue Ford Corsair, highly polished but with rust on the wings, a black Ford Poplar, a red French Panhard, a grey Austin Westminster with a red stripe and a black Standard Ten. Outside the house opposite Jonny's was a large black Velocette Venom on the pavement, tucked in close to the wall under the window so folk could still get by on the pavement. Five noisy, excited boys were undecided whether to play, knobs, marbles or cigarette cards, in the end it was marbles. Four of them were 'smoking' pretend sweet cigarettes, their knees and the toes of their shoes scuffed and dirty as they knelt on the pavement.

"Here it is, number forty seven." It was identical to number forty six and forty eight, a dark green door and front window with net curtains. The entry ran between forty six and forty seven giving access to forty eight and forty five.

Jolyon pulled over and parked. The two young men sat for a moment as the five boys and three gossiping women stared at them.

"Think we'd better put the hood up Jonny, get the bags out of the boot and give me a hand."

Jonny frowned. Jolyon understood.

"Sorry, it's this environment, brought out the very worst in me."

"No, It's the way things are and that's it. I'll get the bags, you put the hood up."

"Yes Sir!" They both laughed.

"I take it your Mum knows we're coming?"

"No, it's a surprise."

By now several more women had appeared on doorsteps. The car and their clothes set the young men apart, something special, rich men in a poor neighbourhood. Something of interest. Jonny knocked on the front door.

"Haven't you got a key Jonny?"

"Yes."

A fat lady with grey blue rinse curly permed hair, red rimmed plastic glasses and a floral pinny opened the door.

"Hello Mum."

Her face just dropped before almost bursting into a huge joyful smile.

"Jonny, Jonny! What are you doing here? Why didn't you tell me? Look at me in my pinny, not even a puff of powder on my face and my hair a mess."

"You look wonderful Mum, this is Jolyon my friend from Cranwell, i've told you about him in my letters. Are you going to let us in or have we got to stand here all day?"

Irene gave her son a long hug before turning to Jolyon with her outstretched hand.

"Come in, Come in, so very nice to meet you. Jonny's always mentioning you in his letters."

Jolyon shook Irene's hand, it was warm, soft and plump. By now the boys had given up their game and were clustered around Jolyon's car, stroking the smooth metal body and feeling the fabric of the hood. Jolyon glanced at them from under his eyebrows and they backed away.

"Very nice to meet you Mrs Conrad."

"Call me Irene, or 'Mum' if you like."

"I've never called anyone 'Mum' before."

Irene gave him a quizzical look.

"It's always Mother and Father." Jolyon's voice confirmed the reason why. Irene didn't need to ask.

"I'll call you Mum then." Jolyon laughed.

The small front room wasn't used much. It was cool even on a sunny summer day. Decorated with traditional wallpaper the walls were simply a nondescript backdrop for photos of Arthur and Jonny. They hung from three of the four walls, the fourth was the front wall with the large sash cord window alongside the front door giving no room for photos. A large dark wood sideboard also displayed photos. There were two different easy chairs facing the small fireplace. Cream painted built in cupboards either side of the chimney breast contained family stuff and a few bottles of whisky. Arthur liked a dram now and again, it was untouched since he'd passed on. Along the inside wall was a brown velour settee, In front of the window was a small table covered by a lace cloth, the telephone and an Airfix Gloster Javelin model were on the table. The front nose wheel had fallen or been knocked off, it was carefully positioned underneath the clear plastic stand. Waiting for Jonny to fix it back on.

"Come through, come through, it's cold in here. I've got the fire on in the kitchen to take the chill off." Irene was all of a fluster.

The kitchen was small but it sufficed for Arthur, Jonny and her, now only her. A small drop leaf table backed up to the understairs pantry. The stairs and the pantry divided the front from the back. There was a white Belfast sink under the window with a cold tap and a Gas miser water heater on the wall to the left of the window. One bar of a two bar electric heater glowed cherry red in the corner.

"Sit down! Sit down! Irene went through back into the front room to get a third chair. Jonny noticed that she looked fatter than the last time he'd seen her, her face looked whiter and puffy. It made her eyes look smaller. Both her knees were now bandaged with varicose veins escaping from the bandages.

"Now, you must be famished, what can I get you?"

"A sandwich will be fine Mum, we had a big breakfast before we came." Jonny said.

"A bread and dripping sandwich if you've got one Mum." Jolyon relished calling her 'Mum', it felt so safe.

Irene looked at him.

"Since when have posh folk eaten bread and dripping?

Jolyon didn't deny being 'posh'.

"Since Jonny gave me one. Plenty of brown jelly and salt please." They all laughed.

The sandwiches, cakes, tea and conversation went on well into the afternoon, every so often Irene would nip into the front room and peep around the net curtain to check on Jolyon's car.

"I'd cook you some nice tea but I've arranged to go to bingo tonight at the 'Legion'.with Mavis from next door but one. If I'd known you were coming I'd have cancelled but it's a bit rude if I don't go now."

"We'll come with you." Jolyon instantly responded, not giving Jonny a say. "In fact we'll take you there in my car."

Irene beamed.

"Don't be silly, Bingo's are for old folk, not for the likes of you."

"I'd love to come, never gambled on anything before in my life."

"Well it's hardly gambling, Bingo at the British Legion with a load of old women."

"Can't think of anything else I'd rather do." Jolyon smirked at Jonny. "Can I have another cake Mum?"

Irene reached for the tin with the butterfly sponges when a knock came at the back door.

"It'll be Veronica." Laughed Irene as she struggled up from her chair. "She can't resist it. She's guessed it's Jonny and can't wait any longer. She's had a crush on him since he was eight. Tried to kiss him once, he rushed in and dashed upstairs in hell of a state. Very funny for all of us, except Jonny here." She put her hand on her son's shoulder.

Irene called out.

"Come in Veronica."

"How did you know it was me?" She said as she came in through the door. Her eyes immediately settled on Jolyon and then moved to Jonny.

Jolyon stood up but Jonny remained seated.

"You look well Jonny, all that RAF food must be doing you good. Who's your handsome friend?"

Veronica had changed since Jonny had last seen her, gone was the really annoying girl next door who was always pestering him. Here was a confident young woman.

Jonny had to stand up.

"Veronica, this is Jolyon Clay, my roommate from Cranwell, a pilot cadet like myself. Jolyon, this is Veronica, the really annoying girl next door i told you about."

Veronica gave Jonny an icy stare. Jolyon offered his hand, she took it enthusiastically.

"She doesn't look that annoying." Jolyon smiled. "What do you do Miss Veronica?"

"I work in a library."

"She's a librarian." Jonny butted in.

"I'm not, I'm a research assistant." Veronica was indignant. " I work for 'The working Class Movement' Library in Manchester."

"Good Lord, how interesting, do you commute everyday?"

"Yes, it's only a couple of hours on the train. I like traveling on the train, it gives me time to think."

"And what do you think about?"

"Work. Whatever I'm researching."

"What are you researching at the moment?"

"Margaret Llewellyn Davies, she led the Women's Cooperative Guild between 1889 and 1921."

"Fascinating, I'd love to talk to you some more but we're off to Bingo." It wasn't a sarcastic comment. Jolyon really was interested.

Veronica glanced a 'WHAT' glance at Jonny. Jonny just shrugged his shoulders.

"How about tomorrow?" Jolyon asked.

"I have a visitor tomorrow, a lady called Hetty Betts, she's an activist for the British Communist Party. Not your type at all."

Jolyon's face lit up.

"Exactly my type Miss Veronica, I'd love to meet her, would that be possible?"

"What about your voice, your clothes, your car, your very obvious money?" Veronica asked seriously.

"Does that preclude me from compassion, caring, fairness and love, Veronica?"

Veronica stopped to think. Jonny and Irene looked at each other.

"I suppose not." There was silence in the little kitchen.

"She, she, She's met Karl Marx's daughter." Veronica almost stammered to break the silent moment.

"I would be honoured if you'd allow me to meet her." Jolyon put out his hand again. This time she shook it with both her hands.

"Now Mum, what time are we off to bingo, can't wait."

" Where's the toilet?" Jolyon whispered to Jonny. Jonny nodded towards a glazed door in the corner.

It seemed like half the street was watching. Jonny and Mavis struggled into the back whilst Irene fitted herself onto the front seat. Jolyon winced a bit as he saw the seat take the strain but nothing broke. The front passenger seat was the only possible position for Irene. The journey into town was uneventful but an experience nevertheless for Mavis and Irene who'd never been in an open top car before. In Mavis's case she'd never been in a car before. It was pleasantly warm in the evening sun. On Irene's direction they pulled into a large bus station with an expansive open tarmacked apron and surrounded by old nondescript buildings of all shapes and sizes. The 'Legion' was up a flight of wooden steps affixed to the side or a building. Inside it was just one big long room with a bar at one end and a small stage at the other. On the stage sat 'the caller' with all his paraphernalia. The room was set out with rows of long benches and corresponding chairs. It was two and six entry and cards were threepence a go. The place was packed with old women, a few middle aged women and even fewer young girls who were selling the cards. It was a place of community and excitement. A place of something for nothing, - if you were lucky - if it was your night.

"Here." Irene slipped an old tobacco tin into Jolyon's hand as they got out.

"What's this?" Jolyon looked at the tin, almost all of the writing and pictures had fallen off with the paint.

"SHhhhhh! It's Arthur's bingo bit box, sometimes when we were on holiday he'd come to a bingo with me. Don't want Jonny to see."

"Why what's in it?"

"Bingo bits, actually they're buttons I cut off Arthurs old shirts before I made them into hankies. Jonny doesn't believe they're lucky but I do."

"What do I do with them?"

Irene gave him an 'Oh Dear' look,

"You cover your numbers on your card with them as the numbers are called out. If you get a complete line you put up your hand and shout 'house' or 'here' or just shout anything."

The hum of undulating conversation fell to almost nothing as Irene, Mavis. Jonny and Jolyon walked in and took a place. After they'd been looked at, the conversations resumed. Men were a rarity at 'Legion Bingos', especially young handsome men.

The microphone crackled into life.

"Right! Eyes down, look in. two little ducks - twenty two - quack quack! Knock at the door, number four." By now the visitors had been forgotten, silence had descended as the serious business took place. Within a minute a hand shot up with a shouted 'HERE'. The conversation of near misses and disappointment immediately resumed. Jolyon was transfixed, comparing notes with Mavis. It was though a river of communal warmth and shared enjoyment, was flooding his parched desert of correctness and formal distance.

The evening went quickly, the break at eight forty five was cheese and onion / egg and cress sandwiches, packets of crisps / pickled eggs/onions, pork pies and pop or tea, no beer. The fun ended about ten o'clock. Jonny had two lines, Irene, one, Mavis two and Jolyon four.

"Reckon you're in line for a prize." Mavis squawked to Jolyon before giving him a nudge with her elbow. A young girl came a long and took Jolyon's four winning cards away to be checked. She asked him to write his name on one of the cards. She had the sort of figure only a teenage girl can have. She didn't want to look sexy, just 'pretty' like in the magazines but she was.

"Ten wonderful prizes for tonight's lucky people. Number ten is Agnes with a dozen farm fresh eggs. Number nine is Doris Miller, a packet 'Quality Street' just what you need for your diet Doris." The caller laughed. "Number eight is.- " There was a pause whilst he showed the sheet to his wife to ask how to say the name. "Mr. Jolyon, who gets a fantastic bottle of Madeira Sherry." Everybody clapped as Jolyon went up to get it. His face beaming with pleasure.

It was dark when they arrived back in Henry Street, laughter, sarcasm and jokes had accompanied their short journey. Jonny was pleased to see his mother smiling and carefree for a while, her present removed from past memories.

Veronica was waiting.

"How come you didn't take me?" She demanded with false indignation.

"ERRR! You weren't here." Jonny replied. "Anyway I thought you had a guest, someone visiting?"

"She doesn't get here 'til tomorrow. Did you win Jonny?" Spotting the sherry.

"No, Jolyon did. Beginner's luck mum says."

"We could try it, see if it's any good." Jolyon shouted from around the back of the car.

"Jonny can you give me a hand to put the hood up please?" Jonny moved to the side of the car. Irene opened the front door and went straight to the sideboard for some small glasses, She had a new box of them at the back. They were a present from Prestatyn a long time ago, she'd never had call to use them 'til now.

It was eleven thirty before Veronica finally went home. Her and Jolyon had been deep in conversation over several sherries, the bottle was almost empty.

"Would you like a spot of supper before bed?" Irene asked Jolyon.

Jolyon thought for a moment. "A bread and dripping sandwich?" He cocked his head to one side in a quizzical way.

"Coming up." Irene was so happy to be a mother again. "You and Jonny can have the big bed in the front bedroom, I'll sleep in Jonny's single bed."

There was an awkward silence.

"Can't do that mum. Can't sleep in Dad's bed. You sleep as usual, Jolyon can have my single and I'll sleep down here on the settee."

Irene looked at her son.

"Are you sure?"

"Yes, it's not right."

The back room was dark and cool, Jolyon slipped between the tight crisp sheets. He thought how lucky Jonny must have been as a boy to have his mum come tuck him in and give him a goodnight kiss. The sherry made him fall asleep quickly.

Irene got up early, her sleep was all over the place since Arthur went. She immediately went to the front window, drew the curtains and checked the car, it looked alright. Jonny was still flat out on the settee, 'only the young could sleep like that' she thought to herself as she went back into the kitchen to make tea and breakfast. It felt so right to have a family to care for.

A mug of hot tea was delivered upstairs, bacon, eggs, fried bread, black pudding, beans, tomato and mushrooms were waiting downstairs. Jolyon relished in the warmth and love that went with their food.

"What's this black stuff?" Jolyon asked.

"Black pudding, it's a Midlands thing." Jonny replied between fried bread and beans.

"It's delicious."

"Made of pig's blood, fat and pearl barley."

"I don't care. Is there any more mum?"

Irene laughed and put two more slices in the pan.

"So. What's the plan today Jonny?"

"Summer Saturday in Walsall. You have the world at your feet Pilot Cadet Clay."

"Well actually Jonny I've sort of promised to take Veronica to the station at twelve to pick up Ms Hetty Betts."

Jonny looked at Jolyon.

"I might take mum out for lunch then."

"Ooh! That'd be lovely." Irene chirped. "Where shall we go?"

"Apparently 'The Albion' do a good lunch, we can walk it, and it's by the canal where me and dad used to go fishing."

"Did you ever catch anything Jonny?" Jolyon's cut glass voice somehow made it more facetious.

"Tell him mum, tell him how I was always bringing home huge fish for you to cook."

"He did bring home a nice Perch once. Lovely it was, not as good as your dad's trout though." Irene replaced their mugs with fresh mugs of tea and some toast, marmalade and best Lurpak butter.

Chapter. 7

"Tell me all you know about Hetty Betts." Jolyon said as Veronica directed him towards the station.

"Well she currently works for The People's History Museum in Manchester, we met through my work. She's wonderful, fighting and campaigning for equal pay for women. I admire her immensely."

"What about your work Veronica? Isn't that to be admired?"

"Me? I'm too scared to stand up to anyone for anything."

"I don't believe that for an instant."

"We're here. Turn right here, into the car park."

"Yes Miss." They both laughed.

The local train from Birmingham was due in at twelve thirty. Jolyon suggested they wait on the seat at the bottom of the footbridge as she would either come in on the platform they were on, or, have to come over the footbridge anyway.

"What's it like?" She sat just close enough to him that their clothes touched.

"What?"

"Flying a jet?"

"Well I haven't actually gone solo yet, Jonny has, mine's next week if things go well and I don't mess up. But, in answer to your question I don't really know. The RAF wants qualified pilots as quickly and cheaply as possible so when you're flying you're thinking about everything, no time to look at the view. Jonny does, he's a natural, everything's easy for him, for the rest of us it's a struggle."

"Here's the train." Veronica stood up. Jolyon followed.

"You didn't tell me much about her."

"Sorry. Here she is." Veronica moved smiling towards a diminutive small woman with light brown curly hair and glasses. Jolyon followed a few paces behind and waited whilst they exchanged greetings.

"Hetty, this is Jolyon Clay he's a friend of my neighbours son Jonny."

Jolyon put out his hand.

"Good afternoon Miss Betts, I've heard a little about you but not much, I would love to hear about your campaigns and activities." The precision, confidence and elegance of his voice took her back. She wasn't expecting it on Walsall Station. Her hand was limp and hesitant.

"Pleased to meet you Mr. Clay and what is it you do?" It was a strong Northern Lancashire accent disguised as a small woman.

"I'm training to be an RAF pilot."

"Ah! So you'd like to drop bombs and kill people?"

"No, I'd like to protect good people from bad people."

"But you'll be a Flying Officer?"

"Yes, I consider the flying more important than the Officer."

"I think you're already an Officer Mr. Clay, Oxford or Cambridge?"

"Cambridge, same as Guy Burgess, Donald MacLean and Kim Philby."

"Friends of yours?"

"Before my time but one has to admire them. At least they were true to their beliefs."

Hetty Betts didn't know exactly what to make of Jolyon Clay, her initial impression, now in doubt.

"Would you allow me to buy lunch? Somewhere nice Veronica, out of town, in town, I don't mind. You must be hungry Miss Betts after your journey?"

Veronica floundered, desperately trying to think of somewhere grand enough for Jolyon but unpretentious enough for Hetty.

"How about The Gamecock on the Wolverhampton Road?" She suggested.

"Lead the way Miss---------- I don't know your surname Veronica."

"Smith, Veronica Smith."

"Lead the way Miss Smith." All three laughed in the sunshine as they came out of the station.

Hetty Betts became more confused when it became apparent they were heading towards the sporty light green tourer.

Veronica deferred to age, experience and reputation and sat in the back. Hetty sat, rather uncomfortably, next to Jolyon.

"Miss Smith tells me you're an 'activist' Miss Betts, what are you currently campaigning about."

Hetty Betts didn't know what to do. Sitting next to a very handsome, amenable, obviously rich young man who was a member of the Armed Forces and was asking her about her activities. It was different with Veronica, she was her admiring subordinate but he was something else. She didn't know what.

"I work at the People's History Museum in Manchester."

"Yes but what do you do?"

She couldn't resist the challenge.

"I campaign for Women's Rights and Peace."

"What do you think about The Campaign for Nuclear Disarmament'?"

"I'm a founder member."

"We're here, turn right here Jolyon." Veronica tapped his right shoulder.

Jolyon slowed, checked his mirror and pushed the small lever above the horn push to the right. The Gamecock was a no nonsense large pub made of light yellow and red brick with a conveniently large tarmacked car park. There were about ten cars in it. Jolyon got out quickly and within seconds was opening the car door for Hetty and Veronica, who didn't really know how to respond to his 'gentleman's manners'.

"It's a matter of trust isn't it?"

"What is?" Hetty questioned.

"Nuclear disarmament, if you disarm you have to trust the other country, power, government, whatever, will also disarm otherwise you look stupid and weak and lose your job."

"Well obviously you have to put in place stages and checks to make sure that happens."

"Yes but somebody has to move first."

"So what do you suggest Mr. Clay, we all blow up the world because somebody refuses to blink?"

"I suggest we go inside and have a really nice lunch and change the world whilst sitting down." Jolyon laughed as they all made towards the large canopied entrance.

Inside was practical enough to cope with Saturday night spilt beer but soft enough to not be a canteen. The chairs were covered in a stout brocade, the tables, oak with a faux leather inlay. The large room smelt of cigarettes and dettol. On one wall was a silent upright piano. The lunch menus were stood up on end on each table. It was an M&B pub.

Hetty chose a chicken salad, Veronica a gammon mixed grill and Jolyon fish and chips with mushy peas. They all settled on shandy to drink.

"I'm surprised you know what 'mushy peas' are Mr. Jolyon."

"I don't but I guessed from the adjective and the picture on the menu. Are they nice?"

"Delicious."

"That's two things today, black pudding and mushy peas. I'm becoming quite bohemian."

"I doubt that Jolyon, I doubt that very much." For the first time Hetty Betts dropped the Mr.

"Have you read 'Das Kapital' Miss Betts?"

Hetty was visually astounded and taken back.

"Some of it, it's a long heavy read, I dip in and out of it now and again, use it more as a reference book really. Have you?"

"As you say, three volumes is a long read but yes I've read it. Do you really believe that societies can only develop through class conflict?"

Hetty looked at him through hooded eyebrows, impressed yet annoyed by his knowledge. The rich didn't normally concern themselves with social development.

"Of course, the elite are hardly looking to change anything, they just want the working classes to be educated enough to operate their machines."

"Here's our food." Veronica piped up from the sidelines. "Tell us what life is like in the RAF, Jolyon, it must be incredibly exciting." Trying to steer the conversation back down to a level she could participate in.

"It's just work Veronica, the RAF wants to educate people just enough to operate their machines. In mine and Jonny's case the machine just happens to be able to fly." He glanced at Hetty and her salad.

Jonny looked at his mother sat on the high backed wooden chair.

"Will you be OK walking to 'The Albion' mom? We could get a taxi."

"No! No! It's only ten minutes, I'll be OK, I'll bandage up my knees and be fine. I do the shopping everyday so I'm OK."

His mom was fatter, only to be expected he thought. On her own, no family to fuss over and see to, just the telly. Bingo, cooking and eating. Maybe he should have bought old Frank Tomb's shop and settled for Veronica. Hardly comparable to a Jet Provost and Calypso though, wherever she was.

A chilly wind had got up. Irene put her best coat on as they headed out the front door.

"Haven't been to 'The Albion' for years. Last time was one hot summer's evening with your dad. He liked 'Bessie Bulls' by the canal bridge but he knows I can't abide flies and midges so we went to 'The Albion'. I had a port and lemon, well two actually, your dad had two Mackesons. Lovely it was. It was dark by the time we got home."

Their walk took them past St Pauls church where they'd had the funeral service for dad. Irene went quiet, finding it hard not to cry.

Just before the Albion the road crossed the canal. There on the right was the spot where Jonny had caught the large Perch with his dad. He remembered the urgent tugging of the fish, his sheer excitement and dad's coolness, touching the flapping fish, dad telling him to be careful of the sharp spines of it's fin. What a day it was , taking it home proudly to mum to cook.

"Not far now mom." Jonny could sense his mother struggling. "What do you fancy to eat?"

"Shall we go mad and have steak and chips? Mavis said they do a really nice one here."

"Here we are, come on, take your coat off and sit down. Steak and chips sounds great."

Jonny ordered, it was a Marston's pub so he had a pint of Pedigree. Mum had a port and lemon,

The chairs were studded red leatherette, quite large and comfortable. The Albion was a big pub that sat with the Banks of the canal at the front and Marston's Brewery at the back. The beer didn't have to travel far, somehow it tasted different, better.

Jonny took a large swig of the beer, it had a light frothy head on it that remained on his top lip. Mum pointed at it for him to wipe it.

"In about six months I'll be passing out as a pilot, all being well I'll get my 'wings'. There's a special parade to get them, will you come?"

Irene was holding her glass. He could see she was struggling as she slowly put it on the table.

"I'd rather not son." She only ever called him 'son' when it was a serious issue. "You know I don't travel very well. I'm fatter than ever, the doctor and everybody says I should diet but I've always struggled with my weight as you know. I feel so alone since your dad passed on and you left, the only comfort I have is a bit of Bingo, a flutter on the horses and eating. The worlds full of couples, people alone just don't fit in so I'd rather not. I'm so proud of you, your dad would be over the moon. An RAF Flying Officer, who'd 'ave thought for a boy from Grange Street Primary and 'The Tech'.

"Most pilots come from very rich families mum, Jolyon's family are extremely rich, have their own estate and a mansion in Herefordshire, it's beautiful."

"How come he wants to be your friend then?"

"His families been rich for over five hundred years, i think he thinks it's a bit unfair and sort of unstoppable, once you're rich you're always rich unless you're totally stupid and Jolyon isn't, he's incredibly intelligent, fascinated by Communism, Marxism, stuff like that. It's as though to him, his obvious wealth is a bit of an embarrassment in a world where there are so many poor people."

"I wouldn't like to be rich, you wouldn't be happy worrying about all that money."

Irene finished her port and lemon.

"Can I have another, the food's taking a long time."

"Think they cook it mum."

"If dad was alive he'd insist you came."

"He's not son and I'm lost without him, please don't make a fuss about it, all the people will be smart in expensive clothes, I'd just be fat and ugly."

Jonny got up, put his arm around his mom and kissed her.

"The food's here, looks good, hope you're hungry?" He laughed as he sat down.

In the end Irene had three port and lemons, apple pie with cream followed the steak. It was two thirty before they left the steps of 'The Albion', two canal boats were passing under the bridge, Irene nearly stumbled as her right knee gave way. She took Jonny's arm. He felt so safe.

As they turned into Henry Street they could see Jolyon's car parked outside the house. Jolyon, Veronica and her friend were sat inside it. The occupants of the street and the little boys had, by now, got bored with staring at the shiny car and the people inside it.

"Hello, been waiting long?"

"I've been waiting forty five minutes. These two have been discussing the difference between communism, socialism and capitalism so they've no idea of the time." Veronica moaned.

Jolyon quickly got out to open the door for Hetty and Veronica.

"I could get used to this." Hetty laughed. "Just don't tell my manager at the museum that my new boyfriend is a founding member of the 'bourgeoisie'." She laughed again.

Jolyon failed to notice or most likely chose to ignore her joke enshrouded innuendo.

"Come on in Veronica." Irene said. "I've bought a Victoria cream sponge cake especially for tea." Jonny wondered how his mum could be so enthusiastic about food after such a large meal and pudding.

"How was your lunch?" Jonny asked Jolyon as he helped put the hood up.

"Can't remember, the company and conversation were too interesting." He winked at Hetty who quickly turned away. Girlish pleasure not befitting her socialist activist image.

"So what's the plan for the rest of your day with the proletariat Jolyon?"

Both Hetty and Jolyon looked at him. Veronica didn't quite understand.

"Actually, if you don't mind, Hetty and I are going to nip into Birmingham to look at the statue of Boulton, Watt and Murdoch."

There were three blank faces.

Hetty filled in the blanks

"They're credited with developing and improving the steam engine. A device that allowed us to create an empire and dominate the world."

"Well, made life a bit easier for some of the working class, let's say." Jolyon added.

"Didn't do much for women." Hetty hit back at Jolyon.

"Made travel possible for both men and women."

"Yes, if you could afford it and as like today, men control the money."

"Not always, take Calypso for example."

"Who's Calypso?" Veronica immediately felt challenged.

"A very rich girl that myself and Jonny know."

"Come on, tea and cake." Irene could sense trouble and diverted it.

It had cleared to a lovely summer's evening as Jolyon and Hetty cruised towards Birmingham.

"Are you a communist Hetty?" It was a question he now felt was OK to ask.

"Used to be but resigned due to the invasion of Hungary."

"What are you now?"

"Member of the Labour Party. You?"

"Nothing. Member of the confused but rich party. If I fought on your side it's tantamount to shooting myself in the foot."

"Do you really need all that money?"

They slowed for lights.

"No, but there's a mind set that implies that if you show any sign of weakness then you'll be destroyed or even worse, simply lose."

Forgetting to double de-clutch, he crunched first gear as they set off.

"And where does the RAF fit in?"

"I want to do something other than just go to the City to protect and increase the family jewels. Something exciting, something patriotic."

Hetty laughed and gently punched his leg.

"Then do as I say, turn left here."

"Are you sure? Women can't read maps." He said. She glowered.

"Of course they can."

"No they can't, hold up your right hand."

Hetty held up her left.

"There you go, you can't even tell your right from your left, how on earth can you possibly read a map."

Hetty hit him a little harder on the leg.

Hetty insisted she take a photo of Jolyon in front of the newly gilded statue. She had a new Kodak Brownie camera and wanted to complete the film so after Jolyon had taken one of her she persuaded an unfortunate passer by to take the final two shots.

"Come on, put your arm 'round me. A unique photograph, an elite member of the bourgeoisie and a left wing proletariat. What a combination!"

Hetty was not pretty, she wasn't remotely sexy. Jolyon felt safe putting his arm around her and smiling for the photo. Wherever the photo surfaced in the future no one would presume they were a couple. That was correct, they weren't but Jolyon liked her conviction, her strength, her struggle for fairness.

"How about fish and chips in the car on the way home?" Jolyon suggested as they cruised out of Birmingham.

"That will be perfectly acceptable to a research fellow of the Manchester People's Museum." She squeezed his arm and for a moment lent on his shoulder.

"Ah! It's all coming out now, you're not the cleaner who wears curlers, a headscarf and blue dungarees. You're a secret weapon. Come on, out with it? What are you researching?"

"American nuclear ballistic missile submarines at Holy Loch."

The mood in the car immediately descended into sombre serious silence for a while. Jolyon thinking about his career as an Officer in the armed forces. Associating with a serious activist and the photo. Hetty thinking about her credibility as a socialist if her associates could see her now.

"There's a chip shop." She exclaimed. Jolyon pulled up outside and gave her some money. The chip shop was full, there was a queue. 'Always a good sign' Jolyon thought as he waited in the car. It took Hetty fifteen minutes before she reappeared with the chips wrapped in newspaper, the vinegar already seeping through the print. 'Another good sign'. They were hot and delicious, the batter on the cod was crisp, it enveloped the white cod that broke away into natural slices. They felt at ease and comfortable despite their disparity.

"Ummm! Delicious." Jolyon commented screwing up the greasy paper into a ball and throwing it into a bin hanging from the concrete lamp post. "Let's go home shall we?"

Hetty screwed up her paper, she hadn't quite finished but she had had enough anyway. She handed it to Jolyon to throw into the bin as he was nearer.

"Yes let's, I'm getting tired." She quietly wished to herself that they were indeed 'going home'. Then quickly filed it, thinking that she could never reconcile someone like Jolyon with her life. She'd be seen as a total hypocrite.

Jonny was dozing on the sofa. Mum had gone up to bed ages ago. Veronica had hung around for ages before she finally gave up on Jonny and went home to bed. It was ten past eleven when he heard a car pull up outside.

Jolyon turned the engine off and sat for a moment. It ticked and clicked as it cooled.

"Hetty?"

"What?"

"If you ever need any help, you know, a bit of money or something for any of your projects, let me know?"

She looked at him in the dark.

"What, you're offering to fund a socialist project? You, a Pilot Officer of the RAF."

"You'd have to be completely discreet."

"What if I rejoin the Communist Party?"

"You'd have to be even more discreet."

"I'm researching potential sources of funds for a women's refuge in Manchester, you know, somewhere safe for women to go to when their blokes get pissed up and knock them about. How about that?"

"What, you mean men physically hit their wives?"

Hetty looked exasperated.

"All the time Jolyon. All the time."

"Good lord, that's terrible. Let me know how much you need. Write to me at Cranwell, I'll be there for at least another six months."

Hetty reached over and kissed him on the cheek before opening the car door.

It was eleven on Sunday morning. Irene was a little tearful standing on her front door step waving goodbye to her precious son. She wasn't alone, with her was Veronica from next door and her friend Hetty. It had been a wonderful Sunday breakfast, the five of them huddled around Irene's little drop leaf table, the leaf up with a nice lace edged tablecloth. It was lovely, best bacon and sausages from Dewhursts, field mushrooms from Ray next door, poached eggs on toast and some lovely big fried tomatoes. The tea pot was never empty, toast and marmalade afterwards filled everybody up. The conversation and laughter, like the tea pot, never dried up, Jolyons posh accent now a part of the little kitchen. Now it was time to go, Irene thrust a large parcel of bread and dripping sandwiches into Jolyon's hands.

"Just in case you get peckish on the way." She gave him a hug.

"Thanks Mum." He emphasized the 'mum', she beamed. He'd never been hugged before. Hetty put out her hand.

"Goodbye, very nice to have met you." Jolyon shook her hand. They both knew it was an act. She was fascinated by his wealth and position though she could never admit it. He was charmed by her intellect and staunch socialism.

The two young men broke away from the women. Half the street were out watching as Jolyon and Jonny lowered and stowed the brown canvas hood. It was windy but the sun was shining as they drove out of Henry Street into Casey Lane and the road back to Cranwell.

The two young men watched the working class town change slowly into a classless city and then to affluent suburbs then to rural idyll. Jolyon with interest and fascination, Jonny with acceptance and hope.

Chapter. 8

"How many pillars on the front of the hall?" Jonny asked after at least thirty minutes of pleasant silence, just the noise of the journey. It really was a beautiful car.

"Good grief Jonny, I've no idea." He paused. "You'll be able to count them in-------."
He glanced at his watch. "Approximately thirty eight minutes."

"Approximately's no good, has to be exact." Jolyon glanced at his watch again.

"We'll be going through the gates at five past four. Is that exact enough for you?"

"Yes." Jolyon speeded up the car to give himself a margin. 'He could always slow down again,' he thought.

"Let's have a guess. I reckon twenty." Jonny said.

"Well let's make it worthwhile the loser bulls the winners boots for tomorrow's parade. Are you on?"

"Yes OK, I'm sticking with twenty."

"I reckon there's more, there's double pillars at each end and double at each end of the canopy.I'm going for twenty two."

"You had any word from Calypso?" Jonny asked, as casually as he could.

Jolyon glanced over at him.

"You've got it bad haven't you? No I haven't and not likely to either unless something social crops up, you know a wedding or some big party."

Jonny quickly changed the subject.

"What are your views on the poor working class now you've experienced it first hand?"

"No change, It's bloody unfair, it's abuse really, smart people are rich, not so smart people aren't. That's what it comes down to. But where it gets really unfair is when you have really smart young people who get nowhere because they can't afford the opportunities, the education. You're a lucky exception. Hetty and Karl Marx have got it right."

"Your solo tomorrow are you nervous?" Jonny changed the conversation again.

"A little but really it doesn't matter does it? If I fail miserably and get kicked out I just run back to my family and their money. So it's different, almost as though it's just an amusing hobby." Jolyon glanced at the clock on the dash. "Here we are, five past four and we're entering the gates."

Jolyon stopped the car just inside the gates.

"There are twenty two, I'll give you my boots when we get to the room." He laughed and hit Jonny on the arm.

Tim Barnes stopped shaving and looked in the mirror. Fifty three, a small paunch and deep lines, how had that happened? All these young fresh hopefuls looked up to him with reverence, he knew all the tricks, all the subtleties of flying the little jets, the badges, the wings, the zips, the pockets, the paraphernalia that embellished the glamour of being a pilot. It was all there, what they had, and he didn't, was the speed. The speed of thought, the speed of reaction, the speed and ease of movement. He intentionally walked fast and disguised his stiffness as he climbed into cockpits but it took more effort these days. Jenny was always going on at him to use the camp gym and to watch his diet but, it just wasn't him. He liked a pint before dinner, a cigar and brandy afterwards. He'd need a new blade tomorrow.

"Morning Jonny, Good weekend?"

"Went home to see my mum."

"And Dad?"

"He passed away a few years ago."

Tim was expecting the usual 'they're divorced' answer.

"Oh sorry to hear that, how old were you?"

"Nineteen." The moment was somber. Tim moved it on.

"Come on, first day on the instrument flying. Have you done your homework?"

"Yes, should be OK."

Tim knew it would be OK, Jonny was a natural, an uncanny empathy with the machine. One of the easiest students he'd had for a long time.

"Let's do a few touch and go circuits to fill in the time Jonny." Jonny did a shallow bank to line up with the runway and cleared with the tower.

"What would you rather do after here, Gnats or Hunters?" Tim asked.

"Gnats, they look so small and maneuverable."

"The Hunters are more versatile." Tim crackled back.

"I'll go wherever they send me. I want to be operational, a front line squadron."

"You'll go wherever I recommend Jonny, that's how it works, it's the only bit of influence this old man has."

Jonny glanced at his teacher.

"You're not old, just experienced."

Tim looked towards Jonny. The eyes were the only real visible part of his face, the oxygen mask and the helmet concealing his greying hair and 'laughter lines'.

"Old, Jonny, take it from me. Old. Now take us back home just using the instruments, don't look up." Tim partially covered the canopy in front of Jonny with some black cloth.

"Yes Sir."

"How did it go?" Jonny asked Jolyon as he walked into their room. Jolyon was lying on his bed with his shoes still on. His hands behind his head staring at the ceiling.

"Passed it, no problems at all, the observer said he'd recommend me for fast jets, whatever that means."

"It means you're bloody good. Congratulations."

"Weird feeling isn't it?"

"What is?"

"Up there, on your own in a jet plane, It's like you're an angel, wherever you want to go you can. No traffic lights, no hills, no rivers, no Zebra crossings, nothing. Oooh that looks interesting, I'll go and have a look, caress the stick and rudder and there you are. It's like magic."

"It is magic Jolyon." Jonny took his shoes off and threw himself onto his bed.

"Do you think we're missing the point?" Jolyon asked.

"What point?"

"Well here we are immersed in tradition, rules, regulations, shiny boots, shiny brass buckles, books, manuals, exciting machines, new experiences, work, work, work, study, study, study, get a nice gold badge at the end if you're lucky. Nobody talks about 'it' do they?"

"And what exactly is 'it'?"

"That one day we'll be expected to use our magic to kill people. We'll be so used to pressing a button or flicking a switch that one more means nothing, even if seconds later people die, one person, ten people, ten thousand people. We're so autonomous that we just do it. Our only concern is that we do it properly, at the right time and on target at the right place."

Jonny turned, propped himself up on an elbow and looked over at his best friend.

"If you're thinking things like that perhaps you should leave, get a job with B.O.A.C if you want to fly, or just go into the city if you don't." There was a long silence.

"Actually, Father's just bought a Cessna six seater. He's had the pasture at the back of the house flattened for a grass strip, even bought a wind sock."

"Whatever for, he can't fly."

"No but in a few weeks we will be able to."

"You mean you."

"No I mean we, I want you to stay in my life Jonny. I've never had a proper 'best friend' before."

Jonny took his socks off and threw them at Jolyon.

Jolyon sat up and threw the socks back.

"Listen, how about after we graduate, after the passing out parade, when we're pilots, we take the Cessna down to the South of France for a week? We're due two weeks leave prior to our postings, we could take Veronica and Hetty."

"Not sure, said I'd spend some time with mum, she's very lonely these days."

"Just four or five days Jonny, come on, we could share the flying, tell you what I'll invite Calypso as well."

"If you do that you can't invite Veronica, there'd be world war three."

"Have to, Hetty wouldn't come without Veronica."

"Is Hetty that important?"

"Not sure, maybe? Come on let's go eat."

"It's like being a member of the 'where the fuck are we tribe.' "

"What are you talking about?" Jonny asked as Jolyon dumped his silver helmet and gloves on the bed.

"Night flying, a bit scary til you get the hang of it, having to rely totally on instruments is the really scary bit."

"You need to eat more carrots."

"Don't be daft."

"Seriously, apparently carotene is really good for night vision."

Jolyon looked at Jonny trying to work out if he was conning him.

"Had a letter from Calypso today, she said she'd be up for the South of France jolly on the twenty fifth. You coming?"

Jonny went silent. Mum would be so disappointed but then again he'd have a week with her.

"What if we don't pass the course?"

"Oh come on Jonny, we're the two best pilots on the course, stop being so bloody negative. Calypso, yes or no?"

"Yes." Jonny wondered how he was going to break it to mum. Calypso wasn't the sort of girl he could take to Henry Street. In fact mum wouldn't like her at all. What about Veronica? She'd undoubtedly report back to mum. He'd have to play it very cool with Calypso, try and make out she was Jolyon's girlfriend.

"Jolyon?"

"What?"

"On the trip could you sort of pretend that Calypso is your sort of girlfriend?"

Jolyon looked at him.

"Difficult, the chemistry between you two is almost explosive and I don't want to give Hetty the wrong impression."

"You're hardly going to marry someone like Hetty, just as much as I'm not going to marry someone like Calypso, the social distance is too great."

"Suppose you're right but I do feel very comfortable with Hetty and I love her politics."

"Turn out the lights will you? I'm done in." Jonny pulled the blankets up.

"Jonny, If I guarantee that Calypso will come along to France will you bull my boots for the passing out parade?"

"Yes." Jonny pulled the top blanket over his head then poked his head out again. "You're such a shit, do you know that?"

"Yes. Goodnight."

"I've bought two."

"Two what?" Jonny asked as they walked to the student room for breakfast.

"Two swords and scabbards, they're over five hundred pounds each, you can't afford it, I can and you need one."

Jonny stopped walking and tugged his jumper to stop.

"I could hire one like everyone else does."

"Yes you could, but it's not the same as owning your own. Come on breakfast, I'm famished. Anyway you've promised to do my boots, you know I'm no good at that sort of thing." Jolyon slapped him on the shoulder as they headed towards breakfast.

It was full English followed by toast and marmalade, they had the same every morning, by now the seats were allocated but unspoken. It was familiar and comforting nourishment prior to a days flying.

It was the last landing in the little Jet Provost, it was by now a very comfortable space and Tim a very easy man to share it with. The jet gently kissed the apron as the hum of the wheels was felt in the cockpit.

"Well that's it flying Officer Conrad. You're on your way."

"Yes but on my way where to?" Jonny released the oxygen mask that fell away.

"My guess is RAF Valley, conversion course then fast jet training in the Gnat, beautiful little aircraft."

"Is that what you've recommended?"

"Yes, but I haven't said that, everythings a secret til after the passing out parade when you've got your wings and you've swapped the white tag on your lapels for a bar on your shoulder."

"What about you, move on to the next student?"

"No, I've had enough, you're my last, and most certainly the best. I'm calling it a day. Started out on bi-planes, finished on jets, that'll do. Time for some gardening."

Jonny looked at Tim climbing out of the Provost, he couldn't disguise his stiffness after two hours in the cockpit. He was stiff and slow. He was right.

They walked to the green painted wooden crew room come office together. It felt good to take the helmet off and feel the wind in his hair. Tim couldn't do that.

After they'd signed off they shook hands and that was it.

They practiced for the passing out parade five times. Marching around the square, halting, turning into line, open order, closed order, dressing, about-turning, standing at attention, standing at ease, standing easy, the whole thing had to be positioned to the inch and timed to the second. H.R.H Prince Charles was rumoured to be taking the parade but no one would actually say.

"Here's your sword, thanks for my boots, they're brilliant, I could never have got them to look like that, how on earth do you do it?"

"Spit and polish, same as everyone else. Oh and quite a lot of time." Jonny took the gleaming new sword out of the box. The handle was gold plated except for the white skin of the grip. He drew it slowly out of the scabbard, there was some writing down the blade just under the handle.

'To my best friend Jonny - Reach for the Sky. - Jolyon 1963.'

Jonny looked at Jolyon.

"I've got nothing to give you. I feel bad."

"Jonny, you've given me your unconditional friendship and shared your family with me. Don't you understand I've never called anyone 'mum' before, never been hugged before, we just don't do that sort of thing in my world."

"Thank you for the sword, it's beautiful." Jonny threaded the scabbard onto his belt. He reached for the yellow duster, the tin of Kiwi and his right boot.

"What are you going to do after the parade tomorrow?" Jonny asked between spits.

"I'm going home, going to familiarise myself with Father's Cessna ready for next Friday. How about you?"

"I'm going home too, promised to take mum to see her sisters. It's only twenty five miles away but it's two buses and a train, her knees can't manage stairs, bridges and big steps up and down so I'm going to collect my new car then take her."

"You're a deep one, why didn't you tell me about your car? What is it?"

"It's a red 1071cc Mini Cooper S with a black roof, I really wanted twin petrol tanks but the garage said that would have been a special order and would take another two or three months. I couldn't wait that long."

"How come you didn't tell me?"

"Because my dear Jolyon you'd only ask me if I had enough money and offer to give me some. That's why I didn't tell you."

"Can't wait to see it, have a go in it. I love the smell of a new car." Jolyon looked at himself in the mirror on the back of the door as he fiddled with his tunic, the belt and the sword.

The parade was clockwork stiff people, a military band and Prince Charles who turned up in a black Rolls Royce. Swords were paraded, badges pinned and twenty eight new Pilot Officers were commissioned. The weather was mainly cloudy, the odd spot of rain and occasional burst of really bright sunlight. The sense of relief when it was over was palpable as the whole camp relaxed.

"Do you want a lift to the station?" Jolyon was throwing stuff into his weekend bag.

"Yes please, was going to get the camp bus but travelling in style would be better. Do you know where you're going yet?"

"No. I'm going to the office now to find out."

Jolyon left the door open but it didn't matter the excitement of the day kept everyone warm. Warm smiles, shouted goodbyes, running students, noisy conversations were the norm for today.

He burst through the door. "Vulcans at Scampton, only down the bloody road."

"Up the road, it's north of here."

"Up, down, does it matter? You'll be in Wales and I'll be in lincolnshire."

"You won't be there long Jolyon, wait and see."

Jolyon looked incredulously at him.

"How do you work that one out? They're going to spend lots of money on a conversion course to Vulcan's and then waste it by shipping me out. I don't think so."

"OK, OK, but they need the best on Lightning interceptors and you're one of the best. Anyway Hetty won't be too impressed if her beau is the pilot of a nuclear bomber, what with her campaigning against Polaris"

"Well you're wrong, come on, let's go, I feel the need for my Sunbeam Talbot Alpine with the hood down whether it's raining or not. I'd appreciate it if you don't mention nuclear bombers on our little trip Jonny."

The station was only ten minutes away. Jonny and Jolyon sat side by side in silence as they came to a halt.

"Well this is it." Said Jonny. "The end of our beautiful romance."

"Only til next Friday. Will you come in your new car?" Jolyon was looking straight ahead at the station.

"All being well, yes. I shall miss sleeping with you, I've got used to your snores, whistles and grunts, oh and the smells."

"That sounds really bad, goodbye."

Jonny got out. They shook hands and said goodbye with eyes before he broke away and headed for the entrance.

Jolyon shouted after him.

"Jonny, get there for lunch on Friday, we can relax and get to know each other again on Friday afternoon and evening. Take off for France at eight o'clock the next morning."

Jonny waved and disappeared into the dark entrance.

"Don't forget to bring Hetty and Veronica, he said quietly to himself, turning the key.

Chapter. 9

"Oh gosh! I just love the smell of a new car and I love the colours Jonny. Where do I put my bag?"

Jonny unlocked and opened the boot of the mini. The ejection seat sear pin he'd stolen from the box of pins on the test rig looked really good as a key fob. Colour matched.

"Not very big is it?" Just enough room for yours and mine, Hetty's will have to go inside with her."

Hetty appeared out of the entry. Mom was standing on the front doorstep.

Goodbyes were waved and shouted, mothers were kissed, then Irene was alone again.

"I can't believe this, driven in a new sporty car to some mysterious mansion in Herefordshire - wherever that is - then whisked away in a private aeroplane to the South of France. Sounds like something out of a movie."

Veronica squealed in delight from the passenger seat of the Mini-Cooper.

"I can't believe I'm allowing myself to be exposed to the shallow delights of elitism. Bet all the other residents in your street never get to sit in decent car never mind an aeroplane."

"You don't have to come Hetty. I can drop you off at a bus stop if you want." Jonny smirked.

Hetty shrunk silently into the back seat thinking about an appropriate answer.

"Jolyon's offered to help me fund my women's refuge so It would be good to have the chance to talk it through."

Jonny pushed the choke fully home as the water temperature climbed. He'd looked at the map and it seemed simple enough but he hadn't paid much attention when Jolyon had driven them there. Too preoccupied with the beauty of the countryside. Then it was summer now it was March, spring was only just about getting going.

The last city was Worcester then it was rural A roads, rural B roads and finally just lanes. They didn't stop, and like him before, Veronica and Hetty were mesmerized by the undulating greens, browns and greys that passed before them. Soon they came up behind tractors, some with trailers some not, cattle crossing a road or just muddy roads where crops had been harvested.

"Where here." Jonny said, turning right into the courtyard.

"Bloody hell, it really is a mansion." Veronica exclaimed. Hetty said nothing. Behind the far outhouses Jonny could see a windsock limply dangling in the weak spring breeze.

Jolyon appeared at the top of the steps leading from the rear hall. He waved as he almost skipped down the steps to greet them.

"Hey Jonny, you got it then?"

"Yes, still running in, hasn't done more than a thousand yet. Haven't dared take it over sixty."

"I wondered why we were going so slow." Hetty had come alive in the presence of Jolyon. Her femininity overriding her convictions.

Jolyon beamed and shook everyone's hands.

"Come! Come! Mrs Campbell has laid on a small buffet for us and there's a jug of Ted's cider."

Jolyon led the way up the steps and into a small room between the kitchen and the dining room. Hetty followed very close behind him then Veronica and finally Jonny who kept glancing back at his car, now covered in mud and road dirt. Jolyon noticed his glances.

"Don't worry, Ted'll get the boy to give it a wash. Come, the food's delicious."

Jonny stood next to Jolyon and reached across the table for a pork pie.

"Where's Calypso?" He whispered.

"Seven, tomorrow morning, she's in London at the moment. Have you actually told these two about Calypso?"

"Ummm, not yet, thought you might 'spring it on them' so to speak, that way it will look more like she's your friend."

"She is my friend."

"Yes I know but we've spent the night looking at your listed ceiling, if you remember."

"It's not MY listed ceiling."

"Well it will be one day, it will never be mine"

"Yes but Calypso's yours, she'll never be mine."

"Are you sure about that?"

"Doesn't matter what happens between Calypso and I she'll always be yours."

Jonny grabbed three cherry tomatoes and a large glass of cider.

"Try this Hetty, made from windfall apples on Jolyon's estate, best I've ever tasted."

Jonny handed the glass to Hetty who took a sip.

"I have to admit it does taste very nice, is it alcoholic?"

"Only a little bit, goes perfect with ham and mustard."

"Tell me about being a pilot Jolyon, what aircraft will you be flying?" She asked.

"I've been reading about Leninism Hetty. What are your views on 'dictatorships', how can that equate with socialism?"

"Let me have some more cider before I answer that one."

"Do you think only the rich can afford to be socialists Hetty?"

She looked at him as she took another drink, the question about his flying totally forgotten.

The cider made everyone tired. A maid showed Hetty and Veronica to their room, Jonny was in the listed room. He lay on the bed looking at the ceiling marvelling again at the shades of winter, the skies of winter and the winter sun. Such skill and talent, but after that it was just her. It made him aroused with an urgency that the merest touch would relieve. And so it did.

Although it was March the clocks had yet to change so dusk was still early. Jonny looked out of the window to see Jolyon walking Hetty around the house and gardens. Veronica followed a few steps behind. Daffodils were eager to bloom. He wondered how she'd be when Calypso was here. She was such a force, the brightest of lights fuelled by an inexhaustible supply of money. He returned to his bed to study the Michelin road maps they were going to use for navigation tomorrow. It looked easy, Bovington to Bournemouth, comfort break and refuel, across the channel, La Fleche, then St Julien, and finally Toulouse. A days leisurely flying with stops for coffee and lunch should easily do it.

It was seven o'clock on Saturday morning, bags had been stowed in the little white and red Cessna. There was a stronger breeze today but the sock was blowing in the right direction.

"What are we waiting for?" Hetty asked impatiently.

Jolyon looked at Jonny.

"A friend of mine, she should be here any minute."

The word 'she ' was noted and the conversation dried up.

"Take it you've all got your passports?" We'll need them to get out of Toulouse Airport."

Everyone nodded. Then there was the sound of something swinging into the yard. A dark green Lotus Elan stopped next to Jonny's Mini. The hood was down wind had simply made her tousled hair more excited. Her eyes connected with jonny's as she almost bounced out of the little sports car. She was tiny as was her orange spotted mini dress. She didn't really care who saw her knickers as she got out. It was just fun.

"Who built that for you? You can only buy them as kit cars."

She came close and looked directly into his eyes.

"The Leprechauns, you know, the ones that live with the elves and fairies behind the boathouse on the lake." Her smile was unstoppable but it was only for him. Jonny broke away.

"Calypso, this is Veronica, she lives next door to my mum and this is her friend Hetty, she lives in Manchester. They both work in social justice."

"Well it's a bit more serious than that." Jolyon butted in. "Veronica is a researcher for 'The Working Class Movement' in Manchester and Hetty works for 'The People's History Museum', also in Manchester. She's an activist for women's rights and peace.
Calypso glanced fleetingly at Jolyon who seemed to be beaming with pride at Hetty, then a 'What?' Glance at Jonny.

Calypso put out her hand and backed it up with an irresistible smile.

"Lovely to meet you both, actually Jolyon's told me all about you and his interesting weekend he spent with you." She moved her attention before they had time to respond. "Wow! Is this the new plane your Father's bought? It looks very small, are you sure it will get us all the way to the South of France? Where are we going? Cannes, Nice, Monaco? We were in Cannes last summer for a while, a bit boring really unless you're into weird films." She smiled again at Veronica and Hetty but they didn't smile back. "Let me get my bag."

"You'd better put the hood up, we'll be away for five or six days. It may rain. You get your bag, I'll put the hood up." Jonny said. It was obvious to everyone they were a couple.

"Wish I hadn't come." Veronica hissed to Hetty. Hetty looked positively furious as they walked towards the plane.

Jonny sat on the right, Jolyon on the left. There were two rows of two seats behind, Calypso sat directly behind Jonny, Veronica and Hetty sat behind Calypso. All the bags were piled on to and underneath the vacant seat directly behind Jolyon.

"All the doors shut?" Jolyon shouted above the stuttering engine. Jonny turned 'round to check. Calypso put her hand on his shoulder.

"All doors shut, all passengers strapped in Captain."

Jonny was elated in her presence, the rest didn't matter, he wasn't Veronica's boyfriend. She was just a neighbour. Hetty's scowl had now been replaced by trepidation as the small craft bounced along the field seeking the start of the flat bit. She wished she'd sat next to Calypso so that she could touch Jolyon now and again. Calypso was gently stroking Jonny's neck as the propeller noisily bit into the air. The two men concentrating on getting airborne.

The green grass fell gently away, cows got smaller, the grey slate roof of Bovington Hall got lighter with distance.

"Next stop Bournemouth, for a drop of juice, and maybe a coffee."

"What channel is Bournemouth on?" Jonny asked.

"Can't remember it's on the paper stapled to the map."

Jonny changed the channel of the radio to twenty three.

"Is that a road map?" Calypso asked, looking incredulously over Jonny's shoulder.

"Yes."

"Urmmm, excuse me but this is an aeroplane not a car."

"It's got wheels the same as a car, stop being picky." Jonny laughed.

"I'm sure Jolyon knows what he's doing." Hetty chipped in, not wishing to be excluded. Veronica wasn't comfortable enough yet to participate.

"I haven't a clue what I'm doing," Jolyon commented. "I'm relying on Jonny, he always knows what he's doing."

"I haven't a clue either. I always rely on Veronica, she always tells me what to do." Jonny looked round and smiled at her. "She's told me what to do since I was seven."

Veronica blushed.

"Yes but you never listen or take any notice do you?"

"I do, I know you like red so I bought a red car."

"It's got a black roof."

"Jolyon let me take control, get used to how it handles."

Jonny grasped the figure of squashed eight control stick and Jolyon let go.

Bournemouth came and went, the smooth tarmac of the runway easier on the small wheels.

Calypso's infectious brightness filled the cabin, Veronica's and Hetty's sworn hostility evaporating and joining with the clouds as they crossed the channel. Before long looking down at the passing land and sea was the domain of the men with their maps. Talking about Clothes, hair, makeup, shoes, the holiday, and gossip in general was far more important. Even Hetty managed some smiles and laughter. After All Calypso wasn't after Jolyon, she was head over heels in love with Jonny, it was obvious to everybody. That was Veronica's problem.

The flat dourness of Northern France seemed interminable as the little plane gallantly droned on.

"I need to go to the toilet." Veronica piped up from the back.

"About twelve minutes to La Fleche." Jonny replied studying the map.

"Will I need my passport to go to the loo?" Veronica asked, everybody laughed.

"Only if you need to go for a number two." Jonny jested.

The coffee and baguettes were delicious, the toilets rudimentary.

Jolyon paid for the fuel with American dollars, the bowser driver wouldn't entertain his Coutts card.

"Think we can make it to Toulouse without dropping into St Julien, that is if the ladies can hold off another comfort break."

Calypso, Hetty and Veronica exchanged glances.

"We're absolutely fine with that." Hetty responded. "How many hours will it be?"

"About five or six depending on the wind." Jonny said. "I'll do the take off and the first couple of hours then you can do the rest if that's OK with you Jolyon?"

"That's good I'll sit in the back with Hetty, we can discuss whether the establishment of a revolutionary vanguard prior to the establishment of Communism was an honest strategy or simply a Trojan horse for Lenin the dictator?" Hetty beamed and swapped places with Veronica. Jonny was now in the left hand pilot's seat. Veronica sat next to Calypso and directly behind him.

"Do you know where we're going?" She spoke close to his ear.

"Yes Toulouse."

"Do you know how to get us to Toulouse?"

"No, here's the map." He reached back with the Michelin road map of Central France. "I'm flying due south and we're aiming for Limoges. It's quite a big town."

"There's lots of 'quite big towns'." Veronica replied perplexed.

Hetty piped up at the back "Women can't read maps. Can they Jolyon?"

Veronica ignored it.

"Well look at the map, it's quite a big town with a big river going through it. How many bridges on the map?"

"Four."

"There's your answer, we need a big town, a big river and four bridges." She thumped him hard in the back, so hard the little plane dipped. Calypso noticed but Jolyon and Hetty were deep in conversation discussing equal pay for women.

"So. What's the plan when we get to Toulouse Jolyon?" Jonny shouted over the droning engine.

"Hire a car, head for the hills and find a nice hotel then tomorrow head for more hills and my surprise location."

"Not sure I like your surprises Jolyon, more hills sounds like the Pyrenees. There's wild bears and wolves in them there hills pardner!"

"Let me assure you I don't do camping, one expedition weekend at Cranwell was more than enough for me thank you very much. So we can listen to the howling of the wolves as we marvel at the moon from our Pyrenean hotel."

"Just asking, that's all." Jonny peered at the passing ground nine thousand feet below them. "We've got about a third of a tank left of fuel, should make it OK, only about an hour to go."

Jolyon left Hetty, clambered over the seats and strapped himself into the right hand pilot's seat.

"Take a break if you want Jonny, go aft and sit with Calypso."

Jolyon knew he'd made a 'faux pas' as soon as he had said it. Jonny cast a steely glance at him.

"I'm OK here thanks."

"I want one of these." The strange single spoke steering wheel of the black Citroen DS seemed to turn effortlessly as Jolyon, Jonny, Calypso, Hetty and Veronica headed for the Pyrenean foothills. The three girls in the back had now shed their initial hostilities and were chatting away.

"It is very comfortable." Hetty commented. "Much more comfortable than your Mini Jonny."

"That's because it's bigger." He replied.

"I'm tired, is the hotel far Jolyon?"

"No, about an hour."

"Wish we could have seen the sea." Hetty said.

"We will in a couple of days, smell that air, smells of liquorice."

"Anybody speak French?" Hetty asked from the back.

"Just a little schoolboy French. Un Peu!"

"Is that Eton schoolboy French?"

"Yes."

"We'll be fine then." Hetty relaxed back into the sumptuous seat.

The road suddenly opened up and changed into the centre of a largeish village. Stone buildings lined the wide space. In the middle were open restaurants, tables and chairs, what looked like market stuff and parked cars. The hotel was just a big mellow stone rectangle that faced the square, a large door at the top of some stone steps led to a dark hall come reception.

"How many rooms do we need.?" Veronica asked. Really she meant who is sleeping with who?

"Two, Jonny and I in one room and you three girls in another." Calypso flashed a disappointed glance at Jonny. "Don't worry it's all arranged, you've got a large room with a double and single bed. You'll be very comfortable. Let's ditch the bags in the rooms then head for that open air restaurant. I'm hungry and it smells wonderful."

Calypso sat next to Jonny at the big wooden table. The food was delicious. Blanquette De Veau followed by chocolate truffles. Jolyon had red wine, Jonny had Belgian beer, all the girls had Blanquette de Limoux. Calypso's leg brushed against Jonny's and stayed there. Hetty gradually moved closer to Jolyon as the dusk changed to night and the alcohol eased inhibitions away. Veronica didn't notice, entranced by the romantic sound of French voices and the moon rising behind a high chimney pot.

It was a joint exit, no one said lets' go. Jolyon paid. Jonny offered to share the bill but Jolyon brushed him away. It was dark. Calypso held Jonny's hand as they climbed the five steps to the door of the hotel. It wasn't an entrance, just a big dark wood heavy door, once inside the hall she reluctantly let go. 'Goodnights' were exchanged as they separated. There was no opportunity for Jonny and Calypso. Hetty was still unsure about Jolyon, unsure of her own femininity, unsure of his masculinity, even if there had been an opportunity. Veronica dreamt from a distance.

During the night Jolyon's restlessness brought his body against Jonny, but it didn't matter. Calypso kissed Hetty and Veronica 'goodnight' that didn't matter either, in fact it helped.

Breakfast was in the dining room come front room of the hotel. Strawberry jam, butter and croissants seemed to be the main fare. A table laid with baguettes, cold meats and cheeses was hiding at the back of the room along with some fruit.

Jonny opted for the croissants and struggled to spread the cold hard butter onto the flakey pastries, in the end he gave up and just spread the soft jam. Jolyon sipped the dark strong coffee as they waited for the girls.

"So where's this secret location?" Jonny asked.

"It's a secret."

"Have you been there before?"

"Yes."

"Is it by the sea?"

"No." At that point three young girls noisily entered from the dark narrow hall. There had obviously been a joint decision to wear shorts as all three were wearing them.

"Sleep well?" Jolyon asked.

Hetty replied.

"Well we did until the bloody cockerel started at about four."

"That's a myth." Jonny said.

"What is?" Calypso asked as she spooned strawberry jam onto her plate. God she looked so beautiful this morning. It was as though she could be any nationality she wanted. This morning she was most definitely French.

"Cockerels crowing at dawn, they crow all night, Especially if there's street lights or another cockerel crowing somewhere.

They're so stupid they think a street light is the sun and any nearby cockerel is a threat to his harem of hens."

"How do you know all this Jonny?" Hetty asked.

"Cause Veronica's dad keeps bloody chickens in the backyard, he shouldn't, it's not big enough but mum won't complain to the council. The bloody cockerel crows all night, take it from me."

"I'd love to but there's not much chance." Calypso whispered in his ear then giggled.

It was ten before everyone fell into the waiting Citroen. It looked as though it had sunk during the night. Jolyon started the engine and waited whilst it clicked and rose.

"Do you need the map?" Veronica asked from the back.

"No. I'm an RAF Pilot, we never need maps, do we Jonny?"

"No never." He kept the amusing charade going.

The overall movement was 'up', The Citroen effortlessly handled the twisting, turning inclines as the scenery changed from pastoral to alpine. Although the sun was shining there were still tiny little clumps of snow in the bottom of ditches or behind rocks.

"Here we are, my secret location." Jolyon said as they entered a small village. "We're booked into 'La Mirabelle' Hotel, I suggest we find it, book in, have lunch there then I'll take you for a walk."

"You're the host Jolyon but it doesn't look much of a place, surrounded by mountains as far as I can tell." Hetty commented.

It was the same arrangement as before, a double room for Jolyon and Jonny, a large room with an additional bed for Calypso, Hetty and Veronica. Lunch was in a beautiful stone barn attached to the hotel with views looking out over a well kept but not manicured lawn, a swimming pool and then the mountains with their flecks of snow. The food was perfectly cooked and presented.

Jolyon looked at Calypso's highish heeled shoes.

"They're no good, we're going walking Calypso, not dancing."

"I've got some pumps in my bag."

"Put those on." Jonny noticed that Jolyon's tone when he was speaking to Calypso was almost paternal as though she was a possession he had to look after.

The white wooden arrow sign read 'Abbaye St-Martin-du-Canigou.'

"He's taking us to a bloody church, might 'ave guest it from an Eton posh boy." Veronica muttered. Hetty cast a disparaging glance towards her. Jolyon was now her comrade in arms despite his money.

The small road got smaller before it started to climb. A splay at the bottom housed half a dozen WW11 Willis jeeps fitted out with seats in the back.

"This looks serious." Veronica exclaimed. "Do you think we should get one of those jeeps?"

"Actually, they're quite dangerous, they can't make it 'round some of the hairpin bends, they have to take a couple of bites at it."

"They look quite old." Calypso added. "Would worry about the brakes on the way down."

"There's that too." Jolyon added. "We'll walk, take us about forty five minutes, trust me, It's worth it." Hetty cast an adoring compliant look at Jolyon.

It started as a steep climb and got steeper as they slowly wound their way up a mountain. Stops to rest on low stone walls were regular. Each one a photo opportunity as the trees and views fell away from them. Then it was in front of them. An ancient stone abbey, built somehow on a very high mountain top over eight hundred years ago. The five young people just stopped and stared.

"No matter how many times I see it, it always amazes me." Jolyon spoke quietly to no one in particular. A jeep rattled past them, it's fat female occupants looking red and flustered.

"As you said Jolyon. It's worth it." The girls said nothing, just stood and stared at the magnificent setting that turned old stone buildings into absolute mystical beauty.

"How on earth did they do that all those years ago?" Hetty stared in amazement.

"A horse and a wheel I suspect." Jonny answered.

"More likely a donkey." Jolyon added. "Come on, let's look around, sometimes you can hear the monks chanting or reciting prayers in the chapple. It makes you feel as though you've died and gone to heaven. Just need a few angels to make it perfect."

Jolyon led the way with Hetty almost beside him. Jonny, Calypso and Veronica followed some ten yards behind. Calypso bouncing around with her camera snapping everything. Veronica sticking as close as she could to Jonny.

A monk in a dark brown vestment stood at the closed wrought iron gate. The deep heavy droning of recited prayers said or sung under a high ceiling seemed to creep out in waves. They stood with other tourists transfixed.

Calypso's hand slipped into Jonnys. Silently she led him away to a low stone wall to the side of the chapel. She sat on the sun warmed wall and concentrated on the view as it flowed steeply down the Cady valley to the small town of Vernet Les Bains. She patted the wall for him to sit down next to her.

Calypso kissed Jonny on the cheek and looked directly into his eyes.

"I'm going to marry Jolyon."

The information just didn't register for seconds. He was expecting some words of love, some expression of passion, of lifelong commitment, even if they couldn't be together. 'I'm going to marry Jolyon' just hammered into his brain as though it had come from the barrel of a gun. It ricocheted inside smashing this dream, wrecking this hope pulverising his normality.

"Why? Why?" He stammered.

"Why do you think, money, it's been arranged at family level, we don't have much of a say in it."

"Do you love him?"

"Of course, we grew up together, we've always been best friends but it's you I'm in love with. That's consequential, by the way, not important." Calypso looked away, almost in tears.

"Jolyon's going to announce it tonight at dinner, he knows how you feel about me and how I feel about you but doesn't know how to tell you. This whole trip, his father buying a plane, everything, is just about him telling you in a public arena, hoping you won't blow your top, start a fight, throw yourself under a bus or do anything stupid. He hopes that you'll have time to think about things. He loves you, as well you know, you must know, he's done so much for you. You don't do those sorts of things unless you love someone. I had to tell you, I love you so much, I don't want to see you hurt. It's just business, big business, think of it like that."

Jonny stared down the valley saying nothing, his brain racing away.

"You're right of course, they'd have never have let you marry me, if we ignored them or ran away or something they'd have one of us killed. It's for the best. Come on we should get back before we're missed."

Calypso was a little taken back and disappointed at his rationality.

Now it was different. Now the beauty, the history, the religious gravity meant nothing. It was just a pile of stones on top of a small mountain with a load of singing men. But there was still a role to play. A necessary pretence.

"We should head back down, it's getting on, it gets dark and chilly pretty quickly this high up." Jolyon was a good actor.

Hetty and Veronica had no idea. Jonny could feel Jolyon getting stressed as they dressed in smart casual for dinner. Conversation was difficult, yet neither could, as yet, acknowledge why. Jonny was still reeling from her close face, almost close enough to kiss, delivering the sharp prick that burst him. Still, how could he not love her. He had since the first moment and would to the last.

Dinner started late, it had taken them longer than expected to come down. Jonny, Jolyon and Calypso had made great overtures about the magnificent views, the sunset, the smell of herbs in the air. Veronica and Hetty slouched casually behind moaning about their shoes, being thirsty, being tired. They had taken a nap before dressing, making everyone late.

On the table there were two large bottles of 'Krug'

"Good grief! Are we celebrating?" Hetty said as she pulled out her chair to sit down. Jonny looked at Calypso then Jolyon. Jolyon realised she'd told him. 'That's why it was so strained in the room.' He thought to himself.

Jolyon remained standing whilst everyone sat. There were about four other couples in the large bare stone room. They were some way away. The waiter, a slim man in his forties who looked more Moroccan than French, opened the first large bottle with a pop. a fizz and a smile. Expertly decanting the lively champagne into the five glasses.

Jolyon held up his glass and everyone stood up.

"I am joyously happy to tell you all that---------." He paused for a glance at Jonny who seemed to be playing his part perfectly. "Calypso has accepted my offer of marriage and we are now officially engaged." He beamed at Calypso, her perfect lips parted to a coy smile, as though she was the reluctant star who outshone everyone and everything.

"To us my darling." He raised his glass towards her. So did everyone else. Veronica was beaming effervescent congratulations. So happy inside that Calypso was now off Jonny's radar. Hetty was back to undisguised fury as Jolyon had been lost.

"Where's the ring then?" Jonny asked as they all sat.

"Oh God! I forgot, yes the ring." Jolyon fumbled in his trouser pocket for the small red Garrard box. Turning towards her he opened it to reveal a glittering palest pink large diamond resting in a gold claw.

"I thought the colour would match your lips." Jonny looked at Jolyon. 'Could he really love her?' He thought.

Calypso took the ring and slipped it onto her finger,"

"How did you know the size Jolly?" He'd never heard her call him that before. Perhaps he'd misread it, perhaps she really did love him.

"I checked with mother, apparently you and her had been rummaging through the family jewels and one fitted, so this is the same size. Now I'm famished after all that walking."

Two waiters descended with menus and champagne top ups.

"Apparently the duck is very good." Jolyon said.

"I want to go home." Hissed Hetty to Veronica.

"Just enjoy the food and wine Hetty, it's the best and we're not paying, you won't get this in Manchester." Hetty softened a little.

"No, you're right. The elite never marry out of class. I'm so stupid allowing myself to be swept along by money. This world is not for me."

"You need to be in it Hetty or you won't get any funding for your 'refuge' just go with the flow. Jolyon does seem to be really sympathetic to the needs of the poor working class. See where it goes."

"Yes, You're right, you can't win the raffle if you don't buy a ticket."

"That's the spirit." Veronica held up her glass for a refill.

Jolyon clicked the door shut and locked it.

"It's business, you know that Jonny don't you? It's what I explained before. It's what I'm expected to do. I know Calypso's head over heels in love with you and that hurts me just as much as it must hurt you. I'll knowingly be marrying a woman who is in love with my best friend. I know it changes everything but I don't want it to change us Jonny. Marriages are complicated with sex. Children, money, emotions, they're difficult, whereas friendship is just liking and accepting someone. Please stay my friend. My best friend."

Jolyon put out his hand.

Jonny ignored it, put his arms around Jolyon and hugged him.

"There you go, your second hug."

Jolyon sat down on the bed in tears with his head in his hands. After a few minutes he spoke.

"Will you be my 'Best Man' Jonny?"

"Of course, I'd be miffed if I wasn't."

After breakfast the black Citroen rose up and glided towards Beziers.

Things had changed in the back but their squashed proximity forced them into occasional laughter, sarcasm and jokes.

Things were OK in the front.

"Why do you want to go to Beziers Jonny?" Veronica asked from the back.

"I want to be in a place where thousands of people died at the same time, to see if I can sense anything."

"Don't think I'll ask anymore questions." Veronica whispered to Hetty.

The church of St Mary Magdalene didn't seem special, local grey stone and a red tile roof. Jonny wandered into it on his own. He felt nothing. He felt no connection between life and death, even the mass death of seven thousand Cathars.

"We're going home tomorrow. Let's go somewhere near the sea. This place is creepy." Calypso felt uncomfortable in Beziers.

"Close your eyes Jonny, stick your finger on the map then let's see if the girls can direct us there."

Everybody laughed. Jonny's finger landed on 'La Palme' a small village near some coastal lakes.

"We'll go there, buy some local wine, stay the night then head for home tomorrow. Hetty! Direct me." Jolyon commanded.

The pleasantries and forced jovialities continued but it was false. In the silences everybody examined their own depths. Well everyone except Veronica.

The little plane seemed to labour against a headwind going back, as though it was uphill. Eventually it bumped safely down on the grass behind Bovington Hall. Wearily everyone clambered out to be greeted by Sir Baltimore. Jolyon invited them all to stay the night but no one really wanted to so excuses were made.

Jonny didn't know how to say goodbye to Calypso, a handshake perhaps? No, too formal, one kiss on the side of her cheek was appropriate. Hetty retreated back into her socialist defense and Veronica stood as close to Jonny as she could.

Jonny had to admit, the Mini did seem noisy and uncomfortable after the sophistication of the Citroen but at the moment that helped. He didn't want to talk, he just wanted to think about her. Hetty was sulking quietly in the back. He'd take mum away somewhere for a couple of days to take his mind off things. North Wales perhaps, she loved to go and pray with the nuns at Talacre Abbey, plus they made the most delicious Lemon curd he'd ever tasted. He'd buy a few jars to take back with him. The traffic lights suddenly changed to green. Someone hooted behind him.

Irene heard a car pull up outside. She peeked through the net. Yes it was Jonny. They all looked so young she thought to herself as she opened the front door. Veronica and Hetty headed towards the entry but Irene shepherd them into her house.

"Come on. Come on you must be hungry after that long journey, I've got some nice brawn from the butchers, some lovely tomatoes and a fresh loaf." She offered her cheek to Jonny for a kiss.

After the peace and beauty of the Pyrenees, Henry Street and it's noise seemed vulgar and intrusive. He wondered if his life as an Officer and all that went with it, was changing him. He'd never noticed before how poor it was. Jonny wondered how Hetty could be almost proud of such a condition. So much so that it was a crusade. Even stranger for Jolyon who seemed to want to be part of her crusade. 'Perhaps you could only be a socialist if you were rich? Maybe Jolyon was right.' He thought to himself.

Chapter. 10

Jonny was 'in civvies'. His car warranted him a salute even though there was no sticker or badge on it. Only an Officer could afford such a car. He pulled up on the left just inside the main gate of RAF Valley to ask directions for the Officers Mess. Two red and white Folland Gnats screamed overhead, slowing for an approach circuit.

The incredible 'wildness' of North Wales had taken his mind away from her. He'd thought of telling mum what had happened but had decided against it. Jonny was finding it more and more difficult to talk to his mother about important things in his life. It was as though she was his life as a boy but now he was a man with his own secrets that she wouldn't understand.

It seemed strange to be in an RAF Camp without Jolyon. He'd get settled in then try to ring him at Scampton.

He'd been there six weeks, the nimble little jets had become the focus of his life. Gradually she'd become less painful. Then it came.

My dearest Darling Jonny,

I've tried my hardest to forget you since France, but somehow that trip has made things worse. Being in your company for three or four days made me realise how hopeless things are for me. For us.

When we met at Bovington, it was like a dream, away from Ireland, away from home, I could be myself but going home was like waking up and so I got on with life pretending the beautiful ceiling had never happened.

Myself and Jolyon must do our duty, we have no choice, it is what's expected. The rules of the rich are never broken. The poor have so much freedom.

The wedding is arranged for Saturday July the twelfth next year. Jolyon tells me you've agreed to be 'best man', at least we get a kiss out of it.

I've no idea where life will take us all but please remember you will always be my life even if you are seldom in it.

You are my love now and always will be.

Calypso

PS, I'm getting concerned about Jolyon, he's seeing a lot of that Hetty woman, I'm sure there's nothing physical going on but his room has a lot of books about Socialism, Communism, Marx, Lenin, Stalin as well as flying. Sometimes he goes to meetings with her. It's really not appropriate for an RAF Officer to do that, especially a Vulcan Bomber pilot. Try and talk to him my darling.

PPS. He's given her quite a lot of money for her 'Women's Refuge' in Manchester.

Jonny flung his helmet to the foot of the bed then collapsed onto it to read the letter again.

Chapter. 11

Phill Shaw was late for work, he grabbed his tie and jacket then headed for the front door. It was no good he'd have to go again. Almost throwing his jacket off he raced upstairs to the toilet. Connie was still in bed.

He'd had to go a lot more recently, at first it was very dark brown, almost black but now, occasionally there was fresh red blood. He'd have to get it checked out but it wasn't something he wanted to do and most definitely not today. The Inspectors meeting at the nick was scheduled for eight o'clock. The Super, as nice a bloke as he was - didn't like his staff being late. No, Bernard Alexander was not a man you kept waiting.

The traffic was light - thank God! He'd just had the car serviced, it was going like a dream, he'd make it in time. Feeling more relaxed he listened to the light program on the radio, maybe he'd go and see mum tonight. She was so much happier without dad. He had no compunction about lying about him. He was a nasty vile person, prison was the right place for him, it didn't matter how he'd ended up there. Mum had lost weight, had her hair done and had started going to whist drives and stuff, even a dance at Christmas, course the band wasn't 'The Notes' they'd packed up long ago.

Phill, jogged up the front steps of Walsall Police Station and tapped in the code for the staff door. 'Better just nip to the loo before I go into the meeting.' He thought.

Chapter. 12

It was 'Déjà-vu', Jonny, Hetty and Veronica heading for Bovington hall, only this time the back of the little Mini was cluttered with his Morning Suit, Hetty's and Veronica's posh frocks for the wedding, all hung on the little clips that opened the back windows. The Mini-Cooper was fun but maybe the time had come for something a bit bigger. He liked the new Lotus Cortina's plus Calypso had a Lotus Elan. In his dreams it would make them closer.

"Calypso here yet?" Jonny asked Jolyon as they all clambered out of the Mini. Jolyon hugged all three of them.

"Not yet, She's flying in with her folk this evening. I won't be able to see her of course, bad luck and all that, but you will. I take it you've got the ring?"

Jonny thought of pretending he'd forgotten it but decided it was too tired a joke.

"Stop worrying Jolyon, I've got it."

"Come on, there's some 'eats' ready for you in the kitchen." Jolyon walked alongside Hetty who'd had her already curly hair permed into waves. Their conversation immediately turned to her women's refuge.

"How many people are coming Jolyon?" Jonny asked.

"Not many, only about a hundred, Brockhampton Church is only small so we're limited."

"Why didn't you arrange a bigger church?"

"'Cause it's got a thatched roof and I like it."

"Oh, as good a reason as any I suppose." Jonny pushed Veronica's bottom up the steps. She giggled with delight.

The eats were cold beef, thick slices of ham, still warm bread, butter that had never seen the inside of a supermarket, tomatoes, cucumber and sauces. There was a big white jug of Ted's cider in the middle of the table.

"Jonny you're in your listed bedroom, Hetty, Veronica you're in the big room at the end of the corridor." I'll get a maid to take your stuff up. Do you need anything ironing for tomorrow?"

"No, we've been very careful, we made Jonny hang everything up in his Mini." Hetty always took the lead. Veronica just nodded with her mouthful of ham sandwich.

Jonny lay on the bed staring at the ceiling waiting for the sound of a helicopter. It came about seven thirty. There was no dinner that night, just a buffet in the dining room. He'd go down about eight on the off chance she'd be there. Thinking things through, his thoughts wandered. 'So what if she was there, all he could do was polite conversation. She was to be Jolyon's bride tomorrow, lost forever to the elite he was becoming part of.'

There she was. Glistening brown ringlets cascading down her shoulders and back. Her tiny waist diving into tight black jeans, a thin blue floral blouse tied up at the bottom so it showed her midriff, pink pumps and the merest hint of makeup. When she was in a room the light was different. She spotted him and broke away from the buffet table.

"Hello." He hadn't heard her voice for nearly a year. It was a waterfall of pleasure.

"Hello you. Are you well?" Jonny replied, picking up a plate.

"As well as can be expected. How about you?"

"I'm contemplating suicide." Jonny joked.

"Well can you hang on til after tomorrow, it will spoil my day."

"I can hang on as long as you want." They looked at each other, their eyes lingering as only two people hopelessly in love can linger.

"Good."

Sir Baltimore joined them and the moment was gone.

Jolyon had chosen to spend his last evening as a single man in the local pub with Ted, some of the ground staff and local lads from the village. Hetty was there but not Veronica, she'd chosen to join Jonny walking around the duck ponds and gardens. It was a golden summer evening, the light breeze seemed to skip across the undulating grass. Some cars and people gradually started to drift in, she took hold of Jonny's arm.

"A long way from Henry Street Jonny. What you going to do now she's unavailable?"

"Fly aeroplanes very fast."
"Is that as exciting as her?"

"No. but it's a close second."

"You could marry me, I know the truth and I'd make a good wife even if I was second best."

Jonny stopped walking, a threatened duck quacked indignantly into the safety of the pond.

"You deserve better than that Veronica, he'll come along one day."

"I doubt it." They're all so boring, you're on a different level, as though something has lifted you up."

"Rubbish, let's go in and get a drink, a gin and tonic will do."

"I fancy some of that wine we brought back from France, do you think there will be any left."

"Ask Ted, he's the 'Sommelier', once more round the pond?"

"Oh OK! You've talked me into it." She giggled and held his arm even tighter.

There was a knock on his bedroom door and Jolyon opened the door before Jonny could say 'come in'. He could tell Jolyon had been drinking but he wasn't drunk. He sat on the bed.

"You were right Jonny."

"Right about what?"

"I got called into the bosses office the other day, said he's been ordered to designate his two best pilots to go to Coltishall for a Lightning Conversion Course and I was one of them."

"Told you, you're too good for bombers, they need people like you in fast jets."

"What about you?"

"I'm being posted to Seven Four squadron at Leuchars, we're getting the new Lightning's next year."

"Handy for golf then."

"I don't play golf."
"Well you should, every 'Gentleman' plays golf."

"I'm not a 'Gentleman' Jolyon, you know that."

"You're an RAF Officer Jonny, that makes you a 'Gentleman', you have no choice."

Jonny sat next to Jolyon on the bed and put his arm around his shoulder.

"Jolyon, I've done some really bad things in my life. Believe me, I'm not a 'Gentleman'."

"What, you mean you've been to bed with your best friend's future wife. I know that Jonny, I'm not stupid."

"No you're not, but I am. Bedtime Jolyon and it's my duty as your 'best man' to ensure you arrive at the church on time in a fit state, so let's go."

"I'm OK. See you tomorrow. Don't forget the ring."

It was two o'clock in the morning, he couldn't sleep thinking of her when the almost timid knock came and the door quietly opened.

"I want to look at the ceiling for one last time."

It was a lovely summer's day. The church looked perfect, the grounds with its neat grass and even neater, almost 'ball' shaped cropped trees were waiting like scenery in a theatre. The two families had discussed how she would arrive. The helicopter. A horse and carriage, an old Rolls Royce, a new Rolls Royce were suggested as options but Calypso insisted she drove herself there in her Lotus with father wedged into the small passenger seat. So that is how it was. The dark green sports car with yellow bumpers and yellow stripe arrived only five minutes late. Brian Guinness looking cramped and flustered holding onto his top hat, only too eager to struggle out of the car and resume his normal composed aloof demeanour. Calypso almost floated out, disentangling the voluminous white dress from the handbrake, gear stick and steering wheel before it was grabbed and sorted by her bridesmaids. Eventually, she was ready. Stood at the side of her father, smiling for the crowd. They walked slowly, arm in arm up the path to the entrance and waited for the organist to start 'The Wedding March'.

Jolyon and Jonny stood together, on the right, at the altar. They were both waiting for her. The little stone church with its small square tower and immaculate thatch, sheltering it's sitting and standing congregation, was also waiting. The organist - Mrs. Beasley - had been practicing all week, she didn't want to make any mistakes in front of such important people. She'd done it so many times, she was never nervous, but today she was.

Jonny fidgeted with the two ring boxes in his pocket and in his mind recited his speech. He'd never made a speech before.

The priest was a woman, Hetty commented to Veronica that was very 'Avant Garde' for such a rural society. Veronica shhhhh'd at her.

The service was short and rather sweet, which was good as it was starting to get hot with so many people in the little church. Soon, they were man and wife, Jonny had dutifully handed over the correct ring at the correct time without looking at Calypso. He'd looked at her as she came down the aisle with her father, slight, almost like a fairy, her tiny waist trapped in exquisite lace. The rest of the dress cascading away from her body. When they were just lying, looking at the ceiling, she'd told him that mother had had it especially made and flown in from Gozo, Malta.

Then it was time for the 'Best Man' to claim his traditional kiss. Jolyon had lifted her veil which now draped and framed her so soft face.

He couldn't make a big thing of it. So a small peck on her right cheek was all it was. Jonny knew what was going through Jolyon's mind and didn't want to hurt him in any way. Not even the slightest emotion or sign other than the required congratulatory smile.

The local villagers and uninvited press were waiting outside to shower Jolyon and his new bride with confetti and take as many pictures as they could, All hoping that one of them would be good enough to sell. After all, it wasn't everyday two elite families came together, one a dazzling socialite the other an RAF Pilot. The stuff of dreams or at least a tabloid picture. Everybody headed back to Bovington Hall. This time it was Jolyon in the passenger seat of the Elan. Calypso drove.

Unlike the wedding anniversary, there were no marquees, no circus animals or special effects. Everything was in the main hall of Bovington. Jonny had never been shown the hall before, it was splendid and very large running almost the whole length of the building, it easily accommodated the guests. The food was Herefordshire Beef, Rack of Lamb or Wye Salmon, the drink was of course, Champagne. Then it was finished. Jolyon had shown him what to do. Stand up, tap the wine glass with a spoon but don't break the glass, wait for the room to quieten, and then----.

"Ladies and gentlemen, honoured guests and of course, Bride and Groom.

Jonny turned towards his best friend and the woman he loved.

I am honoured to be standing before you today as the 'Best Man' of Mr. Jolyon Clay and his brand new bride Mrs. Calypso Clay.

Jolyon and I have only known each other for three years and so i cannot tell you any rude or naughty tales of his boyhood, I'm sure there are those here who can.

A humorous murmur spread throughout the room.

"I've got a few tales." A young man shouted from down the room.

Everybody laughed and thumped the table.

What I can tell you is that Calypso is a very lucky woman to be married to such a loving and caring man. You may have noticed that I have an accent. It's not from Eton or Cambridge, it's from Walsall. It meant nothing to Jolyon who befriended me, when to be honest, I was out of my depth. Who supported me in all ways, as I learned different ways to behave and appear. Mind you he was no good at bulling boots at Cranwell whereas I became quite an expert at it.

There was a polite laugh.

Our shared experiences- some of them pleasant and exhilarating, some of them downright scary- in the RAF have brought us even closer together and he is without doubt my true 'Best Friend'.

All that is left for me to do is to sincerely wish them a lifetime of happiness, and hope that it is a fruitful one blessed with joy.

Please be upstanding for a toast to our brand new bride and groom, Mr. and Mrs, Jolyon and Calypso Clay.

The guests all stood and toasted the Bride and Groom. Jolyon grasped Jonny's hand as he sat down, giving it a squeeze.

"Short and wonderfully sweet Jonny. Thank you, I know how much you've been worrying about this, but that was fine."

Jolyon stood up with a champagne glass in his hand and turned towards his new bride

.

The afternoon gradually moved over for the evening. The formal dinner became less so and eventually became a dance in the large reception room at the side of the hall where a bar and a band had been installed. The band reminded Jonny of 'The Notes' and all that went with it. If he drank a lot of champagne it helped with everything. Mainly he was left to dance with Veronica and Lady Edwina. Jolyon and Calypso disappeared about eight. Jonny never danced with Calypso, he'd thought about it and decided not to. Around about midnight folk started to go to bed or to make their way home.

It was one thirty, Jonny was lying in bed staring at the ceiling, but he didn't see it, and it meant nothing 'cause she wasn't there. Then there was the sound of helicopter blades biting into the night air, so noisy at first, then fainter, then it was gone, they were gone, she was gone. No longer even near him.

Breakfast was laid out in the kitchen, toast or fried bread with whatever you wanted. Jonny waited for Hetty and Veronica to finish.

"You OK to drive back, you had a lot to drink last night?" Veronica enquired spreading butter and marmalade onto her toast.

"I'm fine." Jonny lied. The thought of three hours bouncing around in the raucous Mini didn't enamour him to pleasantries over breakfast. "We'll stop for lunch on the way, I know a nice hotel."

"We need to say our goodbyes and thanks to Sir Baltimore and Lady Edwina." Hetty said.

Jonny was surprised at Hetty addressing them that way, almost as though she'd seen through the privilege and elitism to see the real people behind it. People with real problems, feelings and emotions, just like her.

Jonny said goodbye to Ted and shook his hand. There was an understanding. The Mini had been washed and packed with bags, frocks and suits. It headed out of the yard and turned left. The summer hedgerows were just starting to look a little weary and tired, their job done for the year.

It was the black and white hotel at Droitwich for lunch. Jonny thought about the night there with Jolyon on his first trip to Bovington Hall.

"I wonder where the honeymoon is?" Veronica asked as they were waiting for soup. Nobody could face anything alcoholic so it was an orange juice for Jonny, an elderflower cordial for Veronica and plain water for Hetty. Her hair was now discarding her carefully arranged 'waves' and returning to her tight curls.

"Nobody knows." Jonny replied.

"I know." Chipped in Hetty. There was an awkward silence as Jonny and Veronica looked at her.

"Do tell us Hetty." Jonny almost commanded.

"Russia, St. Petersburg to be more precise. Jolyon's desperate to visit the Hermitage and the Tsar's Winter Palace."

Jonny looked at Veronica.

"Wow! bet Calypso will enjoy that." Veronica quipped.

"Here's our soup." Jolyon decided to be more direct with Hetty. "Are you sure it's just the art and culture Jolyon's going for or is he having secret meetings with Burgess and Maclean?" Jonny tried to make it sound like a preposterous joke.

"For God's sake Jonny, they're on honeymoon." She fobbed him off but didn't deny it.

Mum was peeking through the net curtain before he had time to turn the engine off.

"Was it good?" She asked ushering them in through the front door.

"It went very well mum. I've bought you something you'll like."

Irene's face lit up as she kissed her son.

Jonny took out something wrapped in greaseproof paper and a plastic carrier bag.

"There you go, some thick slices of best Herefordshire cold beef, a rack of Welsh lamb and some wild Wye Salmon."

"Oooh! That's lovely, your dad would have loved the Welsh lamb with new potatoes, runner beans, mint sauce and gravy." She said it as though he was still with her, sharing every moment.

Veronica and Hetty made to leave and go next door.

"Jonny will you run Hetty to the station at eight tonight for her train?"

"Of course."

"Sit down Jonny let's have a slice of this beef on a sandwich with some mustard, it looks lovely."

Irene was happy with Jonny at home.

"Shall we go to the Arboretum and feed the swans later mum?"

"That'll be nice. I'll wear my new coat."

Chapter 13.

It wasn't nicknamed 'The Frightening' for nothing. High and almost mighty it was a large aircraft. Made as a stroke of genius by an English company that made fridges. Jonny looked at the gleaming polished aluminium machine he was expected to fly. As yet there were no trainers so the classroom and the basic simulator was all there was. The simulator didn't do landings and take offs, just emergencies and cockpit drills.

He couldn't wait, with every new challenge he spoke to dad.

"What do you think of this? A bit faster than the Javelin dad, hope I can handle it."

The English Electric F1 could travel at twice the speed of sound and climb like a rocket. Jonny walked around it touching the sleek panels. It would be at least a month before they let him loose, the only drawback was the fuel, it used a lot of it very quickly. It just did it's job of intercepting dangerous invaders and then came back home for a top up.

Leuchars was in the East of Scotland. It had St Andrews to the south and Carnoustie to the north. Jonny was surrounded by golf. He'd taken Jolyon's advice and was taking lessons but compared to the lightning it was dull as dishwater. It would take at least six months before he became operational. It was a world away from the gentleness of Wales and the forgiving Gnat, this aircraft was brutal and bit you as soon as you didn't give it one hundred percent attention. It was a very demanding mistress, a dominatrix of a machine but if you got it right. WOW! When he was flying, everything else disappeared from his life, including her.

Now, she was very much on his mind, she wrote to him every few months, he never replied, it was too risky, the last thing he wanted was to hurt Jolyon.

It was on a long sweeping right hand curve in the road between Dundee and Arbroath. There was no hedgerow or fence, just a large grass splay leading onto an old cottage with some neglected outbuildings. On his days off, when it wasn't persistent heavy rain, Jonny would drive from Leuchars to Arbroath to order a pair of Arbroath 'Smokies'. His mum loved them because his dad loved them. They'd go on the overnight train and she'd get them the next day. Dad loved everything Scottish, every couple of years he'd catch the train up to Glasgow or Edinburgh for the Scotland - England international football match. He always supported Scotland even though he was English. He always bought Jonny a surprise, the last one before he died had been the Gloster Javelin,

It was light blue and the tail of it was just sticking out. It wasn't exactly a garage, more of a free standing wooden lean to, covered in sheets of felt. It was an old cottage set well back off the sweeping curve. He'd noticed it on two or three occasions, the car never seemed to move. Today he'd knock on the door and ask.

The showers were short and sharp, moved in and out by a strong cold breeze.

The door was answered by an old man, well into his seventies, Jonny thought. There was no point in beating around the bush.

"Hi, good afternoon, I was wondering about the car."

"And what exactly were you wondering?"

It was a 'craggy' Scottish voice that said it. The man himself was 'craggy', baggy brown trousers held up with braces, a fleecy shirt and greeny orange pullover, his hair was almost gone as were his teeth. A female voice called from the back 'Who is it James?'

"Some young fella, curious about me car. Do you know what it is young man?"

Jonny could just see the rear valance and twin exhaust pipes sticking out from the hanging sheet of felt.

"I'm guessing at a Porsche 356."

"Four cylinder or six?" The old man's eyes were beginning to light up.

"I'm guessing again at four as the exhaust pipes are pretty small and the six's are very rare."

Satisfied he wasn't dealing with a nincompoop the man went inside, coming out moments later with a bunch of keys.

"I don't want to look if it's not for sale. I don't want to waste your's or my time."

The old man was a little taken back.

"It's for sale sonny but only to the right person. Are you interested? Yes or no."

Jonny nodded.

It was beautiful. Light blue, low, aerodynamic, stylish, everything the Mini wasn't. Sensibly he'd part exchange the Mini for a Lotus Cortina, much easier for mum, but this! This was something else, this was art on four wheels, four quite big wheels actually, especially compared to the ten inch rollers of the Mini.

"It's only done twenty thousand miles, I've had it from new, m'wife thinks I'm barmy hanging on to it as I canna get in or oot of it now. Bloody arthritis, dunna get old lad. It's shite."

Jonny just knew, everything would work OK and the Porsche would drive like a jewel.

"So what's the price?" Jonny asked.

"Not cheap, and don't make offers, it's what I want or nothing."

Jonny could see the man didn't really want to sell but he was Scottish and what his wife was nagging him about did make sense.

"Five hundred lad, take it or leave it."

"I've got fifty pounds on me, will you accept that as a deposit til I sell my car and get back to you?"

"And how long will that be?"

"Two or three weeks, should do it, I'm from Leuchars so someone on the camp will probably buy it, it's quite rare."

"You flyin or spannerin?"

"Flyin."

"Thought so, one of them Lightning's?"

"Yes."

The old man took the fifty pounds, checked each note carefully then held out his hand.

"Soon as you can young man, soon as you can."

Jonny shook his hand and left, there was no need for any paperwork.

The two letters lay unopened on the front passenger seat of the Mini. He knew who they were from, one from mum and one from Calypso. Arbroath quayside was always wet, backed by large three storey houses, built of granite bricks and concrete, It was a 'working' place cluttered by salt water rusted lobster pots. The small yellow painted office on the quay was the place to order the 'smokies', it only took a minute or two then mum would know he was thinking about her. Leuchars was a long way away so he only got home once or twice a year.

Mum's letter was always just about family and what she'd won or lost on the horses or at bingo. Poor people didn't do exciting or interesting things, they couldn't afford to.

My Dearest Darling Jonny.

I hope you're keeping safe whizzing 'round the highlands in your jet plane.

Jolyon and I have rented a charming old vicarage just outside Coltishall, - I couldn't abide those awful married quarters places - which, coincidentally, has a church with a thatched roof.

Jolyon is still involved with that Hetty woman and it's worrying me more and more, the other day a letter arrived from Russia. I need to go back a bit. When we were on honeymoon in St Petersburg - which incidentally I did enjoy despite my initial misgivings - we had coffee one morning at our hotel with a man called Guy, Jolyon did tell me his surname but I've forgotten it. Anyway, the man was English, rather scruffy and unkempt in a sort of stylish manner, you know, good quality clothes that were neglected and stained. I didn't really take to him but jolyon spent the whole morning deep in conversation with him, God knows what about. I left them to it and went to rest in our room, it had a splendid balcony with views over the river to the palace.

I thought nothing of it, maybe an old Etonian or Cambridge chum, he was wearing an 'Eton' tie, well dickie bow actually, after that we just got on with our holiday but there were some days or half days when Jolyon went off on his own, supposedly to look at the art in the Hermitage, which, by the way is huge, apparently it's the second biggest art gallery in the world. Once again I thought nothing of it. To be honest I was grateful for a few hours on my own.

Jolyon left this letter on his desk so I happened to have a peep at it. Nothing interesting in it, just going on about Karl Marx and how Khrushchev was changing things for the worst by squandering the legacy of Stalin.

What worried me was the end, it was signed, 'all my love Guy.' I've never considered his sexuality, I mean we do it, now and again but it's nothing like you and I. Now i'm getting worried. He's an RAF pilot for God's sake, one day he might have to shoot down a Russian bomber or something. Will he be able to do it? I'm not sure?

Sorry to off load on you but you're all I've got in the real world,

Always your love

Calypso xx.

Jonny put the letter down on the red and grey seat, he looked at the grey and grey sea for a while crashing into the solid quay wall, thought about the beautiful Porsche he'd just agreed to buy, thought about James Dean then read the letter again. It wasn't his problem. Jolyon was Jolyon, he'd come out the other end of this and do the right thing, he always did, after all he married Calypso.

Dear Son,

Thank you for the Smokies, they were delicious, I keep them for Sunday breakfast with a poached egg. That's how your dad liked them; we only had them about once every four years when the match was at Edinburgh.

Aunty Win visited with her lot last week, we had a lovely day, tea and buns at Lyons in the town and Bingo at night, they came on the train but Janet's new boyfriend has a car so he collected them about ten. A late night for everybody.

There's some blackies moved in at the end of the street and at the top end there's some paki's, the youngsters seem OK but their old folk dress funny, course they don't speak English but they send their kids to Grange Street anyway. Expect they'll pick it up quick, knowing kids. The cooking smells coming from their houses are strong, you can even smell it when you walk by and they're not cooking, It must stick to the curtains or wall paper.

My knees are getting worse, it's my weight, started eating 'allbran' and grapefruit for breakfast but it doesn't seem to help. I might save up and buy some of those bathroom scales.

I'm so lonely without you and dad, I really look forward to you coming home, I know Scotland is a long way away but try your best, you can bring your friend Jolyon and his new wife if you want, we could all squeeze in.

Ok got to go to the Co-op and do some shopping, it's drizzling so will take my pac-a mac and my rain hood. Going to get a nice fillet of plaice for dinner, there's some parsley growing in the back so that will be nice.

Do take care in your aeroplane, you're all I've got.

Love Mum x

Jonny looked at the two letters, one was on quality embossed paper and written in ink, the other. on pages pulled from a book and written in smudgy biro. He thought that it summed up his strange life quite well. A larger than average wave hit the wooden stanchions of the quay and sent up a wall of spray that found it's way onto the windscreen. Jonny started the engine and watched the Smiths tachometer twitch up and down as he revved. Flicked the switch down for the wipers and pressed the button to wash the screen. He could sense that the wiper bottle was nearly empty, the midges and flies that had flattened themselves on the Mini's screen took a lot of washing off.

Chapter. 14

"There's no nice way to say this Mr. Shaw. You've got bowel cancer."

It was just brutal confirmation of what Phill had suspected anyway. He couldn't eat, he felt full all the time, if he did force himself to eat he was usually sick afterwards, when he did manage to go to the toilet there was always blood. Folk were beginning to notice he was getting thinner. Connie was worried sick but didn't like to push the issue, fearing something nasty. 'Thank God they hadn't got any kids' Phill thought to himself.

The doctor at the hospital sat behind his desk protected by brown manila.

There was a long silence whilst Phill took it in.

"How long?"

"Who knows, it can be very quick, can take months, every case is different."

"Can anything be done?"

"Yes we can cut away the colon and give you a colostomy bag but the prognosis is not good."

"OK I'll think about it. Thank you Doctor." Phill rose to leave the clinical office. He wondered why on earth he'd said 'thank you Doctor' to a man who'd just handed him a death sentence, it wasn't his fault, it just felt like it. He wanted to blame someone, something.

He sat in his car deep in thought. He'd have to tell Connie, that wasn't the problem, work was the problem.

People said hello and good morning as he walked up the steps towards his office. The removable sign on the door read 'Inspector Phillip Shaw.' He wondered how long it would take to remove it and put a different one in it's place, five minutes, maybe ten.

Two offices along was signed 'Superintendent Bernard Alexander' Phill knocked on the door, went in and handed a piece of hand written paper to Bernard.
'Please turn off the tape recorder in your draw.'

Bernard wasn't very pleased, he frowned from under his glasses. The recorder wasn't a secret, he just didn't publicise it much. He reached into the second draw down on his right and clicked it off.

"Sit down Phill, what's the problem." Bernard could sense the problem was important.

"I've got to go off sick for a while Bernard."

"Sit down Phill, sit down. Now how long do you need? Is it stress? things have been pretty demanding these last few months."

"It's not stress." Phill sat down and took a deep breath. "I shan't be coming back Bernard, it's bowel cancer." That was the first time Phill had said those words to anyone. Bernard fell silent.

"Are you sure? You're very young, thirty five is young these days, how about a second opinion?"

"I'm sure, I've been putting things off for a long time dreading this moment. There are some very important things I have to tell you, things that will put you in a difficult situation Bernard, that's why I asked you to turn the tape off."

"Wait." Bernard pushed back in his chair and reached into the bottom left hand draw of his desk.

"Think we might need this." He poured out two shots of Glenlivet whisky into two chunky glasses.

"As you know my father is in 'The Green' for Frankie Fletcher's murder."

"Yes, we know Phill, it's no reflection on you."

"It is Bernard." Phill took a swig of the clear pure whisky. "It is Bernard because he didn't do it."

"He was found guilty Phill, how do you know he didn't do it?"

"Because I followed him home that night, he was playing in 'The Notes', he'd regularly drink eight to ten pints during the night, the more he drank the better he played. I'd promised mum I'd keep an eye on him when I could, so she'd let me know where and when he was playing. If I was off duty I'd follow behind him in my own car. If I was on duty, I'd make some excuse and use an unmarked car to follow him.

I was working that night, he couldn't have done it, I followed him all the way home."

Bernard took another swig and rolled it around his thoughts before swallowing.

"This is serious stuff Phill."

"So's dying Bernard."

"Why didn't you say this at the time? I remember asking you if you knew anything?"

"For my mother, prison is the best place for him Bernard, he's a monster, he'd come home pissed, use his belt on her then bugger her. He wasn't interested in normal sex. I did it for her, she's happy since he's been locked up."

"Why are you telling me this Phill? What do you want?"

"What I did was wrong Bernard. Frankie Fletcher's murderer is still out there wandering around scot free, probably because of me. I made a false statement and condoned the actions of a drunk driver. Dereliction of duty. Taking without owners consent of a police vehicle, miscarriage of justice. Dismissed from the service for gross misconduct I would think. That means Connie won't get her widow's pension."

There was a long silence. The whisky tumblers were now empty.

"Here's what you do Phill. Write down what you've just told me in a statement form, include the reasons that you did it. Put it in a sealed envelope and give it to your solicitor marked 'to be opened after my death'. Eventually it will end up on my desk. To reopen the enquiry I'll have to expedite the release of your father on the grounds of new evidence. I don't think you can be posthumously dismissed so Connie will get to keep her pension."

Phill got up to leave.

"How long before it ends up on my desk?"
"Six months maximum, according to the doctor. Worried what will happen to mum once he's released."

Bernard Alexander got up and walked around his desk. He hugged his inspector.

"We could ask for conditions for his release, if she'll make a complaint."

"Thanks Bernard." Phill said, almost in tears.

"This conversation never happened Phill. Go home to your wife."

Phill left the room. He didn't go home to Connie; he went to see his mother.

"Hi mum." He hid his feelings.

"Phill! What a lovely surprise, wasn't expecting you today. Sit down, I'll put the kettle on, do you want a sandwich? It's nearly dinner time, I've got some nice cheddar and Branston."

"Sit down mum, I've got a bit of bad news, well two bits actually."

A worried look spread across Brenda's face as she pulled the chair out and sat down.

Phill sat down opposite her and took her hand.

"I'm ill mum."

"I thought you'd not been yourself recently, you're thinner, I put it down to Connie not feeding you properly, she's a lovely girl but she can't cook for tuppence."

"Mum! Mum! It's nothing to do with Connie, I've got bowel cancer!"

There was a long silence.

"Well I'm sure they can fix it. They can do wonderful things these days, operations, chemo, drugs, tablets, that sort of thing."

"Mum, they can't fix it, I've got about six months maximum."

Tears started to well up in her eyes. She turned away and started to sob into her cupped hands.

"It's not natural, kids shouldn't d----." She couldn't say the word 'die'. "Pass on before their parents. Look at your bloody father, fit as a fiddle in prison, why couldn't it have been him who's ill?"

"That's another thing I need to tell you mum, soon after I've gone dad'll be released from prison."

"Whatever for, they gave him life."

"Because mum, he didn't do it. He didn't kill Frankie Fletcher. It's my doing he's locked up. I did it for you. I didn't tell lies but I didn't tell all the truth either. I followed him home that night. He couldn't have done it."

"Oh Phill! What am I going to do without you? Especially if he's around. I can't live here. I can't go back to that. I'll have to move back in with Irene, she's lonely now Jonny's not there. Are you sure? You don't look that ill, just a little gaunt. Get a second opinion, go to another doctor."

"Mum, I know myself there's something drastically wrong, I don't need a doctor to tell me. I'm going home now to tell Connie. I've finished with the Police now, officially just off sick, but my boss knows."

"Stay for a bit Phill, please? At least stop for a cup of tea, you can't just destroy my life then walk off, just half an hour Phill please."

"How about we walk into town mum and have a tea and cake at Lyons?"

She brightened up, after all he was with her now, walking, talking, chatting and touching. He'd be alright. There'd been some sort of mistake.

"I'll get my coat, shall I take my brolly?"

"Better had mum, just in case of a shower."

Chapter. 15

Today was the day. Jonny's first solo in 'The Frightening' The sleek silver missile gained the nickname mainly because of its very high landing speed. The nimble little Gnats in Wales seemed positively sedate at one hundred knots but the razor thin wings of the Lightning demanded at least one hundred and thirty knots, one hundred and fifty miles per hour just to make it safely down, his little blue Porsche could only manage just over one hundred and that seemed ridiculously fast. He'd spoken to Jolyon on the phone last night. Jolyon at least had access to T5 two seat trainer Lightning's, but like Jonny, had yet to go solo, they'd laughed at Jonny buying a 'sports beetle'. Jolyon called it a 'Hitlermobile' and swore never to sit in it. Jonny retaliated that Jolyon was getting old swapping his stylish 'Alpine' for a 'family' Rover three litre Coupe. Their conversations carefully avoided the contentious two subjects of Hetty and Calypso and mostly centred on the challenges of flying the enormously powerful fast Jet.

Life at the camp centred on the Officer's Mess and flying. Jonny didn't want to socialise or meet women. There was only one woman he wanted and she was separated by culture, background, money and marriage. She was the one who was always in his thoughts at every quiet moment. Flying a demanding rocket like the Lightning took all his faculties and made her go away. Another month and he'd be 'operational' but for now he had additional duties. Inspection of the lower ranks quarters, Divisional Officer to the 'armourers' section, duty officer three times a month and one weekend a month. When he became operational, some of these tedious duties would fall away.

Tonight he was on duty as 'Officer of the Day'.

"Sir, we have a problem."

Jonny looked up from his flying notes to see the young sergeant behind the voice.

"Go on."

"We've had an incident at the shooting club, a young aircraftman has been seen to have hidden away a .22 target pistol."

"I have no knowledge of the shooting club Sargeant where is it?"

"It's in one of those old green painted nissen huts at the bottom of the camp. There's an indoor range in the middle one and members can go there and shoot .22 target pistols."

"And who supervises this?"

"One of the RAF Regiment Sergeants, whoever's on duty, but usually, it's a sergeant who's keen on shooting."

"And what's the name of the Aircraftman involved?"

"Aircraftman Patrick Quigley."

"Is he Irish by any chance?"

"Yes Sir, Belfast. His mates call him 'Paddy'."

"Religion?"

"Non stated on his record Sir, but his family are believed to be Catholics."

"What are the circumstances?"

"Just a normal Wednesday club night, all the pistols are locked in the cupboard, the keys are kept in the guardroom and have to be signed out by a Regiment sergeant. Come nine o' clock Sergeant James collected in the weapons and locked up as usual. The pistols are kept in their boxes. It seems Quigley had filled his box up with lead fishing weights he'd brought in with him in his pockets, had hidden the pistol, a Smith and Wesson semi-automatic behind one of the brick walls that run the whole length of the range either side. Presumably his intention was to somehow get back into the range later and retrieve the weapon."

"And how do we know all this?"

"A corporal happened to see him hiding it."

"Why didn't the corporal challenge him at the time?"

"Don't know Sir, possibly he thought it was too serious an issue."

"Presumably Sgt. James doesn't check, inside the boxes."

"No Sir, he usually goes along the line of shooters, checks that their weapon and magazines are empty then unlocks the cupboard and everybody walks up with their box and hands it over. He then locks the cabinet."

"Where is Quigley now?"

"In a holding cell in the guardroom."

"Has anybody spoken to him or interviewed him about this?"

"No Sir."

"Where is the pistol now?"

"I have it here Sir, complete with a full magazine." The sergeant took out the pistol from his briefcase. It was in a sealed polythene bag. He put it on Jonny's desk.

"OK Sergeant, leave it with me. Go back to the corporal and have him write out a statement of everything he saw at the time."

Jonny stared at the pistol for a while then locked it in his locker under his new flying overalls.

Group Captain Graham Dangerfield had the most inappropriate name for an RAF pilot. He was renowned for being the safest man you could possibly be with in a plane. Inflight safety was his thing. Now he was a desk pilot in charge of Leuchars.

He arrived, as usual, at about eight twenty and was surprised to find Flying Officer Conrad waiting for him in the lobby of the building.

"Morning Conrad. Problem?"

"A small one Sir, it's been dealt with but requires your advice as to the resolution."

The Group Captain looked at Jonny from underneath his hat before taking it off. He was tall and pencil slim but age and gravity were just beginning to round down his shoulders. The ubiquitous moustache was also pencil thin and immaculately manicured. The uniform loose and stylishly worn.

"Better come in Conrad, sounds as though we'll need some coffee for this."
He hung up his hat and coat and gestured for Jonny to sit down in the chair opposite his desk.

"OK, tell me."

Jonny recounted the details of the incident.

"As I see it Sir, we have two options. The first is we report the matter to the local police with an allegation of attempted theft of a firearm. The fact that the corporal saw him hide it coupled with his act of filling the box with lead fishing weights should be enough to ensure a conviction."

"And the second?" The laconic camp commander sipped from his china coffee cup.

"No report, no enquiry, just 'dishonourable discharge' a travel warrant to Ireland and gone by five this evening."

"Which do you favour Conrad?"

"The second option."

"Why?"

"Well if we involve the police that means it will be in the public domain. The question may arise as to why the RAF is recruiting people from Catholic Belfast in these times of I.R.A. troubles."

Graham Dangerfield considered his coffee cup.

"OK number two it is. Have a report complete with your recommendation and reasons on my desk by two this afternoon. I'll endorse it and as you say he'll be on his way as a civilian by five."

"Yes Sir." Jonny rose from the chair.

"Jonny." The Group Captain's tone was now softer.

"Sir!"

"After you've been operational for a few months put in an application for Flight Instructor. We need the best to teach the rest. I've been hearing a lot of good reports about you." He winked at Jonny.

"Yes Sir, thank you."

"Oh and Jonny, store that pistol somewhere safe, don't want it getting mixed up with the others at the club, might need to produce it as evidence if things don't go to plan."

"Yes Sir. Will do."

It was Easter, The weather in Scotland had been awful all winter. The flying had been intense, instructing, normal training, learning about the new 'Firestreak' missile and Quick Reaction Alert (Q.R.A.) duties had taken their toll. The Russians had been aggressively persistent in just breaching UK Air space. So much so that they now had a good rapport with the Russian bomber crews who regularly waved, flicked the V's or held up some pornographic material. It was tiring and stressful, every time the horn sounded and the telephone jingled adrenalin flooded into his body. Minutes later his body would be pinned back into his seat, his tight straps suddenly loose as the silver rocket thrust upwards on hotpower reheat making him feel as though someone had suddenly pulled away the earth. Was it the real thing this time? You never knew but either way the adrenalin still pumped.

All the talk in the crewroom was of the new belly mounted fuel tanks which were coming in and the new Ferranti radar which could look down as well as forward. It was top secret, still only in the trials stage, only fitted to one aeroplane and that was at Coltishall.

And so it was with relaxed relief that Jonny threw his bag onto the front passenger seat of the light blue Porsche, - some of his colleagues said it was 'powder' blue and asked if he wore make up when driving it - but it wasn't, it was sort of toned down 'cornflower' blue. He turned the key and headed south. It was a long journey but he enjoyed the challenge, stopping for tea, petrol and food was a pleasure, there was always somebody admiring or commenting on his car. It would be great to spend some time with mum. Jolyon and Calypso were heading for Bovington, he wondered if they'd visit mum's, maybe if Hetty was there. If that was the case it would just be Jolyon. A large truck in front of him brought him back to the present as he braked heavily. The little car made no complaint, the tyres didn't even squeal.

Within five minutes of sinking into his dad's chair in front of the fire, Veronica was knocking on the back door with some eggs.

"Oh hello, long time no see, how are you?" She'd heard the sound of a different car pull up and guessed who it was.

"Hello Veronica, I'm good. Only been here ten minutes, you were quick."

Veronica was pretty but not sexy, some women were really sexy without being pretty. Jonny looked at her as Irene fussed in with another cup and a plate of chocolate biscuits. She liked it when they were together so she put the plate and cup down then made an excuse.

"You still working in Manchester?" Jonny asked dunking a chocolate digestive for exactly three seconds.

"Yes but I'm getting tired of the travelling, thought I might marry you and have a couple of kids." It wasn't the joke she pretended it was.

"Sorry I'm taken."

"Yes I know but she's married." Veronica looked directly into his eyes. "I don't mind being second best."

Irene came back into the room with some toasted tea cakes.

"Got these this morning, I know they're your favourites Jonny so tuck in."

"How long you here for?" Veronica asked.

"Til Tuesday then back to Scotland, I'm getting worried, I'm beginning to like haggis." Jonny joked.

"You'll be wearing a skirt next." She teased.

"Haven't got the knees for it. What about Hetty?"

"She's here tomorrow night, so you never know Jolyon might happen to pass by."

"You never know." Jonny looked at the Gloster Javelin on the table by the window. Two wheels had been knocked off, he'd glue them back on tomorrow.

Mum was glowing and happy but somehow she didn't look well. He'd take her out tomorrow, Malvern, she liked Malvern. Dad used to take her there to walk on the hills, not much, just a little, her knees weren't good even then. She'd never been in the Porsche, he hoped she could manage to get in and out Ok, it was quite low, he hoped her weight wouldn't break the seat. She looked fatter than before.

Hetty turned up on Saturday morning. She hadn't changed at all, still little with bubble curls for hair, still a ferocious socialist, still in undeclared love with Jolyon, who, she said, might pop by that night.

Come the evening Jonny took mum and Veronica out for a meal at 'The Bell' on the Birmingham Road. Hetty declined saying she was 'Tired', everyone knew it was a lie.

It was ten thirty when Jonny turned the little Porsche into Henry Street, the front passenger seat was straining under mum's weight and Veronica was squashed sideways on the little bench seat in the back.

As they turned in they saw a large dark coloured Rover Coupe parked outside the house.

"Jolyon's here." Chorussed Jonny and Veronica together.

"That's nice." Mum said.

Jolyon and Hetty appeared on the front doorstep of number forty nine as Jonny switched off the lights and engine. There were smiles all round.

It was good to see Jolyon, he hadn't seen him for over a year.

"Hey Biggles how are you?" Jonny and Jolyon hugged.

"I'm good but so much better for seeing you." Jonny looked at Jolyon, he looked even more handsome, somehow his thin face had changed into a firm ruggedness, his thin shape was now triangular, he looked stronger.

"You look good Jolyon, married life is obviously suiting you."

"Rubbish, it's good old RAF breakfasts and lots of alcohol. Calypso can't cook, I have to draw her a map to find the kitchen, she doesn't eat, she pecks, I'm sure she's really a chicken." Everyone laughed.

"So you can manage a dripping sandwich then?" Mum said.

"That's the only reason I came mum, you know that." Irene relished in 'mum'.

"What's the real reason?" Jonny whispered as they filed into mum's little house.

"Said I'd take Hetty to a CND rally on Monday."

"Where is it?"

"Aldermaston."

"For God's sake Jolyon, that's an RAF camp, you can't go there, if you're clocked by the police or special branch or anybody, you're out, all your dreams will be in the clouds but you won't. You're an RAF officer, a Lightning pilot, the front line of Britain's defences. You can't do it Jolyon."

"I've promised Jonny, and one thing you've learned about the privileged elite is we never break a promise."

The lights came on and everyone sat down. Mum disappeared into the kitchen happy as Larry with a 'family' to fuss over.

"Jonny, make me a port and lemon will you?" She shouted from the kitchen.

"Yes Mum."

Jonny had a Mackeson, Dad liked those. Jolyon had a whisky, Veronica had a port and lemon with Mum and Hetty had a lemonade.

"I'm only the taxi Jonny don't worry, I'll stay out of things."

"You need to be careful, things are building up, what with the Vietnam war and everything."

"I know, I know, and thanks for your concern but I'm not a member of the Communist Party yet." Jolyon laughed as he swirled the whisky around the heavy tumbler. Mum only had one of those glasses. Dad liked to drink out of a proper glass.

"How are things with Calypso?" Jolyon looked at Jonny deciding whether to trot out the company message or tell his friend the truth.

"Don't you know?"

"No." Jonny lied.

Jolyon took another slug of the whisky.

"Sort of separate lives really, and we're both happy with that. Calypso puts on a show for the RAF and I put on a show for her folks, but she doesn't really understand me. Understand why I support Hetty's women's refuge, understand why I want to try for a fairer safer world."

"Does that still bother you then?"

"Yes of course, I live a life of luxury as a direct result of colonial abuse and oppression, in the past people have died and now I'm rich. Most if not all of my type never think of it, but for me, it never leaves me alone. I need to at least try to change things. Look at Tony Benn, if he can do it, so can I."

Jonny poured him another whisky. Mum brought in his sandwich. Jonny thought about asking him about the letters from 'Guy' in Russia but decided against it.

The journey back started in the sun and gradually became cloudy and cold. He was worried about Jolyon, he was in his thoughts as he drove north. Maybe there'd be another letter from Calypso when he got back, she hadn't written for months. She knew why he never replied they'd spoken once on the phone after Jolyon had told him he was away at a rally with Hetty one weekend. He headed diagonally eastward to pick up the M1 just before Nottingham. Then it was just a long drone north, the services were abysmal so he only stopped for fuel.

Jonny was looking forward to a break from operational duties, as exhilarating as they were in the ultra powerful Lightning's it did exhaust you and the QRA's were tedious, lounging in the crew room fully kitted out for twenty four hours soon lost it's glamour after the first couple of stints. Going to the loo was a pain, so coffee and tea, drunk mainly through boredom became a problem. No, the Flight Instructors course would be a welcome change.

As it turned out, it wasn't. The course was mainly in a classroom, learning in considerable depth about the Lightning's numerous systems and alternative ways to respond to faults and emergencies. The new simulator now included landings and take offs so routines and procedures could now be learned without leaving the ground.

The squadron now possessed two T4 trainers, the additional side by side seat bulking out the purity of the fuselage, as though it had been to the gym. One scary moment did take place when they were slowing from supersonic to subsonic. Andrew Roberts deliberately yanked back both throttles and both engines immediately flamed out. The rocket like Lightning did not make a good glider so inflight restart was required very quickly. Fortunately for Jonny and his instructor they started OK,the windmilling of the turbines as they dived towards the ground helped. As the power came back on, Andrew exhaled and laughed.

"Always throttle back gently, one engine at a time coming down from supersonic, keep an eye on your air speed indicator. Apparently if you do what I just did it causes some kind of pressure blow back which causes the engines to flame out."

"Thanks for telling me." Jonny crackled through the intercom. "Are there any other gems you wish to share with me?"

"No. Let's go home. I'm hungry." Andrew said.

Jonny's landing, as always was perfect, he cut one engine out and the other to idle as the silver aircraft nose dived on it's brakes to it's spot on the hardstanding. Things went quiet when the second engine was cut.

"Well It's been a pleasure walking you through this course." Andrew said as he offered his hand.

"Just a final interview with the boss and you're a Flight Instructor, not too many of those around, you should be proud of yourself."

Group Captain Graham Dangerfield's office was at the front of the new building. Apparently he insisted he had that one for the view of the hardstanding and the flight approach onto the main runway.

"Come in." was the response to Jonny's knock.

"Ah Jonny, sit down, sit down, coffee?"

"I'm OK Sir, thanks."

"Glowing reports from Andrew Roberts, welcome aboard. You'll get your own office just down the corridor, not much of a view I'm afraid but a step up nevertheless."

"How did you find the course?"

"It made me realise how much I didn't know."

"Yes, not an easy simple machine, the Lightning, we tend to expect everything to work and sometimes it doesn't. Just one question, If you had to press the button, a bomb, a missile, a nuclear weapon. Would you be OK with doing that?"

Jonny looked at him and considered, he knew the answer immediately but it seemed more appropriate to 'consider' such a question.

"It's a bit like caving someone's head in with a very heavy iron bar, you see the impact, feel the damage it causes, hear the result but you're OK. It doesn't actually hurt you, so maybe it's not real. At a distance, if you understand Sir."

"An interesting analogy Jonny, I take it it's a yes then?"

"Yes Sir."

"Calypso had spoiled it, there were balls, mess dinners, Christmases, birthdays, girls and women in their finest. Hair, makeup, best frocks, sexy frocks, pretty frocks, it didn't matter. None came near her. Her tiny young girl's waist that dived into whatever she was wearing, leaving a gap all around, her shining cascading tangled beautiful hair, her devil-may-care smile that lit up his world, her big brown eyes he could almost swim in. His dedication to flying and being the best, partially genuine but also a convenient screen for his 'Calypso' reclusiveness. On high days and holidays he'd head south to mum, she was also an excuse. She was a widower he had to look after, no time for courting. Then there was Veronica who always turned up with eggs soon after he'd turned off the engine or whenever she came home from work and spotted his car.

Now he was a Flight Lieutenant Flight instructor. Popular with his bosses, conscientious, never late, never made a mistake, the best of the best. The right stuff. Bound for Squadron Leader one day. He could afford to pay Jolyon back for his clothes and sword. He'd offered several times, almost begging him to allow him to repay his debt but Jolyon refused saying his friendship was payment enough.

Calypso's letters were full of worry and concern. Jolyon was planning another holiday in Russia, He wrote to that 'Guy' fellow in Moscow at least once a month. He'd become an almost obsessive fan of Salvador Dali and was desperate to view his famous painting called 'dream of a bee buzzing around a pomegranate' or something silly like that. Apparently it was on loan to 'The Hermitage'. Saying that he wanted to stand and look at it for hours to try and understand why the elephant had flamingo legs. She worried about his mental state. He was working very hard, he was the pilot doing all the tests on the new radar, apparently his was the only aircraft in the UK with it fitted. She was bored silly at Coltishall and spent a lot of time at home in Ireland, leaving him alone or even worse with 'Horrible Hetty'. That was another big worry!

'Beside all that it looks as though his squadron is relocating to Germany, some awful place called Gutersloh, or something like that, it's a fate worse than death, even the name of the place sounds awful. We've talked it over, we'll keep the house on here, most of the time I'll stay with Mother and Father at luggala and Jolyon will use his father's Cessna to fly into here at the weekends, that is if the camp commandant here will let him. What a mess!'

He'd read her letter many times, it was months old but he liked to touch something she had touched. It brought him closer to her.

Jonny hurriedly stuffed the letter back into it's envelope as the horn and the telephone went at the same time, it was three in the morning, the dead zone, when everything, including his body was at it's lowest.

It was difficult to hear and concentrate on the phone with the klaxon type horn blaring away.

"QRA 1 here." Jonny shouted down the phone.

"Unauthorised take off from RAF Gutersloh. Aircraft heading towards the Russian border and failing to respond to radio transmissions. Intercept and destroy. Repeat this aircraft must not enter Russian Airspace. Repeat Intercept and destroy. Permission granted to go supersonic overland if required."

Jonny had a million questions but questions took time, he raced towards the tall silver dart. the ground crew were already there pulling away the ground locks and covers. Nobody was walking. Starting was instant, Jonny used both engines to taxi as fast as he could then, up and away.

What was wrong with the Gutersloh QRA, crews? Why didn't they use them?

It was right on the edge of his range at supersonic speeds even with the belly tank fitted.

Who was the pilot?

What speed was it doing?

Was it supersonic?

What altitude was traveling at?

Why?

Jonny used full throttle hot power to thrust his plane into the cold black air leaving the throttles there until he was in excess of Mach 2.

"Update me please."

"The aircraft is a T2A Lightning fitted with a top secret radar system. It must not fall into Russian hands." The female voice on the radio had no idea of the impact her message had.

'Surely not Jolyon, it must be some Soviet agent who's stolen the aircraft for the radar. Jolyon wouldn't be so stupid, he wouldn't forsake his birthright, his duties, his family, Calypso? For some socialist dream. He was far too intelligent. No It's a Russian pilot.'

"Was the take off observed?" Jonny asked.

"Yes."

"Was reheat used for takeoff?"

"Yes but it seems only on one engine, only the upper engine seemed to be using it."

Thoughts raced through Jonny's mind. 'That was impossible, you couldn't select reheat on just one engine. There must be a fault maybe the aircraft was flying on just one engine or two with one engine on cold power only.'

"How long before it enters Soviet airspace?"

"Nine minutes."

In his head he calculated at least eleven minutes before he sighted the aircraft.

"Do I have permission to enter Soviet Airspace?"

There was a long silence. Jonny knew there would be Senior Officers with possibly members of the diplomatic service standing around the radio.

"This aircraft must be destroyed at all costs. You do not have permission to enter Soviet airspace."

It was the company line, all the world loves a winner, break the rules to win but don't get caught. When they played the tapes back the correct procedures had been followed.

Jonny was closing rapidly on the runaway Lightning. There it was, no nav lights but it's single reheat clearly visible in the still blackness as it rocketed into Russia.

Surely it wasn't Jolyon. He decided to ask?

"Do we know the identity of the pilot?"

"That information is restricted at this stage."

Yes they did but they weren't going to tell him. That made Jonny more worried, if it was some type of agent they would have just said no.

"Oh God." Jonny muttered to himself as he armed the missiles. The 'Firestreak' missiles were notoriously inaccurate with a kill rate of below fifty percent. Jonny decided he'd fire the missile outside of the twenty degree firing arc, thirty or even forty degrees should do it, the missile would fire and miss, he'd have to abort due to being in Soviet airspace and dangerously low on fuel. He'd done his best, done his duty, but there it is, nothing more to be done.

The runaway aircraft was quite slow compared to Jonny's. He throttled carefully back as he closed from the rear. The firing vector was clearly visible in his site. The fleeing lightning was exactly in the middle. Jonny pulled his aircraft to the side until it was well outside the arc, closed his eyes and pressed the fire button.

When he opened his eyes there was just the remains of colour, whites, oranges, reds, deep reds, blacks, all writhing together spewing out bits but no ejection seat, no parachute, no pilot.

Warning lights in his own cockpit instantly grabbed him, no time to think, no time for anything other than getting back out of Soviet airspace without running out of fuel.

Surely they would have put up a tanker for him. He throttled back more to save what little fuel he had, then there it was. The large white Victor, trailing it's lifeline floated way above him. Jonny mentally deflated with relief as he pushed forward to climb and engage. There was no radio traffic as he headed for home. The silence inevitably led to thoughts and silent questions. It couldn't possibly have been Jolyon, he was dyed in the wool, one hundred percent British aristocracy. He'd ring him this morning and tell him about it. Then the radio cut in.

"Leuchars QRA1 upon landing taxi immediately to holding point Zulu for fitting of replacement of stores."

The QRA hangar was visible from the road, sometimes enthusiasts and occasionally the press would come and take photos. Jonny guessed that it was going to develop into a denied diplomatic incident.

It was still dark when he landed at Leuchars, but the whole camp seemed to be twitching. Office lights that weren't normally on were on, traffic was moving, there was a sense of crisis.

"Boss wants to see you." Andrew Cavendish had spent the last two hours strapped into QRA 2 but hadn't moved out of the hangar. Now he was making coffee in the crew room.

"Here you had some excitement."

By now Jonny was sinking into despair. He didn't answer.

Group Captain Dangerfield seemed to look the same whatever time of day it was, only now there was no faithful secretary.

"Come in Jonny, sit down." Jonny was still in his flying overall. The Group Captain went back to his phone call. After three or minutes of Ummms and Yes's he put it down.

"Well it looks as though you've saved the day Jonny, so far the Russians have said nothing. Our line is that one of our Lightning's crashed into the north Sea during a night flying exercise."

Jonny looked at his boss.

"Then the pilot was one of ours then?"

"Unfortunately it was."

"Please tell me Sir it wasn't Jolyon Clay."

Group Captain Dangerfield's attitude immediately hardened.

"How can you possibly know that. It's highly sensitive and secret information. It appears that Flight Lieutenant Jolyon is missing, that is correct, why? Do you know him?"

"He's my,----------He was my best friend. I was 'best man' at his wedding."

Dangerfield softened to his normal self.

"There's nothing appropriate I can say Jonny. I can't think of a worst scenario for a young pilot. I Know it's an inadequate offer but there is support available if you need it."

"Thank you Sir, but it's for me to cope with, as you say words are inadequate." Jonny forced himself up to leave, his head swirling, unable to come to terms with events. Now, standing in this office just didn't seem real. How was he ever going to rationalise this, tell people what he'd done, what dreadful awful thing he'd done. Why the hell did that missile work, they were useless, a joke, they hardly ever worked.

"On the business side of things Jonny, no mentioning to anyone about this, take some time out, two or three weeks, go and see your mum, I know you're close."

Thank you Sir, I will, if you don't mind."

"Just one more thing Jonny."

"Sir?"

"Did you know?" He didn't have to qualify the question.

"I thought it might be, but convinced myself it wasn't."

"That's terrible. May God be with you."

'God! God! What the blazes had God got to do with it. He'd just blown up his best friend, someone who loved him. Someone he loved. Someone who had taught him how to be an Officer. Someone who had taught him how to eat correctly! How on earth could God help?'

The phone rang in his room, he was lying sleepless on his bed staring at the ceiling.

"There's something happening at the camp and Jolyon's not come home tonight. I'm worried sick." He'd never heard Calypso in such a state.

"I'm coming over."

"Coming over! Coming over, you can't come over Jonny, You're five hundred miles away and what if Jolyon turns up?"

"I'm coming over Calypso, I'll be there before lunch."

"Jonny."

"What?"

"I'm pregnant. I'm six months gone, I thought you should know that if you're coming here."

There was silence.

"Is it Jolyon's?"

"Of course, I'm a married woman and nothing like my mother."

As always the little blue car started instantly. The journey south was on autopilot, he didn't remember any of the usual waymarks, the towns, the cafes, the petrol halts, the everything. It was dawn when he left Scotland and eleven thirty when he eventually found their house. There was a flat field behind the house with a green helicopter in it. Several cars were parked in and around the entrance. The curtains on all the front windows were shut. Eventually, about three hours later they were alone.

"They're saying it was a night flying accident. They're saying his aircraft went into the North Sea, that there was no ejection and that there's no trace of him or the aircraft. I don't believe them Jonny."

He'd never seen her look a mess before. The tears had somehow swollen her face, her shiny tousled hair now looked just unkempt and neglected as though the pregnancy had drained it of its magnificent magic. Her small body, tucked into the easy chair with her legs underneath her was an odd shape, as the interloper grew inside her. He put his right arm around her shoulder and looked at his fingers. It was less than twelve hours since one of them had pressed the button.

Jonny peeped out from behind the curtain, there were a few people hanging around, probably press he thought, but they were being held at bay by two 'regiment' sentries armed with automatic rifles.

He didn't know what to tell her. The truth? He was trying to defect to Russia with a top secret radar or stick to the party line? It was a dreadful accident or he'd shot her husband, his best friend, the father of her unborn child out of the skies. The black cold skies of Russia.

"There'll be an enquiry, let's see what comes of that." He despised his own sincerity.

"What the hell do I do now Jonny? Marry you when it's all died down and people have forgotten. I don't think so, social misalignment never works."

Jonny's heart dropped. He hadn't considered it but her immediate rejection hurt him.

"Do you know the sex of the baby?" He asked.

"Yes, a boy." she reached for more paper hankies from the box, he beat her to it and passed her some.

"Any name decided?"

"We'd joked about calling him 'Salvador' after Dali. In fact during lighter moments we referred to my bump as 'Salvador'."

"Salvador Clay, it has a ring to it."

"Salvador John Clay sounds even better, Jolyon would have understood and agreed."

"Doesn't take long does it?" She sobbed.

"What doesn't?"

"To start referring to someone in the past tense. My husband, your loved friend."

"No it doesn't. Can I have a drink?"

"Of course, the cabinets over there." She pointed to the corner of the large lounge. "What are you having?"

"Port and Lemon."

"Stay with me Jonny, just for a few days until all the official formalities are over, then I'll go back to Ireland."

"OK, but won't folk talk?"

"I don't fucking care about folk." She collapsed sobbing into his arms.

They spent the rest of the day hiding from the press while Calypso answered the phone as the news spread between her family and close friends.

Jonny progressed from Port and Lemons to whisky and dry ginger, he wasn't a drinker but the drink dulled his senses, somehow separated him from reality even though the awful result of his action was sat before him, crying, sniffling and sobbing.

"You don't have to sleep with me but I'd like you to, just for comfort. Jolyon and I didn't sleep together, we slept in separate rooms, the only time we shared a bed was on the odd occasion we were both so horny that we had sex, that's how Salvador came about."

It felt so strange to be in a bed with Calypso and Salvador who was by now kicking and moving. It felt so right to put his arms around her and soothe her sorrow with his presence.

At first dawn the helicopter took off. Calypso answered his unspoken question.

"It's gone to get Mother and Father, they'll be here before lunch."

"I'll make you some breakfast then leave. I don't want any raised eyebrows."

"Ok." she looked up at him from the bed and reached for his fingers. "Thanks for last night."

Jonny bent down and kissed her forehead.

"Poached eggs on toast with a tomato, will that do?"

"Can you cook?"

"Yes of course." Somehow the mechanics of looking after her put welcome distance between his nightmare and now.

Jonny turned the little Porsche into Henry Street and parked outside mum's. He sat in the car collecting his thoughts. The engine ticked and clicked as it cooled. He looked at the little narrow street. The road was filling up with cars, there was still plenty of parking spaces but it was filling up. In Front of him was a Standard Vanguard, it's wheels too thin, it's track too narrow for such a bulky car, behind him, a Riley Pathfinder and at the end of the road on the corner outside the butchers was the red Panhard. Then he saw the curtains twitch and in a moment mum was stood beaming on the doorstep.

"Jonny! What a lovely surprise, why didn't you let me know, look at me in me pinnie, hair a mess, no makeup." She hardly let him get out of the car before she hugged him.

"Brenda's here, she's living with me again for a while. You heard of course Phill died."

"Hello Brenda, how are you? Sorry bit of a silly question really what with Phill passing on and everything. What was it? Cancer?"

"Yes. Everso quick it was, which I suppose was a blessing for Phill. Connie's taken it badly though, well and me I suppose, that's part of the reason why I'm back staying with your mum. Loneliness is a terrible thing Jonny but I couldn't face living with him again."

"What do you mean Brenda, Isn't Harry locked up for life?"

"He was, but apparently there's some new evidence so they've had to release him and reopen Frankie Fletcher's murder enquiry. Phill told me before he died. He didn't say what it was. Harry's back living at home. I've spoken to him on the phone, he says he's an old man now and wouldn't behave the way he used to but he's been in prison a long time with no booze. God knows what he'll be like when he gets the pop inside him again. I can't risk it, he still frightens me."

Somehow everything seemed to lead back to death. What had just happened was horrible, now they were reopening Frankie's murder enquiry. Where would that lead?

Chapter. 16

Bernard Alexander pressed the button.

"Sheila get David to come and see me will you."

"Yes Sir."

Chief Inspector David Borthon was in charge of CID. A pugnacious squat square of a man, busted down the ranks three times but too good to leave there, he was back in charge. Both feared and loved all at the same time.

"David take a look at this letter from Phill Shaws solicitor and the statement that goes with it. Take your time, read it properly, don't just scan it."

Borthon sat down and put his glasses on. It took him ten minutes to read it through twice.

"Fuck me this is serious stuff boss."

"Yes it is David. The issue is that if Phill Shaw hadn't died we wouldn't have known, which reflects very badly on our initial investigation into the Fletcher murder."

"So what's to be done?"

"Well, I'll make a representation for Harry Shaw to be released from prison pending the investigation of new evidence and hope the press don't pick it up. If they do the official line will be that the Police are convinced that the correct man went to prison but a technicality in new evidence makes the conviction unsafe. In the meantime you quietly reopen the murder enquiry, nothing too energetic, give it to some tired DC to sit on for a while, you know just enough enquiries to cover our back should the wheel come off. Don't want anything in the press if we can help it."

"Yes boss. I know just the man, Barney Ingles. He's only a year off retirement, knows every trick in the book of how to not do things. Leave it with me."

They'd given Barney Ingles a CID attachment bloke. 'God that's the last thing I bloody need.' He thought to himself walking in the cold drizzle from his car to the front door of the nick. He really should use the rear entrance but they kept changing the code and he could never remember it. 'Really cramp my style that will having to drag some ultra keen, sharp as a needle, just out of the box wannabe detective around.'

"Morning Barney."

"Mornin." Barney acknowledged as he climbed up the three flights of stairs to the first floor. Walking into the CID office his protégé jumped out of the chair behind Barney's desk.

"Hello DC Ingles, I'm PC Hilary, I've been attached to you."

"God, that sounds painful." Barney said as he took off his car coat and hung it on the stand. "How old are you?"

"Twenty two, why."

"Just wondered. Any coffee?"

"Errrm Yes, shall I get some out of the machine?"

"Not on your life. It's putrid dishwater. The makin's are over there in the corner. One sugar please."

This would be his first test, making a decent cup of coffee, most of them failed at this hurdle.

Peter Hilary didn't.

"That's not a bad brew young Peter. I've decided you can stay attached to me------ for a while anyway. What do you drink?"

"Shandy usually."

"Smoke?"

"No."

"Ah!" He exhaled. "I can see we're going to get on like a house on fire."

Barney took off his coat, there was no room on the rack so he dropped it on the floor beside his desk. After a moment he lifted it up to rummage through the pockets for his fags and lighter then dropped again. He stared at the untidy piles on his desk whilst the nicotine reached his brain. The large CID office was buzzing with people all engrossed in files, papers or conversations. He pulled out a large thick manila file and plonked it on the desk in front of Peter.

"There you go, just the thing for you to make a name for yourself. A murder, or to be more precise the murder of one Frankie Fletcher, bookies runner, saxophonist and dodgy transport bloke for all the local criminals, never got his hands dirty himself, no convictions but always around if you know what I mean. That is until someone caved his head in with an iron bar and shoved him under the ice when the cut was frozen over. Bloke called Harry Shaw went down for it but it appears that he didn't do it. He's been released with a very big 'Oops Sorry' and now we, or rather you, have to find who did do it. But first we'll have another coffee."

Peter Hilary fingered the aged brown file before going over to make more coffee.

"Look at that in your own time Peter, after we've finished our coffee we're going walkabout to see a man about an MOT and Car Insurance."

Peter looked bemused.

"Aren't those types of enquiries for uniform DC Ingles?"

"His wife's just got pulled in her Range Rover, It's a ringer, there's no doc's so we're going to have a chat and help him out by fixing the producer. And it's Barney."

"Isn't that a bit illegal------Barney?" Peter looked worried.

"So is a ten thousand pound booze and fags job from the back of The Welsh Club and Reggie Dixon might just give us a pointer as to who we need to talk to."

Peter Hilary looked aghast.

"By the way, you make good coffee, you can definitely stay. Come on young fella grab your coat, after this we'll visit The Welsh Club to inspect the scene. They sell Brains there, it's quite a nice pint."

Chapter. 17

The news about the reopening of Frankie's murder had unsettled him, but now he was rationalising it and calming down. There was nothing to link him to it, or they'd have spoken to him at the time and nobody had. No, there was nothing to worry about at all but at least that concern, that worry, had moved his mind on from Jolyon and Calypso.

Brenda had gone to bed. Mum was watching 'Armchair Theatre', she liked that. That and westerns, her favourite was Rawhide, she was really miffed it was coming to an end. Dad used to tease her about fancying Clint Eastwood.

Mum had moved Dad's urn from upstairs to the small table next to Jonny's Gloster Javelin and the TV.

"You need to get up very early tomorrow mum, we're going somewhere." Jonny said.

"I get up very early every morning these days Jonny, ache too much to lie in bed and my sleeping isn't good. Where we going?"

"Dovedale."

"Oooh! That was your dad's favourite place, he always wanted to go fly fishing there but never did, you really needed a car to get there. There's no bus you know."

"I know mum, We're going to take dad's ashes and put them in the river at the stepping stones."

There was a long silence as Irene stared at the TV.

"That'll be nice. What time shall we go?"

"It gets light about six thirty so I thought about four, don't want anybody around when we do it. It's private and personal."

Irene looked at Jonny from her chair. Both her knees were supported by crepe bandages.

"He'd like that Jonny, mind you, do the same with me when I go. I only went fishing with him once, too many flies and midges for me. I hated them, but when we're together again at the bottom of the river there won't be any to bother me."

"I'm off to bed mum."

"OK, your bed's made up, it always is."

There was nothing moving in the street. The clatter of the engine as it started up seemed noticeably loud. Irene eased herself into the seat which strained backwards as her weight transferred to it.

"Can't you get a nice big car like your friend Jolyon? That's so comfortable and easy for me to get in and out of. Last time he was here, going to some meeting or other with Hetty, we went into town to that new Chinese Restaurant. Lovely it was. So quiet and comfortable."

"Jolyon's dead mum." It took a while for it to register.

"Killed a few days ago when his plane crashed." Jonny half lied. "That's why I'm here, my boss knew we were best friends, very close, so he's sent me on leave for a couple of weeks."

"Oh Dear.----------- I'd better tell Veronica when we get back and she'll tell Hetty. They were good friends you know, nothing in it, just good friends."

"Yes I know mum."

Irene sat clutching Arthur's urn for the rest of the journey saying nothing.

It was the perfect dawn for the moment. Steely grey high clouds allowed just a hint of frost that sprinkled the hills in dark places. The river was cold and clear, so clear the pebbles and rocks at the bottom were somehow magnified. There was no wind, often at dawn there wasn't. Irene was visibly nervous crossing the stepping stones to the middle of the river. There weren't many, only about six, but she wasn't a country woman.

"Shall I do it, or you do it mum?"

"I'll do it. Shall we sing a song?" Irene asked.

"What song?"

"Lena Horne, Someone to Watch over Me'." Your dad loved Lena Horne, listened to her all the time, that's why he bought the stereogram. Used to listen to her with his headphones on. I could tell by his face when he was listening to her, he usually had his eyes shut."

"I know how it goes mum but i don't know the words."

Irene gave him a paper from her pocket.

"Copied it from the LP cover."

Neither Jonny or Irene were good singers but there was no one else in the cleft of the hills through which the river flowed.

-------- *there's somebody I'm longin' to see,*
I hope that he turns out to be,
Someone who'll watch over me.

I'm a little lamb, who's lost in a wood,
I know I could, always be good,
to one who'll watch over me.

In tears, Irene sprinkled the dust of Arthur's life into the pure fast water.

In tears Jonny put his arm around his mother.

They stopped at The Green Man Hotel in Ashbourne for breakfast. Lovely it was. Now there was some distance between the Peak District and black Russian Airspace, between Derbyshire and Salvador John Clay.

Chapter. 18

"How are you feeling?" It was a sincere question asked by Group Captain Dangerfield and by Graham.

"I'm OK Sir, spent some time with my mother, sorted a few things that needed to be sorted."

"Good." There was a pause as he gestured for Jonny to sit. "Jonny, I'm putting you forward for a DFC, obviously we can't disclose the details of your action so you'll be in the same boat as members of the SAS and secret services. What you did saved the country from acute embarrassment, you had a horrible choice to make, your Country and duty or your friend. You made the correct choice. Your friend would not have been your friend had he landed safely in Russia he would have become your enemy at worst, a traitor at best. Well done sounds totally insufficient, but well done Jonny. Well done." Graham Dangerfield stood up from behind his desk and offered his hand.

"Where were you when you fired?"

"Well into Russian airspace Sir, guess he was heading for Lipetsk."

"There must have been some prior arrangement or they would have shot him down. Have you any clue about that?"

Jonny didn't want Calypso bothered about the letters to and from 'Guy'.

"No Sir, haven't a clue." He lied.

"The Russians haven't said a peep, normally they're shouting from the rooftops whenever we stray over the border. My guess is it was an arrangement that went wrong and they don't want to talk about it. Neither do we for that matter. Were you close?"

Jonny looked straight at Graham.

"As close as it gets Sir without being sexual. I loved him like a brother."

Jonny's frankness took the C.O. back a bit.

"Take it steady out there Jonny, make no mistakes and you'll be sitting in my office chair soon."

Graham Dangerfield shook Jonny Conrad's hand again.this time there was a lot more understanding.

'Jonny Conrad DFC.' Jonny rolled the words around in his head as he made for the office door.

"Oh, just one more thing Jonny."

"Sir?"

"It's a bit premature but the Council from your hometown have written asking if you could lead the Remembrance Day Parade from the Arft College to the local Cenotaph on Sunday the 11th of November. Usually we like to do these things if we can. Your decoration will take place in October at the Palace so you'll be even more popular after that." The C.O. smiled.

"Can I think about that one Sir, I'm not one for pomp and circumstance?"

"Yes of course. Let me know by next Monday."

He wasn't sure if dad, knowing all the facts, would be proud of him or not?.

Chapter. 19

"We've got a problem boss."

"What now Barney?"

Dave Borthon was knee deep in paperwork, he rarely got out of his office, he hated it. His thing was nailing his man despite the lack of any evidence. Just a hunch, nick him on a wing and a prayer then wear him down, blag him, convince him he was a loser until he was. He loved it. Nothing was professional, everything was personal.

"Well I gave the young super sleuth the Fletcher murder file to keep him busy and he's only gone and dug out all the old pocket books of every officer who was on duty that night and low and behold there's an entry in Gordon Metcalfe's pocket book, a sighting of a smoke grey mini stopping and picking up a drunk at one twenty five a.m. on the morning of the murder."

"Stop there. We've no idea if Fletcher was murdered the previous night or in the early hours of the next day. If my memory serves me right, he left the pub, drunk somewhere 'round about eleven."

"That's right boss but Metcalfe's entry places his sighting in Clarkes Lane which is on Fletcher's route home and it would have taken him a couple of hours to stagger that far."

"Go on." Dave took a sip of his coffee which was now almost cold. It went with an exasperated - I don't need this - sigh.

"Metcalfe took a number, 448 DJW, a Wolverhampton number."

"And?"

"Well you've got to hand it to young Hilary, he's a bright lad."

"Yes! Yes! For fucks sake get to the point."

"At the time it was down to a Mr. Jonny Conrad of 47 Henry Street Walsall."

"Jonny Conrad? Jonny Conrad? The name rings a bell for some reason."
"It should do boss. Flight lieutenant Jonny Conrad DFC, has been all over the Express and Star recently, decorated at the Palace, bound for high rank, an RAF flying hero to all accounts and he's lined up to lead the Remembrance Day Parade here in Walsall in November."

"And now he's a suspect in the Fletcher case."

"Yes."

Dave Borthon eased back in his chair and stared out of the window.

"Here's what you do, get that file back off young Hilary, I want it on my desk by two this afternoon, tell him in no uncertain terms that he is to do no more work on this case. Give him something easy to do, ask him to look at the 'White' family, they're becoming a pain in the arse at the moment. Check his pocket books, no, photocopy his pocket book since he started with you then let me have them. Tell him not to speak to anyone about this inquiry, I'll have to refer this one up."

"Yes Boss."

"And Barney."

"Yes Boss,"

"You keep stumm about it as well, you know what you're like after a few pints."

"Keep stumm about what boss?"

"Good, Oh, let me have Metcalve's pocket book as well. Is he still alive?"

"No, he died about three years ago boss."

"Well that's one less worry. Shut the door will you on your way out?"

"Yes boss."

Chief Constable Anthony Bannister was young, tall and slim, His black leather shoes were always bulled, his trousers pressed every morning. Handsome, but not a pretty boy, he had an engaging smile that made most people feel comfortable. There were no grey hairs yet. He loved coming to work. His large office was on the top floor of a very imposing sandstone country mansion the constabulary had acquired years ago. He wasn't quite sure what the next step was, Home Office, MI5, Politics, National Crime Commission? At the moment he was content with the view from his large office windows that arched towards the high ceiling.

It was a lovely morning, the 'Elgar' pastures of Worcestershire rolled away before his window. Life was good. Assistant Chief Constable Patsy Lourdes was sitting in the office waiting for him.

"Good morning Sir."

"Good morning Patsy, no disasters during the night I hope."

"Nothing Sir, a very quiet night."

"Good, let's have coffee while I ring the Minister, then we'll talk about this scheme for installing internet screens in post offices. It seems a good idea but as always funding is the issue."

Patsy Lourdes was 'chunky' without being fat. Dark wavy hair that just about reached her shoulders, she was no beauty but was tough with the razor sharp intuition only a woman can have. On ceremonial occasions she always wore brown leather gloves and carried a swagger stick. There seemed to be no significant men in her life and so there was doubt.

She sat the other side of his large desk sipping at her coffee. Anthony was conciliatory on the phone. When the conversation finished he didn't look too pleased.

"Patsy, about that Fletcher murder, get onto Bernard Alexander after we've finished this morning and tell him that on no account must a Flight Lieutenant Conrad be considered a suspect in this case. This has come from the very top, apparently this chap is earmarked for high rank plus he's about to be appointed DFC, plus he's one of the best flyers the country has got."

"What's a DFC Sir?"

"Distinguished Flying Cross, you don't find those in a packet of Cornflakes."

"What if he's a murderer as well?"

"Lots of people are murderers Patsy, it just depends on the circumstances. Some are officially sanctioned murderers, they're called heroes. Some are not and we put them in prison."

"Goes against the grain a bit, the least we can do is interview the guy." Patsy grumbled.

"No, in fact, have Bernard get the file and any connected documentation to me. I'll keep it here, I don't want anybody upsetting the applecart, and that includes you."

"What about 'the protection of life and property, serving the Queen, human rights, all that stuff we all swore to do including you."

Anthony Bannister looked at her. He knew once she got a bee in her bonnet what she was capable of doing. That was why she'd climbed the ranks. He could sense the germs of injustice beginning to sprout within her.

"Forget it Patsy, this is one battle you don't need. You're on leave as from next Monday so don't get doing anything ------." He searched for the right word. "Innovative. I'm going to put an entry in my pocket book to the effect that I've warned you off about this, I know what you're like."

His words only made her more resolute. Why was this so important?

"Now, let's look at the cost of --------------."

Chapter. 20

Peter Hilary was a little miffed, the Fletcher file had been whisked away with no explanation just as he thought he was getting somewhere identifying a possible suspect. He'd made a copy of course. Nobody asked about that, maybe he'd go a bit further, unofficially, in his own time. He sipped the shandy slowly as Barney went to the bar for another pint.

The phone rang in Jonny's room, jangling him back from a half asleep, half deep in thought state lying on his bed.

"Hello."

"Hello, is that Flight Lieutenant Conrad?"

"Yes."

"Oh hello I'm Temporary Detective Constable Hilary of Walsall CID. I believe you are in Scotland, is that correct?"

"Yes, I'm in Scotland."

"I just wondered when you would be visiting Walsall again, I'd like to talk to you about the Fletcher case, just to tie up a few loose ends as it were."

"Are you talking about Frankie Fletcher?"

"Yes Sir."

Alarm bells were clanging in Jonny's head as he forced himself to control his voice.

"I'm not sure when exactly I'll be visiting my mother, maybe Whit. If you give me your number I'll contact you."

"Just Walsall Police Station Sir. Just ask for me DC Hilary."

"I thought you said temporary?"

"I did Sir but hopefully that will change soon."

"Will I have to come to the Police Station?"

"Only if you want to Sir, we can meet elsewhere, as I said it's just to tie up some loose ends."

"As I see it Constable if I come to the Police Station it's an interview and I'll need some advice about that. If we meet in a pub it's a chat."

"A pub it is then Sir."

"Ok, I'll be in touch."

"Thank you Sir."

Jonny's mind couldn't settle, he had an important training sortie tomorrow and needed to be fresh but how the hell had the police got onto him? Calm down, they were probably talking to all members of 'The Notes'. He'd wondered at the time why they hadn't done that.

Peter Hilary was pleased with his call, he'd kept things low key hoping to lull Flight Lieutenant Conrad into a mistake. Something, anything, which would take him further.

The file landed on her desk along with all the other dispatches delivered by Bert. He was a retired Rural Bobby, who had never set the world alight but had never upset too many folk either. She wondered if Bert had got things right and she was just frantically expending her life's energy trying to be a little bit better. Better than what? She thought as she stared out of the same tall arched window as the Chief Constable only along the corridor a bit. She felt she was just a sieve for him, 'you might need to look at this Sir', 'signature required', 'for your attention'.

The manilla bound file had stuff scribbled all over it, stuff that had meant something to someone at sometime.

A while back she used to press a button and one of the secretaries would bring her a coffee. She could chat or smile or at least acknowledge a secretary but the machine that now sat in the corner of her office said nothing. Yes it's coffee was OK. but it was the same every time, no variation, she couldn't say that was lovely or that was shit. The machine just didn't care.

She opened the Fletcher file and began to read, no wonder young Peter Hilary was miffed when it was snatched away. The conviction would never stand up today, there was no direct evidence to link Shaw with Fletcher and now there was this strong evidence to link Conrad with Fletcher. Strong but not watertight, a decent brief would drive a bus through that gap, especially if Conrad denied it. She needed more. At the end of the day she was a simple Police Officer, albeit with a few badges. She was on leave as from next Monday.

Assistant chief Constable Lourdes had never been to Scotland, it looked awful from the rain soaked window of her MGA. Dull, grey, cold, windy and wet. Why would anyone want to live here? Even the Highland Cattle with their dripping wet shaggy long orange coats and sharp long horns looked thoroughly miserable as they twisted their heads through the wire fence to get at the longer grass on the verge.

Dundee was eight miles further north than Leuchars. It seemed funny that the man she was really after was probably in the camp as she drove by it.

This was an unofficial wing and a prayer job. It was a long way to come, she wasn't on a wing, unlike jonny Conrad who moved about on two of them, she was on four wheels and it had been a tiring long journey. She hoped that somehow her prayer would be answered. If it got back to Anthony Bannister about her trip she'd need more than a prayer.

The house was just what you'd expect a Group Captain to live in. Stout, grey granite, white doors and windows with roses. It was ten thirty on a Sunday morning, the sun was just beginning to glimmer through breaking clouds. Would he be in?

Graham Dangerfield was in the vegetable garden planting leeks. The garden was walled with red tired bricks and a weathered door that blew back and forth in the variable wind. By the door was an old bay laurel tree that Mary used all the time for cooking. Down the southern wall was an old dilapidated but still usable lean-to, green house that was home to hundreds of small old flaking terra-cotta plant pots, lots of mice and spiders. Graham loved his garden.

He was surprised to see Mary at the gate with another woman.

"Darling, this is -----."

"Assistant Chief Constable Lourdes." Patsy butted in offering her hand. Graham looked at his hand, it was covered in soil He just smiled.

"Yes, she's driven all the way from the Midlands to see you."

"Good grief! An Assistant chief Constable. Shouldn't you have a driver, or perhaps an appointment?"

"I should Sir, if it was official, but it's not." Patsy had decided that truth was the only option.

Graham Dangerfield looked at her. She'd obviously used official channels to locate him yet here she was admitting that it wasn't official.

"I think we'd better have some tea. Ms Lourdes." Somehow Graham knew it was a 'Ms.'

"We'll take it in the parlour Darling, if you don't mind." Mary walked back into the house in front of them.

The parlour was, as you'd expect, gilt framed originals of English artists, pale yellow walls, a fine knotted Kashmir carpet on the floor. An elegant large beige three piece suite, oak occasional tables and a roll top bureau. Graham had discarded his boots at the back porch. Mary made sure his green chord gardening trousers were clean enough to sit in. Patsy Lourdes considered removing her black shoes but decided against it. Somehow it diluted her power.

"Now, why on earth have you come all this way Assistant Chief Constable?"

Graham posed the question as he sank into one of the easy chairs and Patsy perched on the sofa, Before she could answer Mary brought a tea tray through.

"Please call me Ms lourdes or better still Patsy."

"Patsy it is then, come let's have some tea and a biscuit. Normally Mary doesn't allow me biscuits, says she doesn't want a fat husband." They both laughed.

"It's a bit delicate Sir."

"Go on."

"Well about ten years ago a man called Frankie Fletcher was murdered. His body was found in the canal under the ice in Walsall. A man was arrested and jailed for the murder but recently some new evidence has emerged and it appears the original conviction has been called into question. The man has been released and the inquiry reopened."

"So now you've got to find the real murderer pretty quick or there'll be a lot of eggs on a lot of peoples faces. Am I right Patsy?" Graham reached over, took a dark chocolate digestive then offered the plate to Patsy. She took one.

"Well no actually. My Chief Constable has received instructions to do minimal enquiries then shut it down as undetected."

Graham raised his eyebrows over his china cup.

"And that irks you, hence you're here unofficially?"

"Yes, are you always so perceptive?"

"Comes with the job, Why are you here Patsy?"

"A smoke grey mini was seen giving a lift to a drunk in Clarkes Lane Bloxwich, Fletcher was drunk that night and had chosen to walk home, it's about eight miles to his home the route would take him down Clarkes Lane. The Mini was registered at the time to a Mr Jonny Conrad who I believe is one of your Officers. Jonny Conrad was also in attendance at the event Fletcher got drunk at, it was Fletcher's unofficial stag party."

"So what you are saying is that one of my pilots, in fact the best pilot I have and who is about to be awarded the DFC is a murder suspect."

"Yes----------Sir."

"So I beg to ask the question again, what are you here for?"

"I want your opinion, and any information you can give me, about Jonny Conrad."

"Drink your tea Patsy before it gets cold, it's Oolong, not everybodies 'cup of tea', if you'll excuse the awful pun, but I like it. Jonny Conrad is probably the best pilot I've ever met. Shrewd, fast and logical, comes from a working class background so it's not 'in the genes' as it is with most of our chaps. No, there's a certain indefinable element to him as though he's viewing life and all it's problems from a different perspective, a higher plain, that's almost another dreadful pun." He laughed and sipped his tea.

"Has he been earmarked for high rank?" Patsy asked.

"That's not for me to say but it wouldn't surprise me, especially after winning a DFC."

"How did that come about?"

"I can't disclose that to you but I can assure you it came with considerable emotional baggage and loss for Jonny."

"Do you like him?"

"It's very hard not to like him, he does everything correctly and very well, doesn't upset anybody."

"But he's not married?"

"He's totally committed and focused on his flying career, that doesn't leave a lot of room for family life."

"Is there anyone, you know, 'special' in his life?"

"Yes, his mother, his father died when he was a young boy so he's very protective of his mother."

"Is he homosexual?"

Graham was taken back by her directness, almost rudeness.

"Not as I am aware Patsy but that's none of my concern anyway, my concern is the protection of this country from it's enemies or potential enemies. To that end Jonny Conrad is highly regarded."

Patsy took a second sip of her tea then put it down.

"I'm sorry, Oolong isn't for me, but i will have another biscuit before I leave you in peace to plant your leeks."

"Are you a gardener Patsy?"

"Window box and pot plants are about my limit, and sometimes even they die." They both laughed.

"Has there ever been any aspect of Jonny Conrad's history with you that caused you to note, question or wonder about him?"

They both stood up and walked towards the front hall and door.

The only thing that ever intrigued me about him was one day at an interview at the end of his Flight Instructors course I asked him how he felt about pressing the button, you know, releasing a nuclear weapon knowing that without doubt it would kill tens of thousands of people. He replied with an analogy that it was like caving someone's head in with an iron bar, you saw it, felt it, heard it, but it didn't hurt you so maybe it wasn't real." Strange way to look at things but I suppose he was right. He always was."

Patsy shook hands with Graham and made her way over to her turquoise MGA, the sun was now clearing the cloud. She put the key in the ignition.

"Yes!"

Her car seemed happier to be heading south, almost as if it was downhill all the way. She pondered if she should disclose her trip and thoughts to Anthony and try to get the case officially sanctioned. Anthony was so sycophantic he'd just do as he was told and shut her down, no she'd carry on til she had enough evidence, then he'd have to run with it, fearing dereliction of duty. That's what she'd do, she'd blag it, or even wing it. She smiled to herself at the connection. Patsy turned up the radio, Chris Farlowe came out of the speaker, 'Baby Baby Baby, you're out of time!' She sang along - 'I said Jonny Jonny Jonny, you're out of tiiiiiiiiiime.Yes you are Jonny Conrad!' She added.

Jonny reached under four pairs of flying overalls that were in his wardrobe in the office. The box was still there, forgotten by everyone, including Graham. He took it out and looked at it. The full magazine was in a little compartment on it's own. He picked it out and slid it in. it made a satisfying solid click click as it engaged. He got used to moving the safety catch on and off before putting it in his bag underneath his shirts. He never got stopped for a search leaving the camp, everyone knew his light blue Porsche, he was 'de facto' second in command in the camp, no one dared.

He'd been at Leuchars so long the car almost knew it's own way south. It would be good to see mum, she was getting old and frail now, still fat but somehow it hung weakly around her. She struggled more with her walking, the council had put in some rails in the bathroom and toilet. Veronica,- God bless her- had been marvelous, helping with the shopping and laundry. He thought about stopping and buying her some flowers, just to say thank you but he knew she'd take it the wrong way and he didn't want that 'cause of Calypso'.

Salvador had been born on cue, a perfectly healthy young boy with no father, but at least the Clay's had an heir. He saw them about twice a year. He didn't want to become a surrogate dad, especially given the circumstances. He'd never told her the truth. How could he? 'Oh by the way I shot down and killed your husband, now will you marry me 'cause I adore you and for me there will never be anybody else. Oh I forgot, they gave me a medal for doing it.' No. That wouldn't work.

Jonny liked to take the coast road rather than Edinburgh and Glasgow, there was a nice transport cafe just outside Durham that did a good all day breakfast. Looking for the easily missed entrance brought his thoughts back to the present and Temporary Detective Constable Hilary. He didn't want some young hot-shot Dixon of Dock Green on his back, better he was 'consigned' rather than 'confirmed'.

Jonny left the M1 just passed Nottingham and headed diagonally south towards Walsall. Yes he'd risk it and buy some nice flowers.

Mum was at the door before he could get his bag out of the car. God she looked old. The street was full of cars now, he'd offered to rent a better house for her but she didn't want to leave dad. Her warm hug and wet kiss somehow felt undeserved considering what he'd done, what he did for a living and how efficient he'd become within a 'war' machine and what he might be about to do.

"This is Mr. Edmunds here, can I speak to DC. Hilary?"

"One moment Sir."

There was a silence.

"I'm sorry sir, he's not on duty until two this afternoon, can I take a number and get him to ring you?"

"No, it's OK. I'll ring back at two."

Jonny put the phone down. He wondered if all phone calls into Police Stations were recorded these days.

"Hi, DC Hilary, I'm in town at the moment and wondered if you were free?"

"Oh hello Sir, Yes, I'm free, I'm working until ten tonight but that is flexible."

Peter Hilary had recognised his voice after three months.

"I'm having dinner with my mother tonight at 'The Albion' pub, you know, the one just across the canal bridge. We're eating at eight so if you'd like to come along about nine for our chat that would be fine."

"Errrm, yes OK, but the matter I want to discuss with you is a little delicate for company."

"That's OK we can take a walk outside, bit nippy but I'm sure we won't be too long."

"OK Sir, see you about nine in the Albion."

"Just one thing?"

"Yes Sir?"

"Is it still Temporary Detective Constable?"

"No Sir, I'm a Detective Constable now."

"Congratulations, see you tonight Peter."

Peter Hilary couldn't remember giving his first name, but then again he must have. He went to the locker room and dug out his secret file from the bottom under his boots.

What Jonny was intending to do didn't worry him or excite him. It was just necessary. He wanted to become more involved with Calypso and Salvador and could well do without an inconvenient Frankie Fletcher.

Mum had plaice and chips with peas and tartar sauce, Jonny had Lamb and mint sauce.

It was the weather for overcoats, DC Hilary was wearing a dark blue one as he came into the pub looking around for a mother and grown up son. Jonny spotted him and waved. Mother was just about to tuck into some apple pie with cream, Jonny had given the sweet a miss.

"DC Hilary, how nice to meet you." Jonny put out his hand. Peter Hilary was very young, about twenty one Jonny guessed. Not ugly but certainly not handsome, the sort of looks that people found non-threatening but were often misleading.

Peter Hilary shook his hand.

"Can, I get you a drink? Please sit down."

Jonny could sense his uneasiness. He was on the back foot, not used to kindness when dealing with potential murder suspects or their mothers.

"Actually Sir I'm a bit pushed for time, is there somewhere we could talk?"

"Yes of course. Sorry, let's go for a walk." Jonny turned towards Irene."Mother I have a little business I need to discuss with Peter, I'll only be ten minutes, you finish your pie, and get us both another drink."

Irene nodded and wiped her mouth.

It was very dark and very cold. Jonny and DC Hilary stood on the canal bridge looking over into the black slow ink.

"Did you used to own a Mini Sir?"

"I've owned a couple in my time."

"How about a smoke grey one with a white roof?"

"Now that would be my first one 448 DJW, I loved that car."

Jonny fingered the pistol in the large right hand pocket of his coat.

"On the night or rather morning of Fletcher's murder that vehicle was seen by an officer in Clarkes Lane."

Jonny looked at him.

"Come, let's walk down here, this is where I caught my first big Perch. My heart was beating ten to the dozen, I tell you. I was with my dad, a very precious moment Constable, dad's are not forever, do you know that Peter? Is your Dad alive."

"Yes he is Sir, Do you want to comment on the car?"

Jonny walked down the dark slipway, the rough stone and gravel crunched under their feet as though the frost was complaining. They both stood at the water's edge just looking at the deep blackness. Jonny pushed the safety catch forward.

'Phut'

The huge sodium light fixed high up on the factory wall burst the dark bubble, saturating everything with glaring light. A door banged open.

"Oy You! Don't you get letting off any bloody bangers and scaring my dog, I'll have the Police after you! Bugger off!"

It was the night watchman at the factory. He peered through his bottle top thick glasses.

"Oh Sorry, thought it was those bloody kids again throwing penny bangers at my door. Sends the dog mad it does, poor bugger, leaves him shaking."

The factory door closed. Jonny eased back the safety catch. Too late, the moment had gone, they'd been seen. The Perch was off the hook.

"Look Peter, it was my car that night, I'd taken one of 'the Notes' home, Reg, it was his last show, died soon after with cancer. Then I'd gone to Clarkes Lane to see someone."

"Ah, a girlfriend, that's good Sir, if you could possibly give me details of that person I could eliminate you from the inquiry."

Jonny looked at him in the dark.

"No, it wasn't a girlfriend, it was a man." There was silence as they both looked into the water. "It was a long time ago Peter, in those days Clarke's Lane was the place to go if you required that type of service, if you understand me."

Peter Hilary moved back from the water's edge and from Jonny.

"Yes Sir, I understand."

"Good. I've been very honest with you and that's as far as I'm going. I'm a very respected RAF pilot with good future prospects. You are the only person I've disclosed this to, so I expect you to protect my honesty and privacy. Do you understand Detective Constable Peter Hilary."

Jonny suspected that the Police Service was as the military and the command of an Officer would carry some weight.

"Yes Sir." Peter's fast brain was working through the options, there was no evidence other than a sighting of a car to link Conrad with Fletcher, the car was long gone, Conrad had told him a plausible story that couldn't be proved either way. He was onto a loser. "Good night Sir." DC Hilary crunched his way back up the slip and towards the darkness.

"Peter." Jonny called out. Peter stopped at the top and turned towards him

"Yes Sir."

"Would you like to give me your home phone number just in case anything comes to mind?"

There was a silence.

"No, that won't be necessary Sir. Goodnight."

Peter Hilary slung the thick file in the secretary's basket for shredding then went home.

Jonny fingered the gun in his pocket and remembered his dad and the perch. He'd better take mum home, it was getting late. He'd leave it at home now, he'd put it in dad's fishing basket, mum never went in there.

Calypso and Salvador were still living in the Old Vicarage at Coltishall. Jonny presumed she would have gone back to Ireland but she hadn't. She'd told him that the sound of the jets coming and going somehow kept him alive. Salvador was walking now, he loved to look at the planes streaking overhead. Whenever Jonny visited they never slept together, although the deep love and the memories were there, it was just too wrong for both of them. Jonny always brought

Salvador a little present. Irene never asked where he was going, she just assumed it was a woman. She'd seen a red toy crane he'd bought and just assumed there was a child. His child, her grandchild, but he never said and she never asked.

For Calypso, time was slowly healing the pain and hurt. The pain of his death, the pain of no remains, no funeral, nothing physical to mourn. The hurt of her suspicions of Hetty, and Guy and the socialist dream world they had lured him into. She was sure there was a connection with his death but no one said anything.

"For God's sake tell me the truth!" She silently screamed every day.

Jonny stayed for two days. It was lovely, they took Salvador to the park and even though it was November they went on the river, the golden curled up leaves floating like Viking ships on the still cold river. Salvador and Jonny threw conkers at them trying to sink them, the little boat rocked every time Salvador threw and fell over. They all laughed. Calypso looked at Jonny. Jonny looked at Calypso. They mouthed love to each other. Then the moment and the time ran out.

"For God's sake where've you been?" Veronica came out of Mum's front door, Brenda stood behind her.

"Why what's the matter?"

"Your mother's in hospital, collapsed two days ago, everybodies been trying to get hold of you. I guessed where you were, with Calypso, but I don't know her surname or where she lives. Am I right Jonny? Am I right?"

"What's wrong with Mum?"

"Don't know, she's unconscious, not expected to recover. That's all they'll tell me. She's at the Royal. You'd better high tail it there now, I'll look after things here."

"Thanks." Jonny turned to get back into his car.

"Jonny?"

"What?"

"What would you like to eat tonight?"

Jonny looked at her. It was nothing to do with eating, it was to do with caring for him.

"No idea Veronica, something simple." He turned away.

The hospital hadn't really moved on from the fifties, nurses were still white and starched, all the trolleys were cream with chipped paint but somehow the exposed metal didn't rust, it just went black. Everything smelt of disinfectant. It was a world ruled by a matron, doctors were just an inconvenience.

Mum was in a little partitioned room off to the right, next to a window. She lay there in a green gown, her eyes closed, her breathing shallow and quick. Various drips and lines fed her body. Her hair looked thin and tired. In those surroundings she didn't look all that big or fat. It was as though she was shrinking. Shrinking away from him.

The curtain parted.

"And you are?" It was an Indian looking doctor with glasses asking the question.

"I'm Jonny Conrad, I'm her son."

"Ah, would you be her next of kin?"

"Yes, my dad's dead."

The doctor signaled with his eyes and head that they should move outside the room.

"Sorry but the hearing is the last sense to shut down. She's unresponsive, as you see to everything. We've done some tests, it's as we thought, pneumococcal meningitis. Your mother's not going to come through this Mr. Conrad so prepare yourself for the worst."

"How long?"

"A day, two days at the most."

"Is she in any pain?"

"That we don't know but we're giving her morphine just in case."

Jonny sat down in a chair. The doctor made his excuses and left.

It was a long night, Jonny sat in a green leatherette easy chair beside her bed holding her white mottled old hand. Occasionally he dozed off, she never moved other than to breath, which got quicker and shallower.

"Don't know if you can hear me mum, but I hope you can. It was me who did in Frankie Fletcher, I did it for dad, without doubt it was the prison that killed dad and it was Frankie Fletcher that put him in prison, so I killed him. Smashed his head in with an iron scaffold pole then pushed him under the ice of the cut. I've no regrets, I'd do the same thing again tomorrow. I'm not sure if dad would be proud of me at the moment, I'm doing really well in the RAF, but I'm in love with a woman called Calypso, she's the only woman for me, forever, but, she got married to my best friend Jolyon. You know Jolyon, he's been to the house several times, anyway Jolyon had some strange ideas about life mainly backed up and encouraged by Veronica's friend Hetty. He's a pilot, like me, anyway one day he took an aeroplane, a special one with a top secret radar in it and headed for Russia. As bad luck would have it, I was on duty that night and, to cut a long story short, I had to shoot him down. Kill my best friend." Jonny stared out of the window towards the coming dawn of today.

"Bit like Frankie really, it didn't hurt me, all I had to do was press a button, same as Frankie all I had to do was swing a scaffold pole. Didn't seem real, but it was. Anyway Calypso was pregnant at the time with their first baby, he's two now, looks just like Jolyon. His name's Salvador, I see them both a couple of times a year, that's where I've just been. She'll never marry me, different levels of society, she says it would never work, but I couldn't even consider any other woman. There's Veronica of course, she'd marry me tomorrow but you know what love's like mum? Just look at you and dad. Hopelessly in love to the end. Course i've never told Calypso I killed her husband, my best friend. I can say this to you now mum but I really loved Jolyon as well, he taught me the basics of how to behave with the upper classes. I knew nothing when I left home to Join the RAF. That's no reflection on you and dad mum, Henry Street had it's limits."

Irene's legs jerked and her breathing stopped.

"What are you going to do about the house?" Veronica asked.

All the relatives and close friends had left, Veronica and her mum had put on a really good spread, pork pies from Dewhursts, egg and cress, cheese and tomato, salmon and cucumber sandwiches, all with the crusts cut off, followed by cakes from down the town, everybody said how nice it was.

"Nothing, keep it exactly as it is, as her son I can take it on with the council, the rent's peanuts, I'll just use it for quiet times when I want to be with them."

Veronica stroked his hair and the back of his neck. She was like a sister, there from his boyhood.

"Can I live here, you know move out from next door? Nothing official, we wouldn't tell the Council."

Jonny looked up at her.

"What about Brenda?"

"She doesn't stay here all the time, since Harry's been out she's fliited between here and her two sisters. Homeless I suppose, a bit sad really. I can keep the place clean and aired."

"What? Be my Henry Street wife or substitute mum?"

"Both." She leaned over and kissed his ear.

"That sounds OK but don't hang around for me Veronica, get yourself a proper husband, you're a pretty girl with a good figure, should be easy."

"What, you mean someone from the foundry or someone who works in a shoe shop? No thanks."

"You work in a library you must meet some intelligent blokes."

"Have you seen the sort of men that hang around in Libraries? They wear pullovers knitted by their aunts, have spots, glasses and bad breath."

Jonny smiled for the first time since mum passed as he gave her arm a squeeze.

"Can I sleep here tonight, sleep here with you? We don't have to do anything, it's just I've never woken up next to a man, or gone to sleep next to a man for that matter and I want to."

"Shall we have a Horlicks first? Mum never let dad go to bed without his Horlicks."

"I'll make it." Veronica got up and went to the kitchen.

Chapter. 21

Anthony Bannister pressed the button for his assistant.

"Patsy, can you come and see me? Bring that Fletcher file with you."

Patsy lourdes checked herself in the mirror behind her office door. She'd started to wear a new lipstick, it was very pale, almost white looking. She liked it. It went well with her hair and skin. Lily liked it as well.

She knocked and entered. It was cold, grey and raining outside.

"Got a letter here from Hock - Deighton, They're looking for five hundred thousand in damages for their client Harry Shaw. Neglect of duty, unlawful imprisonment and general fucking incompetence! And you know what Patsy? They're fucking right!"

Anthony Bannister was pacing up and down the large office. Stopping at each of the tall wet windows looking out at the rain as though one of them would offer him a glimpse of the sun. steam could almost be seen coming out of his ears.

"How do you think that makes me look with the namby pamby Eton boys at the Home Office?

He sat down at his desk, trying to calm down.

"Patsy, I want you to go and see Shaw, the address should be in the file, see what he's like. See if we can do a deal, I can't go begging to the minister for that sort of money. After that go and talk to some members of that band, 'The Note's or whatever it's called, see if you can get a handle on who did do it."

"Shouldn't that be the work of CID Sir,"

"It should but I don't want it spread all over town that we're trying to get it right. Again! Just do some discreet digging Patsy, I know I can depend on you."

Patsy paused wondering whether to disclose her trip to Scotland. Then decided against it. For now.

"Sir?"

"What?"

"Does Harry Shaw know that he went to prison because his son failed to disclose crucial evidence?"

"No, he's just been told that new evidence has come to light that makes his conviction unsafe. Why?"

"Just wondered."

48 Dale Street Wednesbury looked derelict. Patsy drove around the block looking for signs of life. From the gully behind was an entrance with an old Thames Trader van that looked as though it hadn't turned a wheel in years. Green slime started at the tyres and worked it's way up to the windows. The curtains at the back windows of the house were faded and hanging down, paint was peeling from everything. She drove back around to the front of the house and parked at the end of the street. If Harry Shaw was in she didn't want him clocking her car.

The front windows and door were filthy. The door itself looked unused but she didn't fancy the back entrance. Patsy knocked. She was smartly dressed in a beige mac and was carrying a small leather writing case.

After a short while and considerable effort the door was opened by a man in his seventies. The man looked at her.

"Yo'm from the Council about me van. I'm gooin to get it fixed and use it, just tell that to the bloody complainers."

"No, I'm not from the Council Mr. Shaw, I'm a police Officer. Can I come in?"

"Harry Shaw looked her up and down again."

"Yu dunna look big enough. Got any I.D?"

Patsy got out her warrant card, he looked at it but she could tell he didn't read it.

"It's a bit of a mess, me missus ain't 'ere."

The front room was dark and cold, by a fire grate was an old easy chair, a wheelchair and what looked like an old piss pot was on the hearth, there was an obvious path through discarded rubbish. Rubbish that should have been put out for the dustmen but instead just got piled up in the front room to slowly rot and stink. Patsy held her hanky to her mouth and nose as they walked through into a back kitchen. An electric fire glowed in the corner, the sink and draining board were full of dirty pots. This was an old man just doing the bare minimum to survive at the lowest level of life. Patsy concluded.

There were three chairs in the kitchen, two slat back wooden uprights and a folding metal chair full up with old newspapers, he made space on the other wooden chair, putting some old slippers on top of the papers.

"Sit down, sorry everything's a bit untidy, me missus ain't 'ere." It was the second time he'd said it. She wondered if he knew?

"Now, what's this all about, sorry I can't offer you a cup of tea, got no milk." After a moment's silence he added "Got no clean cups either, me missus ain't 'ere. You're from the police, are yu gunna lock me up again. Me son Phill was in the police yu know, an Inspector he was, died about nine months ago, cancer. Wish it'd bin me and not him."

Patsy looked at him, merest wisp of tired grey hair, a fat face that had now collapsed and hung around his neck, thick brown dirty trousers that were held up over his paunch by braces, a food stained vest and a brown thick cardigan with holes in it and big brown buttons that looked like laced leather but weren't. He reminded her of a fatter version of Harold Steptoe. Just as smelly even if he wasn't.

"To the point Mr. Shaw, your solicitors are asking for half a million pounds in compensation for your ten years inside. The Force can't afford that and my Chief Constable will fight you all the way on it. Even if you win your solicitors costs will be huge for such a case and also it will put your case and all it's details in the public domain. There may be details you may not wish to be public."

"What details, I've got nothing to hide?"

Patsy looked directly at him, considering how to tell him.

"No but Phil did have."

"What yo'm on about? Our Phil's dead."

"Mr. Shaw." Patsy could see the confusion and sadness in the old man's face. "Phil made a statement just before he died that on the night of Frankie's murder he followed you home from wherever it was you were playing. He did most nights you were playing in the band. He knew you'd be well over the limit. He did it 'cause his mother asked him to. She didn't want you hurt or in trouble with the police."

Harry Shaw's shoulders slumped as though someone had just kicked an already dead body.

"You couldn't have done it Mr. Shaw." Patsy said.

"Why? Why didn't he say that at the time. Ten years I've been locked up. Ten years of life I've lost. I've never touched a piano for ten years, never had a pint. Why would my own son do that?"

"To keep you away from Brenda Mr. Shaw, to keep you away from your wife."

He was silent with his chin on his grey haired chest.

"Do you want all that to come out in court Harry, all the horrible details of what you used to do to Brenda, how you treated her mother. Everything?"

"Has Brenda made a complaint?"

"No, but it wouldn't take much."

He exhaled.

"OK, how much can you give me for ten years of my life?"

"Fifty thousand."

"Five thousand a year." His grey watery eyes rose to meet her's.

"It's more than you'd get if you'd been working at the Leyland."

He half smiled.

"Tell you what Assistant Chief Constable Patricia Lourdes, you get my wife to come home and we'll call it quits. Tell her I'm a sad finished old man whose balls have dropped off. Tell her I need her here. Tell her I love her and always will."

Harry Shaw was near to tears. Patsy realised he'd pretended not to read her warrant card, realised he was smarter than he looked, realised perhaps he wasn't all bad, perhaps he lived with a demon inside him.

"I'll see what I can do." they both stood up.

"Sorry I couldn't give you some tea."

"Harry?"

"What?"

"If you didn't, who did?"

"God knows, that's your job. Frankie was a bit of a lad mind, he was the fast transport for some bad people. He'd never actually do a job himself but he had a black Austin Atlantic convertible at the time, quite a racy car, he loved it. He used to transport the nicked stuff around for them, that's how he always had a lot of dosh. Course, it all went wrong with Arthur."

"Arthur?"

"Arthur Conrad, apparently they'd done a job on the Harpers Social Club over Christmas, fags and booze, a lot of money, anyway it was all in Frankie's car. Then the bloke up north, Frankie was supposed to take it to, buggered off on holiday and wasn't back til the first week in January. Frankie didn't want it sitting in his car so he made up some cock and bull story about having a New Years party at his mothers and needing the space, so could he store a few boxes in Arthur's front room? Somehow your lot got to know about it and the next thing is Arthur's in 'The Green' doing time. We couldn't believe it. Arthur was the straightest bloke you could ever wished to meet. Course it affected 'The Notes' badly, he was a really good bass sax player. After he got out 'The Green' he was never the same, then he died, burst stomach ulcer apparently. It affected Irene and young Jonny badly, well, it would, wouldn't it? I must admit I found that a bit strange with young Jonny?"

"What?"

"Well him and Frankie seemed to be quite good mates later on. Jonny had started to play sax like his dad, not bass but tenor, he was quite good and played alongside Frankie who sort of took him under his wing, musically speaking of course. On the night, Jonny was feeding Frankie loads of gin and tonics, it was his stag do, well not officially, but Frankie did pay for the grub. Him and me did have our usual spat, we just couldn't stand each other, it happens don't it? Anyway could never quite figure it out, what with Frankie denying any knowledge about the stuff in Arthur's house and everything. Frankie was the reason Arthur was inside. Take it from me 'The Green's' not a pleasant place to be."

"Did Jonny drink?"

"No, never saw him with anything stronger than an orange juice. Mind you he was still quite young then, eighteen or nineteen."

"How did Jonny get home that night?"

"He had a car by then, a new Mini, he took Reg home. Reg was Arthur's best mate, he had cancer and was very ill at the time, that was the last time we saw him, he died about six months later. Jonny sort of felt obligated to run him around as he was so close to his dad. Arthur and Reg worked together at the foundry, shared an old Ford van that they used to transport Reg's xylophone around in and go fishing in, so he couldn't have done it, anyway, as I've said, they were good mates."

Patsy held out her hand and he shook it.

"I'll talk to your wife if I can, where is she?"

"As far as I know, still living with Irene Conrad in Henry Street. Irene moved after Arthur died, said she couldn't stay in their house without him."

The old man shut the dusty dirty front door and went back inside. Patsy walked to the end of the street. Her car was OK.

"Got him down to fifty thousand Sir, or nothing if I can talk his wife Benda to going back to him." Patsy relayed the news to Anthony Bannister, whose shoes were like mirrors today, he must spend at least half an hour a day getting them like that - she thought to herself.

"Well that's good news, and can you?"

"No idea Sir, have never met her. Have you read Phillip Shaw's statement?"

"No."

"Well Harry Shaw did some dreadful things to his mother Brenda, over the years. That's one of the reasons he joined the force, to get a free house."

"Not the best of reasons to become a Police Officer Patsy."

"No, but then again, life's not perfect and he was a bloody good copper."

"Pass the file to the legal department will you? Get them to draft out the usual letter of agreement for fifty thousand pounds."

"You don't want to wait until I've had a shot at Brenda Shaw?"

"Two weeks Patsy, I'd rather pay up though, there's no comeback then."

Patsy took the file from his desk and left. Metcalfe's pocket book entry, Graham Dangerfield, Harry Shaw, she'd drop it on the Chief, he couldn't refuse her then. 'Jonny Conrad, I'm coming for you.' She thought.

Patsy didn't enter her office, she turned around and headed back up the corridor.

"Forget something Patsy?" Anthony didn't look up from his desk as she entered.

"No, just decided something."

Anthony Bannister took off his glasses and looked at her. He didn't like wearing his glasses anyway, he only wore them when he was alone. They aged him and he didn't want that.

"Go on." It was an ominous 'go on' as though he was worried what was coming.

"Jonny Conrad."

Anthony moved his glasses to the side and leaned forward on his desk.

"You mean Squadron Leader Jonny Conrad, soon to be decorated DFC, ace fighter pilot, local boy makes very good, local hero and all round good guy who's going to lead the Walsall Remembrance Day Parade next Sunday. Do you mean that Jonny Conrad?"

Patsy was taken back at his knowledge.

"How about adding well known murderer?"

"Forget it Patsy, I've been warned off once by the mandarins, you go charging in, upsetting a very important applecart and my career is toast. I'm going to put an entry in my pocket book that you are not to continue any investigation into Mr. Jonny Conrad. Is that understood?"

"Yes Sir." He reached into the second draw down and clicked it off.

"Now, what have you got Patsy?"

"I took a trip to Scotland and had a cup of tea with his C.O, as you said, the best of the best, destined for high office, then right at the end he described an analogy that Conrad had used, it described the M.O, used to kill Fletcher to a 't'."

"Will he make a statement?"

"Doubt it, he thinks the sun shines out of his proverbial, he had no idea of the significance of what he'd told me."

"And?"

"Metcalfe's pocket book entry placing Conrad's car in Clarkes Lane, picking up a drunk in the early hours of the morning directly after Fletcher's stag do."

"And?"

"When I saw Harry Shaw he told me that he found the friendship between Conrad and Fletcher really strange seeing as Fletcher had been the cause of his dad going to prison and possibly his death. Said that Conrad had been feeding Fletcher gin and tonics all night at the pub."

Anthony Bannister pushed back his chair, straightened out his legs and exhaled. He was torn between his career, his office and the fact he was still a policeman whatever boy scout badges they'd given him.

"What are you thinking Patsy? What do you want to do?"

"How about if I lead the Police Contingent next Sunday, engage him in conversation and sound him out, get the measure of him. I'd love to arrest him for murder."

"Patsy, there's nothing, a hearsay reported conversation, a sighting of a car by a long dead officer, and the rambling thoughts of a drunken old man who's just come out of prison. No forensic, no witnesses, not even a statement of any description. You're skating on wafer thin ice Patsy and we both could get very wet and cold. As a friend I'd say forget it, as your boss I'd say forget it. As a policeman, well that's down to you but don't expect me to back you up. I can't."

"OK Sir. Understood."

Patsy got up to leave.

"Patsy?"

"What Sir?"

"Good luck."

She closed the office door and thought about Sunday.

Chapter. 22

The day was cold and steely grey as befits a Remembrance Sunday. It seemed totally bizarre and wrong, standing in mom and dad's small bedroom in Henry Street. His uniform with it's badges and gold sword. His DFC dangling from his chest, his hat with gold braid. He couldn't look like that leaving the house. Of course he'd carry his sword, not wear his hat and wear a gabardine mac over the top. His car was directly outside the front door so it would only take a few seconds and he'd be gone. Veronica and Brenda were fussing about downstairs competing over who would cook his breakfast.

"Wow! Good morning Sir." Veronica looked him up and down before batting imaginary fluff from his shoulder.

"Your mum would be proud of you. Look at you all dressed up." Brenda said.

"What about my dad?"

"He'd be proud as punch of his boy."

Every time he wore the sword he thought of Jolyon and their happy time at Cranwell.

"Ok quick cuppa then got to fly; well not really, got to go in my car to the Art School, flying's next week."

"Good luck Jonny, you'll be famous next week when the Express and Star comes out."

"I'm famous now Veronica, but for the wrong things in the wrong places."

They had no idea what he was talking about.

The participants in the parade were mingling about in front of the Art college. It was a substantial red brick building that had played many roles in it's time but for now it was a refuge of creativity.

Sea Cadets, Air Cadets, Army Cadets, Police Cadets and Territorial Army chaps were all huddled in small groups sheltering from the bitter blowy wind that whipped around the side of the college. A bugler from the barracks at Whittington was trying to blow some warmth into the naked bugle. A couple of Police Officers were on hand to control the traffic when the parade got to the Wolverhampton Road. A few people looked at the Porsche as he pulled up. As he got out someone with a large gold chain of office immediately approached him.

"Squadron Leader Conrad." The small tubby man with the chain thrust out his hand. "Thank you so much for coming to lead our parade today. Scotland is a long way away for such a small event as ours."

"Walsall is my hometown Mr.------------?"

"Phillips, Terry Phillips."

"Mr. Phillips, it's my pleasure to do this; really."

"Shouldn't take too long an hour at the most, last post and the carry on at eleven then we can all go home or to the pub." The mayor said. "Kick off at ten forty five."

A coach pulled up with the band from the barracks, they spilled out from the steamed up coach into the chill of a November morning, moaning, lighting up, fiddling with uniforms, warming up instruments and positioning hats. Jonny fixed his sword to its buckles and straps.

Silently he thanked his best friend for buying him the sword. He was never far away from his thoughts. He'd never get over it, or him.

"Form up! Form up! A T.A Sargeant Major with a loud voice immediately commanded attention. Jonny wondered why reservists always had to be better, smarter, louder, more military than the military.

"Band first, Royal Navy, Royal Airforce, Army and then the Police. Move yourselves we haven't got all day."

By now it was beginning to drizzle.

The Sargeant Major marched over to where Jonny and the Mayor were standing and saluted. After the bellowing orders it was quite a shock to hear a refined quiet voice.

"Think we're about good to go Sir, if you'll kindly lead us."

Jonny drew his sword.

"Where do you want me Sargeant?"

"About ten paces in front of the band Sir. Mr. Mayor, if you'll kindly take up the rear behind the Police Cadets we'll be off. Take about ten minutes to march around the square and position ourselves in front of the Cenotaph. I'll give you the nod Sir when to move forward and lay the wreath. The wreath will be on the first step of the monument. After that the bugler will sound the last post. After the minute's silence I will say the eulogy, the bugler will sound the carry on and we'll march back here then go home."

"You've done this before then Sargeant?" Jonny looked at the immaculate man.

"Many times Sir and every one brings a tear to my eye and a lump in my throat. Death is a bit permanent Sir. Most of the names on that monument hadn't a clue what they were going into or why. Virgin soldiers Sir, Virgin Soldiers." The Sargeant marched off.

For Jolyon he held the sword firm and straight.

Patsy stared at her target. He was tall, dark and handsome, a film star only this wasn't Hollywood, this was Walsall. Two and a half bands on each sleeve, his pilot's wings surmounting his DFC. The gold embellished cap keyed in naturally with the gold of his sword and the shiny brass buckles of it's brown leather straps. He looked as though he belonged in a church. How could he be a murderer?

Two three beat drum rolls and they were off. She quite liked marching, the band struck up with a military march. She'd heard it before but didn't know it's name. She held the silver tip of her swagger stick in her left fingers, the stick clamped under her arm, her right arm swinging. Ten cadets were two paces behind her. It was cold but it didn't matter.

It took the band three marches to get the parade in front of the cenotaph. The T.A. Sargeant Major took over and dressed everyone up.

"--------------------we shall remember them." Somehow the grey day, the red poppies, the uniforms and the silence worked together to make her think how these young people died. Most, if not all, not heroes but frightened youngsters, barely men, away from home, from mums, aunts, grannies and girlfriends. Their freshness and vitality instantly gone or preserved forever depending on your mood.

Flash bulbs popped as Jonny laid the wreath, stood up, looked straight at the monument and saluted. There could never be any connection between death and life, yesterday and today. We were all travelers in time with one way tickets. He'd played his part, his private thoughts were well hidden by his cap.

Patsy snapped back to now as the bugler fluffed the first few cold notes of 'reveille' before his lips and the shiny copper bugle responded. Then it was a more relaxed march back to the front of the Art College. Colonel Bogey, lifted everyone's mood as people mouthed the unofficial words.

"Parade - Turn right - Dismissed." The Sargeant Majors voice cut through the cold air.

Immediately the ordered ranks melted into humming conversations and milling young people. The few veterans moved towards their waiting warm cars.

Jonny was unclipping his sword from his belt.

"Hello, are you dashing off to look dashing somewhere else?"

Jonny turned to look at the police woman standing in front of him. She was short, a little wide with black wavy hair, brown leather gloves and a hickory swagger stick with a silver knob and brass tip.

"And you are?"

"Assistant Chief Constable Pat Lourdes, West Midlands Police."

Jonny curbed his reaction but she picked up something that told her he knew her or at least knew of her.

"For a small town Walsall does pretty well I'd say, a Squadron Leader to lead it's parade and an Assistant chief Constable to back it up. Wouldn't you agree -----?"

He pretended to have not remembered her name.

"Patsy, call me Patsy, and yes I would agree. Would you agree to a cup of coffee on a cold morning?"

Jonny looked at his watch.

"Actually it's a cold afternoon now Patsy and yes I would agree. Do you know anywhere?"

"There's the Red Lion Pub round the corner, they do morning coffees and it's only just afternoon."

"Is it OK in our uniforms?"

"Yes of course, it's Remembrance Sunday, it's almost expected."

"One moment Ms Lourdes I'll just put my sword in the car and grab my coat, it's a bit less formal."

A small, quick, shabby photographer tagged along behind them. 'Why did they always look like rats?' Jonny thought.

Patsy waited for her murderer to put his sword in the car. She told herself to be careful not to compromise the investigation. Nothing that could be construed as an interview. He was so nice and courteous.

"I'll be guided by you Ms Lourdes, I'm not too familiar with this part of town."

They walked together, he walked on the outside of the pavement. It wasn't far to a stout red brick building with tall leaded windows and the ground floor brickwork actually painted a dark red. The door handles were polished brass and the inside smelt like all pubs do, even if they do sell coffee.

Jonny opened the door for her. The photographer snapped their smiles at the door.

"The photographers will snap us." Jonny sang the line of the song.

"And then we'll be seen in a smart magazine." Patsy added another line and they both laughed. "Well at least the Walsall Express and Star."

"Let's sit near the window. I'll go and order." Jonny said. "Just coffee or something to go with it?"

"Just coffee please ----------------."

"Jonny, call me Jonny. Jonny and Patsy at least it doesn't jarr the brain." He laughed.

Patsy tried to conceal her swagger stick, it was OK for a parade but a bit of an embarrassment in a pub.

"So, how old are you Patsy?" His directness shocked her a bit, but it wasn't rude, more professional.

"I'm thirty four, and you?"

"Thirty. When you were a teenager thirty seemed ancient. The slippery slope to death, yet here I am, or rather here we are in a pub in Walsall dressed in grown up boy scouts uniforms."

"I'm a girl, so it would have to be the 'Girl Guides."

"Well blow me, so you are." They both laughed.

"What was your dad, what did he do?" Jonny asked.

"That's a strange question coming from a Squadron Leader. He was a fettler in a foundry."

"Did he make it to his retirement?"

"No, died in his fifties."

"Do you miss him?"

"Terribly, we were very close. I was closer to my dad than my mum. Mum had a bit of a temper and a hurtful tongue when she was cross. Dad was always the one I went to. You? Any kids?"

"Not really, my best friend died in an accident, he had a small son so I spoil him on his birthday and Christmas but not really. Easy isn't it?"

"What?" Patsy enquired.

"Talking about serious personal things to a total stranger."

"I don't feel we're strangers." Patsy put the empty cup down and looked at him.

"How about your mum and dad, still alive?"

"No, mum's recently died of pneumococcal meningitis, at least it was quick that's all I can say. Dad died a long time ago, burst stomach ulcer brought about by stress, he'd had a bit of a bad few years and it'd caught up with him." Jonny finished his coffee. "I can't ever remember him telling me he loved me. I know he did though, you just didn't say those sought of things."

"Mine did, used to tell me all the time. He loved me so much I don't think any other man's love can come near it."

"How about a woman's?"

Jonny and Patsy looked at each other.

"Maybe?" She said.

The bar started to fill up as folk came in from the cold.

"I'm going to make a move now, feel a bit out of place in this uniform. Police aren't the most popular of people. I'll nip to the toilet first."

Jonny looked at her as she crossed the room. He paid for the coffees and stood by the door waiting for her.

"Well it's been very nice meeting you Mr. Conrad and thank you for the coffee."

Jonny noticed that her stick had disappeared, she held her brown leather gloves in her left hand.

"Where's your stick?"

She looked embarrassed that he'd noticed.

"I've hidden it up my sleeve, and taken my gloves off. Don't want people thinking I'm a dyke. Most people think that all police women are dykes."

"Think it goes with the job Patsy, it's a difficult job, why would a woman want to do it? That's the reasoning behind it."

After a few minutes of silent walking they were back at Jonny's car.

"Well goodbye Jonny Conrad."

Patsy held out her ungloved hand.

"Goodbye Ms Lourdes, ----------Patsy?"

"What?"

"If you want to interview me you're going to have to drive up to Scotland,-------again."

"Ah!----- He told you."

"Of course, you didn't tell him not to."

Patsy thought back. He was right, she hadn't asked Graham Dangerfield not to discuss it, she'd just assumed that he wouldn't. Fuck! He'd known all along. She'd lost this round.

"Till we meet again then Jonny." Now the gloves were off but she couldn't help liking him. Feeling safe in his company.

Jonny sat in his car thinking as the engine warmed up enough to blow warm air onto the windscreen. He'd planned to go back to mum's house to change and then head for Scotland but everything he needed was already in his car. He'd head for the M6, Glasgow, Edinburgh, then Leuchars. He could be supersonic on thin wings in the ice cold Scottish air by ten tomorrow. He really needed to do that. Marvin Gaye, 'Heard it through the grapevine.' came on the radio. He loved that song, it made his thoughts turn to Calypso. He thought of diverting to see her but had no idea if she'd be in or not so discounted it.

Grahams and Jonny's offices were side by side. It was usual to tap on the door and walk in. That is what Graham did.

"Jonny, I've got a letter here from the West Midlands Police, they want to interview you. Is it what I think it is? That woman who turned up out of the blue and disturbed my gardening?"

"Yes Sir, It's that woman, apparently my car was seen somewhere and they want me to explain it, officially. I had a chat with her at the Remembrance Sunday Parade about it, said she'd have to drive up here if she wanted to interview me officially, she obviously does. We got on quite well actually, I quite like her."

"She's suggesting December the twelfth is that OK with you?"

Jonny checked his desk diary.

"Well we've got night flying up until the tenth, then nothing then til practice bombing starting on the fifth of January so that will be OK."

"OK I'll get Judy to knock out a reply saying the twelfth is OK" Graham left.

Jonny wanted to spend Christmas with Calypso and Salvador at Coltishall but she was going home to Ireland and he'd never been invited there. With mum gone there was nothing really to go home for, Veronica was becoming the only alternative to a lonely Christmas on camp. Then there was that letter from Patsy Lourdes saying that she would attend the camp between nine and ten on the morning of the twelfth. It was something and nothing but it played on his mind, a distraction to his usual one hundred percent commitment to his squadron.

Chapter. 23

Scotland was the same as the last visit, wet, grey and cold. At least this time she got to see the sea. Anthony had offered her a car and driver seeing as this visit was official but she'd declined. It limited her freedom. This time she went up the M1 /A1 and then onto the new Firth of Forth Road Bridge, it had only been open a couple of years. The little MGA almost scampered across it whilst she kept looking at the prone lattice diamonds of the railway bridge. She was a little apprehensive, a little nervous and a little excited about interviewing Jonny Conrad. You didn't come from nothing and reach the rank of Squadron leader before you were thirty by being 'Mr. Niceguy'. No, there was something else, something he hid, some inner steel, just something.

She'd booked a bed for the night at St Michaels Inn, just to the North of Leuchars. She wanted to be fresh tomorrow, it wasn't going to be the friendly chat they'd had in the pub, this was going to be a mental battle with a formidable foe. She hadn't got enough to arrest him, in fact she hadn't got anything really except a twelve year old pocket book entry from a dead police constable, an off the cuff comment from his boss and somebody who said that he'd bought the victim a few drinks on his stag do. As Anthony had said, 'very thin ice'.

She'd decided It was going to be contemporaneously recorded so it wasn't going to be quick.

St. Michaels Inn was a nondescript black and white place on a corner of a road junction. Patsy had taken considerable care not to dress like an off duty police officer, her hair was untidy, no makeup and casual clothes. She just wanted warmth, decent food and a comfortable bed. Tomorrow she'd be entering Jonny Conrad's world. A world where talented, gifted men played with very dangerous toys. The old wartime song 'coming in on a wing and a prayer' somehow seemed to apply to her.

The morning was just like yesterday evening, a dour heavy greyness that compressed you.

Patsy came to a halt in front of a red stop pole with jointed metal rods that hung down from it. A sentry box come control centre was on the left. A Spitfire was mounted on a stand behind the box, then came huge dark voluminous buildings. On the right was a big light blue RAF sign. A sentry wearing a beret came towards her. She produced her warrant card.

"Assistant Chief Constable Lourdes to see Squadron Leader Conrad."

The damp cold sentry inspected her card and then her. Then saluted.

"Please park over there Ma'am I'll get an Airman to accompany you to his Office."

"Would that be in my car or walking?"

"In your car Ma'am, it's quite a way." He nodded towards the box and the pole started to lift. The metal rods obeyed gravity and folded neatly downwards. Patsy drove in and parked in a box.

A very young, very nervous Airman came up to her wet car, she wound down the window and told him to get in. He directed her to a new, brick, flat roofed, rectangular office block with a straight path leading to two heavy wooden doors, one of which was open. A small wooden painted sign planted into the grass read 'Administration Office', around the side were some parked cars, one of which was a light blue

Porsche, it looked small and cheerful compared to the slab sides of the modern saloons parked either side of it.

The Airman led her in and up the stairs to the first floor landing with offices. There was a photocopying machine at one end of the corridor, at the other was an RAF flag and a Union Jack. The carpet was light blue and not made for dirty shoes. On the other side of the corridor were some toilets and an open glazed area with soft seats that gave a view of the main runway. Each office had a name plate.

Patsy knocked on the one marked 'Squadron Leader J Conway DFC.'

"Come in." By the time she'd opened the door he was halfway across the office to meet her. Smiling, dressed in blue grey with a tie and a jumper.
"Assistant Chief Constable Lourdes. How nice to see you again." Jonny held out his hand, she shook it.

"Sit down please. Can I get you a tea, a coffee? How was your trip?"

Patsy sat down in a comfortable wooden semi-circular chair.

"A coffee please." Jonny ordered two coffees and some biscuits on his desk intercom. The office was large, his desk was large. It had an old Airfix model of a Gloster Javelin on it and a new metal model of a lightning. In the corner was a coat stand with his green flying suit and kit hanging on it. Filing cabinets and cupboards occupied most of the walls, above them were maps and photos one of which was a handsome young man with his arm around a beautiful dark skinned girl in front of a light aircraft. Jonny noticed her eyes settling on the photo.

"My best friend Jolyon Clay, he was killed in a tragic accident."

"And the girl?"

"Calypso Fortnum." She pounced on Jonny's silence.

And the girl?"

"Later Calypso Clay."

"He'd recognised the trap and moved out of it."

"So how was it?"

"How was what?" she asked.

"Your trip, it's hardly round the corner to the Co-op, is it?"

"I quite enjoyed it actually, it gave me time to myself. Time to think about things."

"Penny for them, what did you think about?" He asked, offering her a plate of biscuits.

This wasn't the professional serious start she had planned.

"My dad, my mum and Lily."

"Who's Lily? She despaired at his ability to home in immediately on deeply personal stuff.

"My friend."

"Your 'special' friend?" She sipped her coffee and nibbled a Rich Tea biscuit.

"Yes." She looked at him. He was totally relaxed, why shouldn't he be? This was his ground. He was on home turf.

"And you're wondering, if or when to tell them that Lily is more than just a friend?"

He'd seen straight through her as though she was made of glass.

"Shall we get on Mr. Conrad?"

"Yes of course. Sorry, how do you want to do this?"

"I'm going to write down my questions and your answers, when we've finished you read it over and sign each page as correct."

"Good grief that'll take all day."

"It probably will." Patsy reached into her leather briefcase and pulled out a wad of blank statement forms.

"May I lean on your desk?"

"Of course, pull up your chair."

"First of all I must inform you that you are not under arrest and you are free to leave, seek advice or terminate this interview should you wish to and that you are not obliged to say anything unless you wish to do so, but what you say may be put into writing and given in evidence. Do you understand Mr. Conrad."

"I understand Ms. Lourdes." Jonny replied and Patsy wrote it down

"Were you the owner of light blue Mini Saloon number 448 DJW, between December 1963 and June 1965?"

"I was."

"During the early hours of Friday the 24th January 1964 that vehicle was seen by an on duty police officer to stop in Clarkes Lane Bloxwich and pick up an unknown male who appeared to be drunk. Can you explain that?"

"Yes." Jonny wasn't going to make it easy for her. She waited then realised.

"Can you tell me the details of your explanation?"

"Yes." Fuck she'd asked another closed question.

"Please tell me those details."

Jonny looked at her.

"That night it was Frankie's unofficial stag do, nothing much, just a few drinks after a 'Notes' do and some grub Frankie paid for. Frankie and Harry Shaw had their usual spat, Frankie was pretty drunk as everyone had bought him a drink. Frankie decided to walk home to sober up. That's about it."

"What did you do?"

"I took Reg home, Reg was our xylophone player, he'd got cancer, he's long dead now of course. Then I drove to Clarkes Lane."

"Why did you do that?"

"It's personal. I don't want to say."

"I put it to you that you drove to Clarkes lane looking for Frankie Fletcher in order to kill him."

"Now why would I want to do that Patsy. We were mates, we played together in 'The Notes' he helped me out with the difficult bits."

"How many drinks did you buy Frankie Fletcher that night?"

"Good grief, you have done your homework haven't you. I've no idea, two or three, whenever he had an empty glass, which wasn't often by the way, I topped it up. I wasn't actually counting."

"I put it to you that it was your intention to get him drunk."

"You're wrong Patsy, it was just a social occasion." Jonny could see that she was getting annoyed by his use of her name. He moved the plate of biscuits closer to her. She ignored it.

"Who was the man who got into your car in Clarkes Lane?"

"I've no idea?"

"What do you mean, you've no idea, you have a brand new mini, barely a month old and you don't know who gets into it at one in the morning?"

"That's correct."

"Can you explain that?"

"Yes." Fuck another closed question. 'He must think I'm a total amature' she thought.

"Go on." Patsy was writing as fast as she could to keep the flow going.

"I'm not married Patsy, have I mentioned any girlfriend in our previous conversation? You of all people should be able to work it out."

In one reply he'd exposed a previous conversation, inferred that he was homosexual and inferred that she was lesbian but not actually said anything. A defense lawyer would have a field day with that.

"Why did you pick up a man in Clarkes Lane?"

"Oh come on! I'm a Squadron leader, I'm hardly going to admit any misdemeanours, plus I was under twenty one at the time. Anyway I've already explained my motives to your DC Hilary at our unofficial interview in the pub."

Patsy tried not to react. Hilary had been pulled off this enquiry, told in no uncertain terms not to do anything on it. What the fuck was going on? She decided to pretend she knew about that and ignored it. Jonny clocked that she didn't know. She had no idea Peter Hilary was very lucky to still be alive.

"Did you Kill Frankie Fletcher with a scaffold pole and push his body under the ice of the canal?"

"No, obviously not. I hope now the information I've given you is enough to earn us both a nice lunch." Jonny knew she'd have to write out his words verbatim as she'd undoubtedly assume he was recording their conversation.

"Did you blame Frankie Fletcher for the death of your father?"

Jonny was surprised at her knowledge and perception.

"I was a boy Ms. Lourdes, my dad died and life went on."

"Did your mother want you to play in 'The Notes'?"

"She said it was my choice, my decision. I just wanted to be like my dad. To honour him I suppose."

"Did your mother blame Frankie Fletcher for your dad's death?"

"Yes." Jonny knew it was a mistake as soon as he'd said it.

"Then why did you wish to play saxophone, an instrument that would put you directly beside the man your mother blamed for the death of your dad."

Jonny thought before answering.

"I've told you, my dad played saxophone. I just wanted to be like him."

"I put it to you that you deliberately joined 'The Notes' and deliberately chose to play the saxophone in order to get close to Frankie Fletcher and kill him."

"Blimey, that's a very long term strategy for a young boy Ms Lourdes. You don't just 'play' a saxophone, you have to learn, learn to read music and practice, a lot! Of course I deny your allegation." Jonny was smiling at her.

Patsy had run out of angles and questions. Jonny knew it.

"Do you wish to say anything more about this investigation?"

"Yes, Let's go to the Officer's Mess for lunch, the food's quite good, then tonight I'll treat you to a steak at St Andrews Golf Club, the food there is delicious."

"He smiled as she dutifully wrote down his every word. Patsy was furious that he'd managed to infer they were close friends.

"No thanks." She replied as she sorted the papers for him to read through and sign.

"No! Then how about a 'jolly' tomorrow?"

"What do you mean 'a jolly'? What's a jolly?"

"A trip, a flight in one of our aircraft. Let me explain. I'm the Flight Instructor for my squadron. Part of my responsibilities is to test fly an aircraft after any major service. One of our

Lightnings, a T5, a training aircraft, has just had two new engines and a lot of modifications done to it's electronics. The engineers have told me that everything's working OK so I'm going to take it up tomorrow morning. There's a spare seat, come along. The chance of a lifetime Patsy." He smiled from behind the sheath of statement forms. "'Think of what you could gain from a trip in my plane', or so the song goes."

"What's the song called?" She was starting to warm to the idea, what a chance, a trip in the fastest Jet fighter the RAF had.

"You'll fly high in the sky." I think, I'm not a hundred percent sure.

"What would we do?" She stood up to collect the signed papers from him.

"Go out over the North Sea, go supersonic, go inverted so I, or maybe you, can collect all the bits and pieces that will fall into the canopy, do a few tests then come back home."

"What do you mean? bit's and pieces?"

"You know, bits of lockwire, washers, nut's, sometimes bolts but not often, stuff they've dropped during the work."

"What would I have to do?"

"Nothing, turn up here about nine tomorrow morning do a dummy run in the seat shop, a bit of instruction on the flying suit and it's connections, airborne by about eleven back for lunch at twelve. I would advise you to give breakfast a miss though." He laughed. "Just tell your Chief I was unexpectedly unavailable today and you had to stay on another day. Easy, just tell lies."

"What like you do? I make no bones about it Mr. Conrad, should I get the slightest bit of evidence about this case in the future, I'll be back, not to interview you in a nice comfortable office but to arrest you and interrogate you in a police station."

"That's not very friendly Patsy."

"I don't like being made a fool of or being lied to, and that's just what has happened to me."

Jonny looked at her stern face. She could easily have been a man.

"Till tomorrow at nine then."

Patsy turned and let herself out of his office, walked down the stairs and collected the waiting airman.

Jonny watched her leave from the glass gallery. Her exit silenced by the roar of twin afterburners as a silver lightning rocketed into the grey low sky. Everything made him think of Jolyon, some things made him think of Calypso. He didn't want this pint sized policewoman disrupting his life.

Chapter. 24

It was nine o'clock when Jonny left the Officers Mess and got into his car. He sat there thinking for a while, the ejection seat sear pin on his keyring was beginning to look a mess, scratched, with most of the red paint gone, it's swinging movement on the dash was beginning to wear the blue paint away. He took it off and put it in his pocket. It was another constant reminder of Jolyon and the day they'd both blasted off up the rig.

"Well hello! What an unexpected pleasure. You couldn't resist it then?"

The man or boy in her had won, it was, as he had said, a once in a lifetime chance.

Jonny pressed the intercom "Coffee for two with some biscuits Carol please, Oh, and let the seat shop know I'll be attending in thirty minutes with a civilian for a dummy run."

He clicked it off without waiting for an acknowledgement. She was a lot more relaxed this morning, smiling to cover her nervousness and excitement. She was about to take to the skies of Scotland with the man she'd interviewed as a murder suspect the day before. Worst still, inside she knew it was him.

"Come on we can walk over to the seat shop, it's only the next building."

"It's raining or hadn't you noticed."

"I notice everything Ms Lourdes but I do have an umbrella."

They both huddled under the umbrella as they struggled against the wind.

"According to the met boys it's going to get sunny in about an hour. Perfect timing."

The ageing kindly Scottish voice told her.

"When you hear the words 'EJECT, EJECT, EJECT, you reach up with both hands grasp this handle here and pull down hard. A fabric cover will come down over your face to protect you from the blast of air. If, for any reason you can't reach up, you reach down and pull the handle between your legs up in one strong movement. Do you understand?"

"Yes Sir." Patsy responded.

"I'm not a 'Sir' , I'm a Sargeant. He's a Sir." He nodded towards Jonny. "And a bloody good one two. You'll be in safe hands."

Jonny laughed as she hung on the rig whilst the metal seat detached in slow time and the roof girder became her parachute.

Freddie Kincaid was the sargeant in charge of the safety equipment and practice seat shop. He was an exact copy of Jimmy Edwards, a pronounced paunch, greying hair and a substantial handlebar moustache. It was a great way to slide towards a pension. He made you think that his seat shop was the most important place in the world and you were special to be in it.

 "Twist and bang it, don't try pressing it, give it a good thump and everything will let go." Freddie demonstrated the harness release buckle to Patsy, then it was next door to kit her out.

"What's this dangling green thing?"

"That's your personal equipment connector, it clips into the side of the seat like this." Jonny took her hand and guided it to the right side of the seat.

"It gives you everything, Oxygen, radio, air, everything."

Touching and feeling close seemed very comfortable and safe to Patsy.

"Right, go to the toilet and then we'll suit you up."

"Yes Dad!" Patsy giggled.

She looked at herself in the mirror, green flying suit, anti-G suit. Mae West life jacket, things dangling everywhere and a shiny white helmet in her hand. She'd told Anthony last night on the phone that she was miserable in Scotland but had to interview Conrad tomorrow as he'd had to fly off somewhere on the arranged day. It was a lie, This was probably the most exciting thing she'd ever done.

"Ok navigator, let's go." Jonny slapped her on the back.

"I did mention you were my navigator today didn't I? You can read a map can't you?"

They walked together towards the high big jet. Sure enough the sun was now shining, the large puddles on the hard standing shrinking in the wind.

Patsy followed him around and underneath RAF Lightning L264. Jonny poked,, tugged and shook things and looked in every hole there was.

"Looks OK Patsy, shall we get in?"

"After you Sir."

"You go round the other side Patsy climb up the ladder and sit in. An Aircraftman will strap you in and remove your seat pins, he'll put them in a little red block on your right. Make sure all the holes in the block are full. I'll check it anyway when I'm in."

Patsy had to pinch herself as she walked around the front of the silver rocket. It did look like a rocket, it's radar cone thing sticking out of the front air intake just like the top of a rocket. The young ground crewman smiled and held her helmet as she climbed up the red ladder and clambered in. He followed her up the ladder and helped her clip in the straps. He tightened them very tight. Jonny said they would feel tight until they started to climb or went upside down, then they would feel loose. She could hardly move, the young man helped her put the helmet on and the oxygen mask. It felt a bit like the ones in the dentist when she was a small girl, smelt like it too.

Jonny smiled at her as he put his helmet on.

He twirled his finger around, pushed a switch forward. The rocket came alive. Instruments jumped, lights came on or flashed The plane pitched forward on the brakes. He did it again and the noise, a cacophony of sucked in air, whining of turbines and whoosh of exhaust, doubled. The canopy closed, it became quieter. The radio cut in.

"Feeling OK Patsy?"

"Fine." She lied. She was so high up, imprisoned in this bubble, surrounded by black and white switches, gauges, instruments unable to move except for her arms. Legs and head.

"Fine." She lied again.

Jonny signaled to the men on the ground 'chocks away.' The aircraft lurched forward a few yards then nose dived to a halt as Jonny checked the brakes.

The two idling engines were too much power for taxiing, Jonny had to use the brakes all the time. The airfield sped and rumbled by. The little lights, the painted lines on the concrete and the short squat signs planted in the grass meant nothing to her then they turned onto the apron of the main runway. It had a big white '25' painted on it with uncountable black tyre skids as planes had contacted the ground and wheels suddenly had to turn.

Jonny spoke to the tower. He looked at her. She gave a small nod.

Jonny Conrad pushed both throttles forward, passed the cold power stop into hot power maximum position. The after burners lit up as he released the brakes.

Patsy's straps suddenly felt loose as an immense hand pushed them forward more and more into the invisible air that would soon lift them up and away from the ground. Jonny kept it low and straight as the undercarriage tucked itself away, then, at the end of the runway the jet plane went vertically up, not clawing at the sky trying to get higher but slicing upwards as though somebody had removed the earth. Her straps now felt very loose. She glanced at Jonny who was grinning like a schoolboy with a new bag of marbles.

"Up Up and away eh! Patsy, in our beautiful balloon."

Dials in front of here were whizzing around as they climbed ever higher, was it ever going to stop, now she could see the coast and the sea. It looked silver. Now they were over the sea. Jonny leveled off.

"Look at the instrument to your left Patsy." Jonny said. "The one marked 'Mach'."

She looked, the finger pointed to one point three.

"A thousand miles per hour Patsy. Faster than the speed of sound. At this speed we could do Lands End to John O'Groats in three quarters of an hour."

"I thought there would be a big bang?"

"There was but we were going too fast to hear it, they heard it below though, that's why we're not allowed to do it overland except in an emergency."

"Would we have to stop for petrol?" Patsy joked wondering at the endless silver carpet that spread before her.

"Probably." Patsy noticed a little tremor in his voice. Almost a sadness.

"OK in a moment Patsy we're going to go inverted, upside down. When I tell you, just hold the stick steady, don't move it, whilst I just scrape up the inevitable flotsam and jetsam."

"So! You want me to control an RAF jet fighter upside down whilst travelling at supersonic speeds."

"Exactly, here we go."

She fell into her loose straps as little things fell into the dome of the canopy. Remembering what he'd said she held onto the stick.

"There you are, told you so, two small washers, a locknut and two bits of lockwire."

Jonny pulled the faded and scratched ejection seat sear pin from inside his glove and slipped into the main breach of Patsy's ejection seat then collected up the debris into his gloved hand.

"OK, I have control." The plane righted itself and she fell back into the seat.

"Time to slow down and head back home."

His voice did sound different, even through the intercom, sort of nervous and hollow.

Jonny looked at the throttles and paused, after a second he yanked them both back to the idle position. There was a 'pop' almost like a powerful balloon then silence.

"Should it be this quiet?" Patsy asked, she was worried, although she knew nothing about aircraft, surely it shouldn't be this quiet.

Jonny didn't answer, he was watching the airspeed indicator come quickly down. Using what little hydraulic power he had left in the system he put the lightning into a steep gliding dive.

"EJECT. EJECT. EJECT." He said quietly before reaching up.

Only one seat ejected before the silver aircraft disintegrated as it smashed into the cold hard sea.

Chapter. 25

Freddie Kincaid had told him one day when they were doing a drill, that the North Sea was the coldest sea in the world. Now he knew he was right. The tiny one man life raft bobbed about like cork, even so it required constant bailling. Freddie had assured him it would still float full of water plus a wet pilot but it wasn't comfortable sitting in sloshing cold water. The distress beacon was working, well the light beacon was, so he assumed the radio signal was, all he had to do was hang on to be rescued. Patsy would be dead now at the bottom of about a hundred meters of cold black sea. Two out three wasn't bad, three out of four if he included Jolyon but that didn't count as it was 'official'. He wondered if mum and dad knew what he'd done. He started to feel quite sick bobbing around. It took two hours for the American rescue chopper to locate him and hoist him out. He sat huddled in a thermal blanket as they whisked him towards a hospital. He didn't want to talk to anyone so curled himself into the corner on the floor. The American crew constantly attended him, worried he might have some internal injury and die.

The ejection had left him with a back that hurt, and an experience he would rather not repeat. The three second clockwork wind down of the breach mechanism seemed to take an age then all hell was let loose. The canopy was literally blown away exposing him to ice cold air and violent movement as drogues fired off and barostats did their stuff, throwing him out of the seat and leaving him dangling on a parachute. All within a telescoped time frame accompanied by uncontrolled movement. He remembered seeing the Lightning smash into the sea, wings breaking off, the fuselage bobbing up for a few seconds before it slid backwards into the dark. He'd hoped the impact had killed her, being crushed by pressure whilst still breathing oxygen from the seat bottle, would not be a nice death. Anyway, it was over now.

"Take some time out Jonny, go home, relax, go visit some friends." Graham Dangerfield pushed a cup of coffee over towards him. Jonny reached from the chair to pick it up. "Officially you're suspended from flying duties until after the enquiry. I suspect you'll get an official reprimand for not seeking permission from a higher authority to take up a civilian. Why do you think she didn't get out like yourself?"

"I suspect she just froze up with fear, I don't know of course." Jonny lied.

"How are you feeling yourself?"

"Physically fine but very bad about her, after the parade and this, we'd become friends despite the fact that she was investigating me for a murder." Jonny sipped his coffee.

"Yes, not a good situation, the Chief Constable of the West Midlands Police wasn't very pleased about losing his assistant."

"What went wrong up there?"

"Not sure, just slowing from supersonic, as you know it's a critical stage you have to be careful with the throttles, suddenly there was a loud, sort of gassy, balloon pop and both engines cut out, tried to restart several times but nothing." He lied again. "I don't know, but I suspect that it's something to do with the staggered positioning of the engines causing some kind of pressure blow back that stops the turbines dead, probably damages them, hence it wouldn't restart."

"Well it makes sense." Graham concurred.

The enquiry was scheduled in three weeks time, all they could do was look at the flight records and question him, there was no wreckage to be examined. Well there was, a piece of wing had washed up in Norway but that wasn't going to tell them anything. He'd never been invited but he'd go and visit Calypso and Salvador in Luggala. He'd just turn up out of the blue and surprise them. He'd go now.

The blue Porsche pushed west across Scotland heading for Stranraer. Jonny hadn't booked anything, he'd just chance it, if he had to wait it didn't matter. He began to wonder what did matter in his life. Dad gone, mum gone, Calypso unavailable, nobody else particularly special. His mood related to the descending cloud as he neared the port. He wondered what she'd say when he just appeared? Was she even there? She'd started spending time in the Caribbean, she might be there. What about Salvador could he be close to him as he grew older? There would always be the horrible dark secret. His DFC, his Dead Fucking Chum medal. What a hero he was, two murders and that. No you wouldn't really want Jonny Conrad as a friend would you?

Belfast, he'd never been there before. He'd never been to Ireland before. It wasn't a particularly safe or happy place at that moment. An RAF officer driving from Belfast to Dublin was a headache the authorities didn't need, so he told no one. The military at the border accepted his identity card and respected his rank, letting him through from one grey drizzle day to another. According to the map Luggala was about twenty five miles south of Dublin, He'd stay another night in a hotel or an Inn and hope he didn't get shot, then again, would that really matter, except of course for the pain. His car helped to set him apart as a little eccentric.

It was just a road with a large double metal gate, nothing fancy, nothing could be seen from that point except the road that disappeared into a gentle green valley. For once it wasn't raining, sun and fleeting, fleeing, flying clouds fled before a strong happy breeze. He shut the gate before driving up the road. It suddenly appeared, as if from nowhere, he must have rounded a bend but he hadn't noticed, It was white and magnificent. Tall, tall, narrow arched windows surrounded it like sentries on duty, the tops of the walls were castellated almost hiding the roof, neat gravel drives and paths surrounded it. There was a huge splayed level area to the side of the house. The white helicopter stood there, it's rotors tethered so as not to flap about in the wind, it looked like a naughty puppy, sulking, waiting to leap up. Jonny stopped for a moment to take it all in, it was such an impressive awe inspiring place, surely important history must have taken place here but for now it was owned by a family of brewers.

He was met at the door by an old woman with a duster and a tin of metal polish in her hand. She was busy polishing brass things that didn't really need polishing. She had a blue and pink loose dress and a pinny to protect it.

"Good morning Sir. can I help you?" She looked out through the open hall door to his car and decided it was an appropriate car to warrant a 'Sir'.

Jonny wondered if he should use his rank but decided against it.

"Hello my name is Jonny, I was in the area, I'm an old friend of Ms. Calypso and her late husband and of course Salvador. Nothing is arranged but I wondered if she was at home?"

Jonny's knowledge of the family gave him access.

She looked him up and down before allowing her face to break into a big smile.

"Oh! That will be lovely, Ms Calypso gets very bored and a bit lonely stuck here when everyone's away. Come, follow me, i'll take you to her rooms, she lives in the East wing, will you be staying?"

"I've no idea, I hadn't considered that."

For a 'mature' lady she still took the stairs two steps at a time.

"What was your name again?"

"Jonny, Jonny Conrad."

She knocked, opened the heavy large wooden door, then poked her head around it.

"A Mr. Jonny Conrad to see you Ma'am." She opened the door wide for him to enter then closed it quietly."

"Hello you." Jonny said.

She stood up from her chair. They stood looking at each other.

"What! What on earth are you doing here? What a lovely surprise." She moved towards him, her arms outstretched her face alight with pleasure.

The large room was a gilded cage, extreme opulence and wealth, people were just adornments. An empty coffee cup, breakfast plate and newspaper lay on a simple wooden tray waiting to be collected. The view from the 'sentry' tall windows was breathtaking, vast lush green pasture dotted with healthy green lavish trees fed and watered by constant Atlantic rain and Irish filtered sunlight. It seemed to go on forever.

Her tiny waist had disappeared. In the room at various points were cut glass decanters with Irish whisky, Russian Vodka and English Gin. Somehow her eyes were slower. The diamond brilliance, now a flickering candle.

It was always there. Never left him. 'Hello, I killed your husband. I shot down Jolyon. I killed my best friend and the father of your son. Do you still love me?' Is what he thought as he looked at her.

"Had to get out of my aeroplane pretty quick, landed in the sea, so they've given me an unscheduled holiday, nothing to do, so I thought I'd come and visit my lover."

Calypso threw her arms around him and kissed his cheek.

"You've made my day, my week, my month, even possibly my year. Are you hungry? Let me order you something?"

"Toast, marmalade and coffee would be nice." Jonny spoke into her ear as he hugged her. "Where's Salvador?"

"They've bloody well sent him away to boarding school in London. He's only seven for God's sake, poor little chap, was awfully upset, so was I, It's like they have to totally destroy you before they rebuild you into something they want. Jolyon told me, that's what happened to him, then he met you and you gave him access to a normal better world. He loved you Jonny. So do I."

Jonny could smell the whisky on her breath. It was only ten in the morning. Her olive skin was now a little flabby with useless fat, Her cascading hair now shorter, more easily managed.

The toast and marmalade was delivered by the polishing woman whose name was Mrs Meredith. They sat on a 'chaise lounge' so they could touch each other.

"What are you going to do Calypso?"

"I've no idea." Her seriousness pulled her down. "Everything is so pointless. They've taken Salvador off me, said they didn't want him to grow up with a drunken mother. Yes I take a drink now and then but I'm not a drunk."

"I'm the same, only I don't drink, everything I do has a dark side to it. I'm the most successful failure I know."

"Are you staying for a while?"

"I hadn't planned to."

"Stay just one night. We can lie on the bed and look at the ceiling." She giggled.

"Is there anything on the ceiling to look at?"

"No."

"Then I'll stay. You'll get bored looking at nothing on your own." she laughed and pulled on his arm.

"Let's go for a walk?" She said.

"It's raining."

I don't care, I want to get wet with you."

His car was where he'd left it. Outside the front door, there was no need to move it or park it somewhere else, there was definitely no need to lock it. Calypso came with him to the car to see him off.

"Do you think we ought to get married then?" She asked.

"You said it wouldn't work, marrying out of class never worked, you said."

"Yes but I'm not wholly the same as them or hadn't you noticed? I could make a break for freedom."

"No you were right, we'd only end up a boring couple. Think I'd rather keep it this way, at least it's exciting." Jonny kissed her on the lips, got into his car and tooted as he drove away up the manicured drive. He looked at her waving in the mirror. The Caribbean was calling her back but Jolyon wouldn't let her go, or him for that matter.

Jonny headed south for Rosslare and a ferry to Fishguard, he'd go to mum's maybe do a bit of fishing with dad's tackle, it was all upstairs in the cupboard, he'd have to get a rod license of course. Veronica was living there now, just keeping the place ticking over, Brenda had moved back in with Harry who apparently was behaving himself now and they were happy.

The Irish Sea looked like milk, no, it looked like thick dark gloop that could easily swallow you up. There was not a breath of wind as the ferry left the lights and headed into the darkness. He stood on the port side leaning on the rails. The power of the undisturbed swell lifted and dropped the vessel effortlessly, as though it didn't even exist. The undulations of a strong beating heart, pushing his chest in and out, slowly, gently, but inevitable.

Fishguard was a pleasant town, breakfast was in a small homely cafe, where most customers spoke Welsh. Jonny was hungry but he settled for two Welsh cakes and a mug of tea. Years ago he'd passed through Llandovery, he couldn't remember why, but he remembered wonderful fish and chips and was hoping to repeat it. It was nine in the morning by the time he left Fishguard so it would be somewhere near lunchtime by the time he got there. Driving through Wales was a pleasure, usually wet mostly green, almost empty roads and lots of curious sheep.

The street was full of cars now, you had to search for a space, gone were the days when he could just pull up outside mum's front door. The only empty place was at the end of the street between an old Standard Ensign and a Mini Countryman. He knocked on the front door wondering if Veronica was in. there was no response so he had to search in his bag for the key. A new neighbour came out of the house the other side of the entry, he was a black man, it made his thoughts fly back to Calypso. Perhaps he should seriously ask her to marry him, she didn't look too happy now Salvador had gone. Perhaps he should settle for Veronica, he could do worse, she was an intelligent capable woman, he'd have no worries with her, he'd have loads with Calypso.

Nothing had changed in the house. Mum and dad's photos hung on the chimney breast.

"Our Jonny's home." He could hear his mother shouting to his dad. He put his bag down and had a conversation with them. Telling them all the bad things he'd done.

Jonny made a weak Port and lemon then sat in dad's chair, thinking, dozing then thinking some more.

Veronica was late, it was nearly six o'clock, perhaps she was working late or out somewhere with friends, then he heard her put the key in the lock.

"Well, what a pleasant surprise, saw the light on and your car so knew it was you." she leaned over and kissed his cheek before he could get up. "How long you here for?"

"Not sure, got some unexpected leave so thought I might use dad's tackle and do a bit of fishing."

"Have you eaten?"

"No, not yet, been waiting for you?"

"Wow! Jonny Conrad, famous pilot waiting for homely Veronica! That'll be a first."

"No it won't. I waited outside a Ladies toilet for you once, when we were out with Hetty. Don't you remember?"

"Toilets don't count. How about poached eggs and beans on toast?"

"Are they from your dad's chickens?"

"Yes, why?"

"Thought so, yes that sounds lovely."

"Some chap called Graham phoned for you this morning, said he'd got some good news for you. Asked for you to ring him when you could, said you knew the number. Sounded ever so posh." Veronica called from the kitchen.

Jonny looked at the time, six thirty, unlikely that Graham would still be in his office but he could try.

"Dangerfield." He was still there.

"Hello Sir-------------."

"Jonny, good of you to ring in, bit of good news. I've had permission to reinstate you back to flying duties. Apparently the Navy have located L264 in about a hundred metres of water and the SAS have expressed an interest in recovering it, some new procedure they have, saturation diving or something like that , they don't breath in air, helium and oxygen or so I gather, anyway they want to try and recover it as a dummy run for what they think is a Russian nuclear sub on the seabed somewhere north of the Hebridese. That isn't going to happen until next summer, so by the time they've got it and the techies have had time to look at it it will be the best part of a year so they've agreed to reinstate you with just a written reprimand on your record for unauthorised passenger. A slap on the wrist basically. I'd like you back here for next Monday if you can?"

Jonny's heart sank, his brain turning somersaults inside his skull, banging against every side. There was no way he could explain a pin in the seat.

"Yes Sir, a few days fishing and I'll be back."

"Good show, see you on Monday." Graham Dangerfield put the phone down on what he thought was a good news call. Jonny Conrad slumped into dad's chair.

"Are you coming into the kitchen to eat or do you want it on a tray?" Veronica's normal, happy voice floated through from the kitchen.

"On a tray please." Jonny was staring at the dead TV set covered with a cloth.

Veronica brought it through and put it down on a pouffe next to the chair.

"There you go, I've got to go next door for an hour, see to mum, she's gone down with a bad cold, it may be flu, there's a

lot of it about and she's getting on a bit now. I won't be long."
Veronica bent over and kissed him on the head. It was a kiss
of tenderness.

Veronica left, it was silent. Jonny got up and turned on the
radio, just for some noise, anything other than his thoughts.

The stairs were narrow and steep, as a boy they were nothing,
as a man they were small and confining. At the top were two
more steps to the left which led into mum and dad's room. He
remembered sunny summer days as a boy after school lying
on their big comfortable bed bathed in warm afternoon rays
and gently but irresistibly falling asleep. To the right were two
similar steps leading into his room, his single bed and dad's
fishing cupboard. In there were rods, baskets and nets. Under
the folded landing net was the box. He took it downstairs and
turned up the radio.

It was a rerun of last weekends 'Two-Way Family Favourites'
with Cliff Mitchelmore in London and Jean Metcalfe in
Monchengladbach.

"------and from Corporal John Gilmore in the third battalion
here in Monchengladbach a message to mom - Sheila, dad -
Robert, and sisters Margaret and Tessa, oh, and poppy the
dog." Miss you all very much and only a few weeks to go
before I'll be home for Christmas. Don't forget my sock! So for
you John Gilmore we have the Judy Garland version of that
ever popular song 'When Jonny Comes Marching Home.'

Jonny turned the radio up as loud as it would go and took it
out the box. He looked at the photo hanging on the chimney
breast. It was of mum and dad at Uttoxeter races. Mum had a
new blue coat on and dad had his binoculars.

" Wait for me mom and dad. Our Jonny's coming home."

"When Jonny comes marching home again ------------------------
----
---Hurrah Hurrah!

The End.

Printed in Poland
by Amazon Fulfillment
Poland Sp. z o.o., Wrocław